Blades Over Breakfast

The Breakfast Murder Club Series

Yvonne Hamilton

Cover Design: Get Covers

Formatting by: Yvonne Hamilton

Developmental Editing: B. Wills and Charletta Benedict

Paperback ISBN: 979-8-9928401-5-5

EBook ASIN: B0FWW6LVF3

Contents

This story delves into dark and complex themes, portraying both the beauty and brutality of human resilience. Readers should be aware that it includes scenes of violence, gunfights, and physical conflict, as well as moments of captivity and psychological distress. Elements of human trafficking and abduction are referenced, though never graphically depicted.

This story delves into dark and complex themes, portraying both the beauty and brutality of human resilience. Readers should be aware that it includes scenes of violence, gunfights, and physical conflict, as well as moments of captivity and psychological distress. Elements of human trafficking and abduction are referenced, though never graphically depicted.

The narrative explores trauma, PTSD, and the lingering weight of loss, including the deaths of secondary characters. Emotional manipulation, betrayal, and moral ambiguity are central to the story's tension, challenging characters to face the consequences of their choices. There are also depictions of consensual yet explicit sexual content, and non-graphic references to past sexual violence.

Alcohol and mild drug use (cannabis) appear in certain scenes, along with strong language throughout.

This book is intended for mature readers who are comfortable exploring emotionally charged material and morally gray characters.

Also, there's a very stubborn cowboy with dimples you can lose yourself in.

For the ones who hid in plain sight, wearing lies like armor and calling

it survival—

may your unmasking be your awakening.

May you find the courage to burn the name they gave you

and reclaim the one that was always yours.

If you've made it this far, thank you. Blades Over Breakfast is a work of fiction. But the pain, trauma and darkness woven through these pages are very real for many.

If you're struggling, please know this:

You are not weak for surviving. You are not broken for feeling it all. And you do not have to walk through the fire alone.

There is help. There is healing. There is hope.

Mental Health &Crisis Resources

-National Human Trafficking Hotline: 1-888-373-7888 or text "INFO" to 233733

-National Domestic Violence Hotline: 1-800-799-SAFE (7233) or

text "START" to 88788

-Suicide & Crisis Lifeline: Call or text 988

-RAINN (Sexual Assault Support): 1-800-656-HOPE (4673)

-NAMI (Mental Health Helpline): 1-800-950-NAMI (6264) or text

"HELPLINE" to 62640

International Readers:

You can find support in your region at https://findahelpline.com

Note from the author:

If this story touches something raw inside you, please take care

of yourself. Take breaks. Breath deep. Reach out. You're not "too

much." You're not "imagining it." Your survival is already a revolu-

tion. This story may be fiction... but your healing? That's *real*.

"Love Me Normally" – Will Wood

"My Blood" – Twenty One Pilots

"Sweet Dreams" – Emily Browning (cover)

"Gasoline" – Halsey

"I Know the End" – Phoebe Bridgers

"People Help the People" – Birdy

"Believer" – Imagine Dragons

"Lose Control" – Glass Animals

"Exile" – Taylor Swift ft. Bon Iver

"Wolves Without Teeth" – Of Monsters and Men

"Numb" – Meg Myers

"Control" – Zoe Wees

"Take Me to Church" – Hozier

"Run" – Ludovico Einaudi (cover by Sleeping at Last)

"Glory and Gore" – Lorde

"Dead of Night" – Orville Peck

"Bad Habit" – Steve Lacy

"Hold My Hand" – Lady Gaga (acoustic)

"I'm Not the Only One" – Sam Smith

"The Archer" – Taylor Swift

"Tear You Apart" – She Wants Revenge

"Bad Moon Rising" – Mourning Ritual ft. Peter Dreimanis

"The Last Goodbye" – The Kills

"Heavenly Father" – Bon Iver

"The Night We Met" – Lord Huron

Chapter 1
Clara

Everything has changed now. Everything. All with one word, a word I've said a million times. But this time it hits different. Goodbye. It rings in my ears as I sit at the table, elbows propped on the worn, sticky surface. A warm cup of coffee rests in my hands, the meandering steam curls and fogs my glasses. All the better; at least now the tears threatening to spill are momentarily hidden. My breath is slow and shallow as I sit in the residue of the word and the conversation.

Did I ignore the signs? Was my head so deep in the sand of everyday life that I took what we had for granted? No. It can't be that. Can it? I shake my head, dislodging the train of thought that threatens to pull me down a dark spiral of blame for his betrayal. He had asked me to meet him at the diner, our favorite booth where we sat every Saturday morning, drinking coffee and eating pancakes with blueberry syrup for the last three years. Where we had our first date during that torrential snowstorm that shut everything else in the city down.

I guess it's fitting that the place of our beginning would also be where it ends. I had a sinking feeling in my stomach ever since he asked to meet, butterflies coiling in my gut and looking for an escape. The familiar feeling I get every time change is coming. I take a sip of coffee and the warm liquid soothes the ache in my chest. The murmur of the diner is a background hum as the scene replays in my head. He had the audacity, the gall, to bring her with him.

I sit in the booth with the front door in view. In walks Travis, wearing a leather jacket that hangs too big on his thin frame, his chestnut hair slicked back. Normally he's all pressed shirts and tailored slacks, the picture of corporate composure. I am equal parts amused and confused when he first walks in, until I see her. Cassandra Belevue, tall, blonde, with legs for days. She is playing the role of sweet treat on his arm in a cream sundress that hits just below her ass. We lock eyes as they round the counter and she gives me this knowing smirk, like she thinks she won. He leads her to the booth, holding her hand as she sits on the inner side. Then I see it before he says anything: a fresh tattoo on his forearm. He consciously folds his arm in, hiding it. This is not the man I left when I went away on business.

"I see a lot has happened since I went on my last trip," I scoff, my gaze flicking between them. He fidgets while she stares straight at me, daring me to say the question hanging in the air.

"Hello, Cassandra," I greet her bluntly.

"Hello." She smiles, drawing the first line. "Cousin."

The word hangs between us, sweetened with venom. His eyes dart to me, guilt plain on his face, while she leans closer to him like she's already won. My jaw tightens, but I refuse to let her see the crack. Without giving her a response, I grab his wrist and pull his forearm into view. Ointment still glistens over raw skin, the black lines of a tattoo raised and tender. A sword runs down the center of a shield, its edge inked sharp enough to cut. Barbed thorns coil around the steel, curling into a vicious knot at the bottom. Between them blooms a dark flower, petals shaded heavy, almost bruised. Beneath it, etched in clean, precise lettering, the Latin reads:

"Sanguine et Spinis."

By Blood and Thorns.

It isn't large, maybe the size of his palm, but it carries weight—too deliberate, too symbolic to be just art. A scowl twists his face as he yanks his wrist back, tucking the mark out of sight again.

"Um… yeah, about that," he mutters, eyes darting anywhere but to me.

I watch as she pats his hand, leaning in to reassure him.

"It's okay, sweetheart," she says sweetly. He glances at her as she flutters her lashes, then leans close to press a chaste kiss to his cheek.

A shock of courage seems to hit him. He sits up, squares his shoulders, and takes a deep breath. Finally he looks me in the eye. There is a determination there, a look he has never given me before. He swallows hard, as if preparing for an argument. I cut the silence.

"Why?" I say flatly, my lips pursed into a thin line. The word hits its mark. He stumbles; no words escape his open mouth as he stares at me with wide eyes. Cassandra narrows her blue eyes at me.

"Tell her," she hisses, dropping the sweetness for a hint of venom as she squeezes his hand.

"It's over," he manages to choke out, fighting some internal battle.

"Why?" I repeat, bringing my coffee to my lips. I look up to see Doris approaching our table. I make eye contact with her and gently shake my head no. She nods once in acknowledgement before pivoting and heading back to the kitchen. I turn my gaze back to them. They have started arguing in harsh whispers. With a final pointed look from Cassandra, Travis huffs and turns his attention back to me.

"I want more," he says finally, running a hand through his slick hair. I scoff. He looks like a greased-up wannabe. "More than this mundane, coma-inducing routine we have." He glances at Cassandra. She gives him a reassuring smile and nods.

"More..." I let the word sit on my tongue, bitter.

"Listen." Cassandra huffs. "He doesn't want your boring life anymore. The day in, day out routine of going to work and coming home. Dinner precisely at six, breakfast here every Saturday. It's just so dullllll." She snarls, dragging the last word out.

He nods once, hard, like her words are his own. "That. We never take any trips. The only time you go out of town is for your job. We've done the same thing for three years without a single deviation."

"You could've gone with me," I counter, fingers playing with the edges of my oversized sweater.

"Gone with you?" He scoffs, eyes wide like I've said the most ridiculous thing he's ever heard. "And do what—sit in the hotel room waiting like a lap dog while you did your inspections? While you went to meetings? I think not."

He pulls his hand from Cassandra's and leans forward, elbows on the table, hands steepled like he's spent weeks rehearsing this speech. It's like watching him load the barrel of a gun, aiming it squarely at me.

"At first, I found it endearing. Your quirks. The way you keep a precise schedule. That everything has a time and a place. But have you ever thought life is more than lists and neat edges? For fuck's sake, even our sex is routine. Missionary. Scheduled. Not a shred of passion dripping from your touch. You live like it's surgical, sterile, every detail controlled. And I'm done living under your thumb. I'm ready for more. I want some spontaneity."

He leans back against the cracked leather booth, crossing his arms, eyes locked on me. Defensive. Waiting. Like he knows exactly how I should react. Like he's daring me to break, to cause a scene he can point to later.

I tilt my head, letting his words sink in, marinate. Anger rises warm and steady beneath my skin. It wants out when I see the smug smile on Cassandra's face, like she has rehearsed this exact moment. She keeps saying we're family, folding the claim into conversations like it's fact. It's unverified, a rumor passed at funerals and on group texts, a name stuck to us by other people's memories. We may be family in that loose, I-know-you-exist-but-don't-call-me way. Today is no exception. I want to yank those extensions and dunk her head in the fryer. I want to see the look on her face when reality gets hot. That's not my task. Not today.

Leaning back, I let the silence grow, inspect the ridges of my nails for them to watch, breath held like an audience waiting for the finale.

Finally I answer, cool and flat, like I'm debriefing one of my inspections. "So let's review, shall we? You think I'm boring, predictable, and that you must leave our three year relationship to find this mysterious 'more.' Some spontaneity? The schedule and the predictability you once told me you craved, for the stability. Because, and I quote, 'we are building a foundation.'"

He shifts in his seat, jaw tightening like he regrets ever feeding me that line. Cassandra smirks, her hand sliding over his like she owns him now. Maybe she does.

I keep my gaze steady, voice level. "So which is it, Travis? Did I suddenly become too sterile for you, or are you just too weak to admit you want easy? Because let's be honest, Cassandra doesn't come with responsibility, she comes with distraction. And that's what you've been craving. A shiny toy to keep you entertained when life got too... real."

His mouth opens, but nothing comes out. He looks at her, then back at me, caught between defense and shame.

"Better dull than dead inside. At least I know how to make them burn," she says, lips curving in a smirk.

I let a smile ghost across my lips, cold and cutting. "Yes, well... arsenic is sweet too. Until it kills you."

The silence that follows is thick enough to choke on. His face reddens. She bristles but does not dare look away. I do not give them the satisfaction of more. I sit back, lift my coffee, and let them stew. Only when the tension starts to itch do I click my tongue and let my gaze drift to his forearm.

"I see you're already experimenting. New clothes. Hair slicked back like some wannabe gangster." I pause and let my gaze linger on his forearm. "Remember, darling, tattoos are permanent."

He tucks his wrist closer to his chest like I burned him. Cassandra's smile thins and goes hard.

"Have your things out in an hour," I say, voice even. "Go. Take Cassandra and that shiny new future with her. She'll amuse you for a while, pick at you like a flea until there's nothing left worth keeping. Enjoy the glitter while it lasts."

"We're done here," he snarls through gritted teeth. His jaw clenches, the muscle twitching like he's holding back more. Roughly, he grabs Cassandra's wrist and yanks her from the booth. She squeals in excitement, thrilled with herself, like she's just won a prize at the fair.

He straightens to his full height, glaring at me like I'm the one who forced this. Cassandra doesn't waste a second—she hooks a hand in the collar of his jacket and drags him down to her. The kiss is all teeth and tongue, desperate to make a spectacle. Her cream dress rides up as she arches into him, flashing the edges of her ass for the whole diner to see.

He grips her ass in response, staking his claim like it's supposed to cut me. When they finally break apart, her lips are swollen, her smug smile gleaming like she's already engraved her name on his skin.

He looks at me once more, eyes hard. "Goodbye."

I tilt my head, sip my coffee, and let a faint smile ghost across my lips. "Good luck," I murmur, just loud enough to carry. "You're going to need it."

Cassandra bristles, tugging him toward the door. He laces their fingers together and marches out, the bell above the diner door ringing a bright, cheery note that feels like mockery in the wake of their exit.

I sink back into my seat. The sounds of the diner rush in all at once, like the spectacle was sealed off in its own vacuum. I run through the checklist in my head. Three years together. The small, quiet moments. The comfort I let myself believe was stability. Each box ticked, each note accounted for. Maybe that was my mistake. I used him as an escape from my real work. A reprieve from the dirty, bloody pieces of my life. A distraction.

And I know too well what distractions cost. Not long after we started dating, everything came crashing down. One breach. One failure big enough to stain my record for good. They shoved me back into the field when I wasn't ready, forced me to claw through assignments with that weight hanging over me. I've been carrying it ever since, a shadow I can't shake, no matter how clean my reports read.

I'm brought out of my thoughts by the sound of a plate being set on the table in front of me. A stack of pancakes sits there, syrupy blueberry compote dripping lazily down the sides. My brows furrow as I look up at Doris. "I didn't order this," I say, though my stomach betrays me with a low growl.

"Oh, I know, sweetheart." Doris smiles at me in that maternal way I wish I'd known growing up. "Compliments of…" She turns to gesture toward the end of the counter. The stool is empty. Just then the bell over the door jingles. Doris tilts her chin toward the window. "That fella. Said there's nothing a good stack of pancakes can't fix."

I follow her gaze.

And there he is, like he's walked straight out of another life. Black Stetson hat, hunter-green flannel stretched tight across broad shoulders, dark denim that fits him far too well for someone that rugged. Boots worn but polished, spurs catching the light as he pushes the door open. Sun glances off his black hair, cut close at the sides, long enough on top to be mussed by the wind.

When his head lifts, gray eyes cut through the glass like storm clouds about to break, and just for a second I forget to breathe.

A cowboy. Right here in the middle of the city.

I slide the plate closer, fork in hand before I even think about it. The first bite melts across my tongue, warm and sweet, heavy with butter. My stomach growls again like it does not care that my heart is still bleeding out on the floor of this diner. Doris was right. Or maybe he was. There is nothing a good stack of pancakes cannot fix.

Almost nothing.

I chew slower with the second bite, letting the syrup coat my mouth while Cassandra's smug grin replays in my mind. Her nails on his sleeve. His words, mundane, sterile, routine, like every moment of our three years was a prison sentence he needed to escape. I wanted to drag her across the tile and remind her just how short my patience runs, but that was not my task. Not today.

Instead, I sit here eating pancakes from a stranger who saw me at my lowest and thought to send me something sweet. Something that made the ache settle for a heartbeat. But I cannot linger. Routine is what he accused me of, and for once, he was not entirely wrong. I thrive on order. I need it. And right now, order means focus. I stab another forkful, blueberry compote dripping back onto the plate like blood spatter. My next assignment waits, and it cannot come soon enough.

Chapter 2
Beau

Greasy spoon diners always offer me the comfort of home when I travel for work. This one is my favorite when I have to make trips to Dallas. Doris is always a peach. I don't know how she seems to remember my order when it can be months before I step back into the place. It's early afternoon, the light trickles in through the out of date blinds by the window booths. The neon open sign buzzes slightly by the front door. I'm sitting in my usual seat at the corner of the counter. It gives me a good vantage point of the diner. I can quietly watch without suspicion and eat in peace. There is one particular spot I always keep an eye on, a booth on the opposite end of the diner in the back corner near the bathrooms.

"Hey darlin'," Doris greets me with a warm smile. Her brown eyes crinkle at the corners. "The usual, Beau?" she asks, setting a cup of coffee in front of me.

"Do you remember?" I tease as I set my cowboy hat in the empty seat next to me.

"Of course," she chuckles. "Two eggs over easy, a short stack extra crispy but not burnt with butter on the side, loaded and crispy home fries with a side of sausage gravy. I also know you like your home fries in a bowl so you can put your gravy and eggs on top before you mix it all together." She raises a brow as if daring me to say she's wrong.

"I can't argue," I say, putting my hands up in defeat. "I shoulda never doubted you." I flash her a smile before I bring the coffee to my lips.

"You should know by now," Doris calls over her shoulder as she heads to the kitchen. Leaning forward, I prop my elbows on the countertop and sip my coffee, savoring it as I let my gaze roam over the other patrons. I let it linger when it reaches the booth in the corner. She's there. But this time she's alone. That's rare; usually there is a man with her.

I catch myself watching her again. Dark hair pulled into a tight braid down her back, sunlight catching the red threads buried in it like sparks in coal. Sage green eyes behind simple frames, sharp even when she smiles. Today it's a cream knit sweater over green leggings and heavy boots. Not flashy. Not meant to impress. Just… her.

Doris stops at the booth, and she gives the woman one of those small smiles that look private, like they weren't meant for an audience. Doris leaves a thermos, and I watch the little ritual that follows—three creamers, three sugars, wrappers stacked neat, cups nested like she's filing a report instead of fixing coffee. There's something about the precision of it, the steadiness. Makes me want to see what else she does that carefully.

I take a long pull from my cup and look away. Doesn't matter. With my line of work, she's not gonna be more than a passing thought. Ranch life doesn't mix with city girls who've never had dirt under their nails. The clink of a plate snaps me back. Food slides in front of me, and my stomach growls as the smell hits. I nod thanks, fork in hand, ready to dig in—until the bell over the door rings.

Her companion steps in, only he's not alone. A blonde's on his arm, smug grin already claiming the room. Cream dress riding high, heels clicking like she owns the floor. Every step's a performance, and the way she smirks at the woman in the booth makes it clear—she's not here for breakfast. She's here to stake a claim.

Him, though—he's no prize. Jacket hangs off his narrow frame, hair slicked back like he saw it in a movie once and thought it'd make him dangerous. It just makes him greasy. He walks like a man trying on someone else's boots, hoping no one notices they don't fit. Fresh ink shines on his arm, too bold for someone who can't carry it.

But the nerves? The awkward shuffle? That feels like an act. His eyes are too alert, hands too controlled when he thinks no one's watching. He's playing at clumsy to lower the bar, to make folks underestimate him. Together, they look less like a couple and more like a performance. And from where I sit, it's one hell of a bad show.

I lean back, chewing slow, watching over the rim of my coffee. Not the first time I've seen her. Usually, she's just background—someone I've clocked and filed away as off-limits. But today? She doesn't crack. No tears, no raised voice, no scene. Just steady eyes, cool and sharp, watching every twitch like she's keeping score. Doris starts toward her booth, but one small tilt of her head sends the waitress pivoting right back. Quiet authority. Hard to miss.

The diner's loud—forks on plates, voices bouncing off the walls—but I don't need sound to read what's happening. His hand cuts the air, defensive. The blonde's all show, tossing her hair, every gesture too big, too bright. Then his sleeve shifts, a flash of fresh ink still raw. She notices. He covers it like it burns.

She leans back, calm as if none of it touches her. Regal in a place built for grease and noise. I'd told myself she wasn't worth thinking about. But watching her now, I can't shake the feeling she's a puzzle I wouldn't mind solving.

He finally storms out, dragging the blonde with him. She makes a show of it, kissing him like she's marking territory, dress riding up too high to be decent. He grabs her ass for the whole diner to see, then spits a goodbye at the woman in the booth before the door jingles shut behind them. I should look away, but I don't. Not when she sits there unshaken, like she knew exactly how this scene would end the moment they walked in.

The silence that follows hums, heavy and uncomfortable. Yet she still doesn't break. She just sits there, calm as stone, staring at the table like she's already moved on to the next thing. I catch Doris as she passes, sliding a bill across the counter. "Stack of pancakes," I murmur. "Blueberry compote if you've got it. Send it her way."

Her brows lift, but her smile is warm. She's known me long enough to not ask questions. I add, "Tell her I said there's nothing a good stack of pancakes can't fix." By the time the plate hits her table, I'm already out the door.

The bell jingles as the door shuts behind me, and the rush of hot Texas air slams into my face, thick with exhaust and sun-baked asphalt. The kind of heat that sticks to your skin, daring you to breathe too deep. I climb into my old red pickup, the seat worn smooth from years of miles, and rumble toward the center of downtown. Concrete and glass rise around me, the skyline etched against the haze. In the parking garage, I weave my way up to the fifth floor and nose between a row of polished sedans—my dirt-caked truck standing out like a scar.

I take the elevator to the lobby of the adjacent skyscraper, the glass and metal reflecting the sun like a magnifying glass. Stand still too long out here and you're a toasted ant. I step through the revolving doors, cool air hitting my face like a balm after the furnace outside. My spurs clink against polished marble as I cross to the turnstiles.

The security guards track me the second I step in, one already murmuring into a headset, the other eyeing the buckle at my waist like it doesn't belong in a place this polished. Truth is, neither do I. Not really. Orion likes its people in suits and ties, pressed and polished. Then there's me—boots, spurs, dust from the road still clinging to my jeans. I belong here on paper, sure, but walking these halls feels like breaking in through the back door.

I dig my badge out of my back pocket, hold it up slow, and make a show of the scanner's chirp. The guards trade a look, disbelief written clear across their faces. "Still works," I mutter, brow lifted, smirk tugging at my mouth as I tip my hat and stride through, disappearing around the corner toward the next bank of elevators. The massive *Orion Group* sign looms overhead, all glass and steel, gleaming like judgment. God, I hate these visits. HQ never changes, except the rookies they keep throwing out front.

Once the elevator doors slide shut, I hit the button for the four-teenth floor. Hands shoved into my pockets, I lean back against the cool metal wall, the whole death trap humming as it climbs. With a ding, the doors part, like they're welcoming me to a place I'd rather avoid.

I step into a carpeted reception area, all staged comfort and stale air. Potted plants sit in perfect symmetry with polished leather couches. The walls are lined with glossy photos—chefs at stoves, janitors with mops, clerks at registers. Every one of them grinning wide, fake smiles plastered on to prove how damn wonderful The Orion Group is supposed to be. Like a shrine, marked across the wall is their motto: *"We create a better everyday for everyone to build a better life for all."*

I scoff. If only they knew what we really did to "better that every day."

The reception desk stretches across the room in a long curve of glass and chrome, tidy as a showroom display. Not a pen out of place, a small vase of lilies tucked neatly in the corner, the kind of detail meant to soften the steel. Behind it sits Beverly, blonde hair pulled into a neat twist, headset crooked against her cheek. She's the one bit of warmth in this sterile place. Big brown eyes, quick smile, and a nervous habit of tucking stray strands of hair behind her ear.

I stop at the desk, smiling warmly, dimples on full display. "Hello, Beverly. How are you, darlin'?" I drawl, watching as her cheeks stain crimson.

"Hello, Beau," she says shyly, fingers brushing back that strand of hair. "You here to see Marcus?"

"I sure am." I wink, pulling a small giggle out of her before I lean against the desk.

She taps quickly at her keyboard, the soft clack of keys followed by the whoosh of an instant message. A reply dings almost immediately. Beverly glances up, smile bright. "Head on back, he's waiting in his office."

"Thanks," I say, giving the desk a light pat before heading down the hall to the last door. It swings open into a corner office with glass walls that overlook downtown Dallas. A sea of steel and concrete stretches below, all sharp edges and noise. I'll take my open fields over this view any day.

Standing with his back to me is a man of understated power. Only a trained eye would catch the balance in his stance, weight evenly distributed, or the way he angles himself to track me through the reflection in the glass. He waits, ready, the only sound in the room the steady click of a silver pen.

Marcus is broad-shouldered but lean, the kind of build earned from discipline rather than show. His dark suit is tailored crisp, not a wrinkle to be found, cufflinks catching the faint light from the window. Salt-and-pepper hair is trimmed close, precise as the man himself. Steel-gray eyes meet mine in the glass before he speaks, calm and assessing, giving nothing away.

"Hello, Beau," he says gruffly, pivoting to face me at last. He gestures toward the sitting area where two couches flank a glass coffee table. At its center rests a single manila envelope.

I nod in greeting. "Marcus." Crossing the room, I take the opposite couch. No sense wasting time. "I'm here for my next assignment."

He slides the envelope across the glass. I ease the flap open, pulling the papers just far enough to catch the heading.

"I've got a special one for you," he says, voice clipped. "Close to home. Red Haven Foods."

My gaze snaps to his. "Red Haven Foods," I echo. He nods once. Right under my damn nose.

Marcus leans forward, elbows braced on his knees. "This isn't just a box to check. The higher-ups want this handled right, and they keep pointing at you like you're the golden boy who can't miss." His mouth tightens. "They're talking full-time again. Promotion. Command. The kind of position you keep running from."

I let the words hang, studying him. He hates saying them almost as much as I hate hearing them.

"Marcus," I say evenly, "you know where I stand. I take the jobs. I do them clean. That's it."

His jaw works, eyes sharp. "One of these days, you're going to have to stop pretending you don't belong in that chair."

I tuck the papers back into the envelope, leaning back. "And one of these days, maybe you'll admit you'd rather be in that chair yourself."

The flash in his eyes is quick, gone in a breath, but I see it. He leans back, face smoothing into neutrality. "Fine. Handle Red Haven. But know this—eyes are on you whether you want them or not."

I rise, envelope in hand, smirk tugging at the corner of my mouth. "Story of my life."

He gives me a brief nod, and I take my leave, the rest of the office blurring around me as I head for my truck. My thoughts spiral. Red Haven Foods. Warehouse #Twenty-Seven sits just outside Harring-ton—the second-largest employer after the university. If they're dirty, it's enough to gut the town. My town.

The place where my roots still run deep, whether I like it or not. Where people know my name, my family, and where every secret bleeds into the next. Orion wants me to dig, so I'll dig. But some stones, once turned, can't ever be set back in place.

Chapter 3
Clara

My mind wanders as I drive through downtown Dallas. The city bustles around me, yet the wide Texas skies beyond it always manage to ground me. Here, it's been easy to slip in, to build a routine, to carve out space that feels like mine—away from the suffocating expectations of my family name.

The sun warms my face as I cruise with the canopy down on my black Jeep. Not my first choice, but necessary. Blending in matters. A vehicle in my preferred color would stand out too much, and I can't afford to be that easy to find. I slow to turn into the parking garage when a beat-up red pickup barrels out like a bat out of hell, missing my fender by inches. My hand slams the horn. "Watch where you're going, you damn hick!" I yell after it, though the driver's already gone.

Heat rushes to my cheeks, anger simmering until I force a steady breath. No sense chasing down an idiot who's never driven in the city. I have bigger matters to focus on. Getting my next assignment will be enough to distract me from this Travis mess.

I pull into the first open spot on the second floor and head to the stairs. I take them two at a time before reaching the lobby of the adjacent skyscraper. Before stepping inside, I drape my badge over my head, letting it rest against my chest. The security guards nod in acknowledgment as I move toward the turnstile. My badge beeps, and the guard beside it greets me.

"Hello, Miss Hayes."

I offer a shy smile, murmuring a hello before slipping around the corner. In the elevator, I press the button for the twenty-sixth floor—Compliance and Procurement Division. The doors slide shut, sealing me into the soft hum of machinery. The ride up feels longer than usual, each floor ticking by in slow increments. My reflection stares back in the steel paneling, tight-lipped, tired. Travis's face flickers in my mind uninvited, along with the mess he's left behind. I square my shoulders, willing the thought away. Work is safer ground.

When the doors finally part, I'm met with a reception area stripped of warmth. Fluorescent lights buzz overhead, reflecting off the white walls and polished tile floor. The faint scent of disinfectant lingers in the air, cold and clinical. Abstract art hangs in even intervals, muted grays and blues, their rigid angles chosen more for symmetry than meaning. At the far end, the Orion Group logo stretches across the wall in brushed steel, perched above the motto: *"Our mission is to improve the quality of life of our employees and those we serve."* I glance at it, a reminder of the work I'm here to do.

I don't stop for idle chit-chat with the receptionist. Instead, I move straight past until I reach an office halfway down the hall. Centered on the door is a polished placard that reads: *Clara Hayes, Lead Compliance Officer, Food Safety and Services Division.* I slide the key into the lock and push the door open. My office greets me in silence, everything precisely placed, exactly where it belongs.

The office is as practical as it is impersonal. No plants, no photographs, nothing that suggests permanence. Just a clean desk, two black monitors, a docking station, and a single filing cabinet tucked against the wall. Even the blinds are drawn to an exact angle, keeping out the glare without disturbing the symmetry.

I set my bag down in its usual spot and pull out my laptop, clicking it into the dock. The monitors blink to life, casting a cool glow across the desk. First, I review the report from my last assignment, scanning for any missed details. Then I turn to my inbox. A dozen new messages wait, mostly noise.

One stands out, flagged and encrypted. My stomach tightens as I open it. *Latte.*

Status steady. Driftwood's quiet enough, though I've got a lead circling that smells like more than gossip. Nothing solid yet. If it pans out, I may need backup. I'll keep you posted. Hope Dallas isn't chewing you up too much.

I read it twice, lips twitching despite myself. *Latte.* The nickname stuck years ago, even though she prefers chai and never let me forget it. That was the point, half a tease and half a reminder that in this work you rarely get what you want. She still signs with it. That is her tell.

The next message hits my inbox like a stone. Handler Fedricks wants me in his office. Of course he does.

Leander Fedricks is one of Orion's golden boys, though no one would guess it at first glance. Blond hair always a little too long, combed with fingers instead of a brush, and blue eyes that carry more arrogance than wit. He wears a suit that passes for professional if you don't look too closely, but the wrinkles at the cuffs and half-shined shoes tell the truth. Details never mattered to him. Decorum never mattered to him.

His office smells faintly of cologne, the kind poured on heavy to cover old smoke. A glass of whiskey sits on his desk, and he doesn't bother standing when I walk in. He just leans back in his chair, hands laced behind his head, grin already waiting.

"Well, well. If it isn't Orion's poster girl." His gaze drags over me in a way meant to irritate. "Always so stiff. Precise. You'd be easier on the eyes if you loosened up a little, Clara. Maybe a brighter dress, hair down. You've got potential. Shame it's wasted on all that discipline."

I keep my face still, notebook tucked under my arm. "You called me here for a reason."

He chuckles, low and patronizing. "Straight to business, as always. That's your problem, Hayes. Women in this work think they can out-stiff the men, and when it cracks, it cracks big." He leans forward, eyes glinting. "Case in point: your little program fiasco. Three years gone, and you're still cleaning up the mess. Maybe if it had been left to someone who knew how to play the game..." He lets the words trail, smile sharp. "Well. Let's just say Orion wouldn't have taken that hit."

I feel the words land like barbs, but my face stays cool. He wants me rattled. He won't get it.

He watches me like he's about to hand out charity and he does not stand. Of course he doesn't. Leander never rises for anyone who isn't part of his audience.

"Clara," he says, slow and too sweet, "I've been meaning to get you back on the board. A little dirt under your nails might do you good." He slides the file across the desk. The tab bears my name. He knows it—my given name, the one that's supposed to be for HR records and family reunions. People like him keep that detail like a blade.

My hands stay steady on the file. Inside, something folds tight and hot. He thinks this is a kindness.

"Victor Leclair," he says, letting the name roll out like perfume. "He's here. He's staying at the university house. You'll have an opening to get close. Search his ties. Follow anything that leads to his son. If there's data, you bring it. If there's a threat that can't be negotiated, you eliminate it. Clean. Public enough that the disappearance draws attention. Quiet enough that the university doesn't get splattered across the front page linked to us."

He smiles like he's doing me a favor. He doesn't bother with softness. He doesn't have to. He knows what broke me.

"You know why you're getting this," he says, patient as a man reading someone's medical chart. "Three years ago, that theft cut a hole through our program. Your operation—your program—was compromised. You took the fall. You were forced back into the field. You're still carrying the ledger on that, in the red." He leans in, voice low. "You only kept your post because of the family name. Don't forget that."

Lucky. The word tastes like ash.

His gaze slides over me, amused and clinical. "If you find the boy, if you find the drive, that hole closes. If you don't—" he lets the sentence dangle, comfortable with threat.

"And if I do find him?" I ask. My voice is steady.

"Then you do what you must. We need this to be seen. We need the son to move. Victor's removal will pull the threads. It will make the headlines. But it has to look tidy—no fingerprints pointing at Orion. You understand how to make it look like an unfortunate, high-profile tragedy rather than an extraction." He taps the file as if that settles it.

He says all this like he's offering penance. He is not. He is arranging leverage. He is polishing the noose.

"Understood," I say. I close the file. The snap of the tab is small and hard. I stand. The heat in my chest is louder than his smugness. This is not mercy. This is the one thing that will reopen the wound he insists on picking at.

I walk out of his office with the assignment tucked under my arm. He watches me go, satisfied. I will do what he asks. Not for him, not for Orion. For the piece of my life they stole and never returned. And if the operation must make the papers to drag a ghost back into reach, I will make it so.

Red Haven Foods — target. Warehouse Twenty-Seven. Acquisition cover.

HQ Billings, MT. Major regional distributor. Tied to university food service.

Objective: Find data trails. Locate any connection to Leclair. Eliminate clean and public enough to draw the son out.

I head back to my office, the fluorescent hum folding around me. The door closes behind me with a soft click. I drop the folder on my desk, let the paper lie face up for a breath. Then my hand goes to the far wall without thinking — a small, practiced motion to a pressure point disguised by a strip of molding. The panel slides on soft hydraulics. Not a closet. A tradecraft cache built for movement and erasure.

Inside, a Faraday-lined rack hums low. A compact server holds encrypted drives. Cables hang on hooks. A bank of burner phones sits in cold storage. A write-blocker and USB dock share foam with soldering tools and a hardware kit. Battery banks, a portable hotspot, and a small signal jammer live in padded cases. Cameras, spare microSD cards, discreet mounts tucked into pouches. A slim ballistic case holds a service pistol and mags. First aid, tourniquet, multitool.

I pack with intent. Laptop and dock first, then encrypted tablet, burner, battery bank. Body cam in my jacket. Evidence bags and tamper seals. Forged credentials in the hidden zipper.

The panel seals with a click. Short list on the screen. No drama.

Move like a buyer. Sweep like I own the place.

Chapter 4
Clara

The drive south stretches long and unremarkable. The Dallas skyline shrinks in my mirrors until it is nothing but haze, replaced by highway lined with weathered billboards and open pasture broken by silos and windmills. Pickup trucks outnumber sedans. Each small town I pass carries the same features: a diner with faded lettering, a church steeple, a hardware store that looks older than the pavement.

By the time the water tower comes into view, its faded blue letters spelling out *Harrington,* I already feel the shift. Slower streets. Fewer people. A rhythm that is rooted, unhurried, and cautious of outsiders. This is the kind of place where everyone knows who belongs and who doesn't, where a stranger's car parked too long on Main Street sparks conversation at the barber shop.

The inn sits on the edge of town, its sun-faded sign promising clean rooms and hot coffee. Gravel crunches under my tires as I pull in. The building rises two stories, brick on the lower half, wood siding above, shaped in a shallow U around a small parking lot. A covered entry leads into a wide glass-fronted lobby where soft light spills through gauzy curtains.

Inside, the air smells faintly of lemon polish and brewed coffee. A brass bell sits on the counter beside a bowl of peppermints, glinting under the soft lobby lights. Two carpeted hallways branch off from either side, lined with framed photos of the coast and neatly numbered doors. The quiet here feels lived in. A place just big enough to keep secrets, but small enough that no one ever arrives unnoticed.

I press the bell once, and the soft chime breaks the stillness. The woman behind the counter looks up with a smile that's just a little too wide, the kind of cheer that feels practiced. A man joins her a moment later, wiping his hands on a dish towel, both of them eager in that small-town way. They ask if I'm visiting family, how long I'll be staying, whether I'll need directions to the university. Too many questions. Too much warmth.

I answer politely, giving only what is required. My name goes into the registry, my card is swiped, a key placed in my hand. They beam at me as if I have returned home. They could not be more wrong.

I take the key and head down the hall, the carpet muffling my steps as the light from the lobby fades behind me. My room is near the end, the brass number worn smooth from years of use. The key scrapes in the lock, and the door swings open on a sigh of stale air. The room greets me with an air of dated hospitality. The wallpaper is faded and peeling at the seams, its floral pattern dulled by decades. A heavy quilt in muted earth tones covers the double bed, the kind that might have passed for fashionable thirty years ago.

In the corner, an old box television with a crooked antenna squats on a rickety dresser, a yellowing microwave perched below it like an afterthought. The carpet has been vacuumed, but the faint musk of long years seeps through, clashing with the artificial sweetness of air freshener. It is the kind of smell that only leaves when the carpet does.

At least they have Wi-Fi.

I drop my bag on the chair by the window and take another slow look around. There is a theme here, though it is difficult to pin down—Western prints on the walls, a ceramic lamp with a cracked shade, faux-wood furniture worn smooth along the edges. It is generic comfort, dressed up as charm, and none of it convinces me.

I sit on the edge of the bed, pulling out my laptop and notes. The mattress dips unevenly beneath me, springs groaning in protest. This will do for now. Not home. Never home. But enough to work from.

The laptop hums to life as I move it to the desk, plugging it into the wall socket with its chipped beige cover. The Wi-Fi connects slower than I like, but it connects all the same. I arrange my notes in a neat stack, pen resting at a perfect angle, the same way I always do before beginning work. Order, even in places that resist it.

A secure tunnel opens with a few keystrokes. I bounce through relays, stripping identifiers until the motel signal is only one layer in a stack of ghosts. Orion systems light up in muted green. I search the usual channels: public records, tax filings, vendor lists. Red Haven's acquisition briefs. Harrington University supplier contracts. Nothing loud, nothing immediate, but I mirror everything into a local cache. Patterns begin to surface in the margins. Same subcontractors showing up in different bids. Shell company names tied to the same PO box in Billings. Little overlaps that look like coincidence until you stitch them together. Worth following.

Then the wall goes up. A corporate proxy, ratcheted permissions, an account flagged for review. A vendor portal refuses my token. A manifest is there and then it is not. The kind of friction meant to slow someone who pokes without permission. I smile without humor and switch tactics.

Social engineering is slower but cleaner. I spin a caller ID, warm a vendor contact with a quick, plausible story about logistics and a pending acquisition. I script my voice to the exact cadence the man on the line expects from a procurement rep. He reads the name off the manifest. I copy it, then hang up before he thinks to ask why I need it. Two small lies buy me a route around a firewall. Old trades, old smells. Necessary.

Even with that, a hardened partition refuses to cough up manifests. It will need hands on site. That means a physical visit to Warehouse Twenty-Seven, an ability to walk around with forged credentials and a cover story that survives casual questions. It also means someone else could already be there. It means risk.

My mind slips while the downloads run. Not the technical stuff. The personal. The breach that happened three years ago. How quickly a life recalibrates around one failure. I taste it the same way I taste metal when I cut myself—sharp and immediate. I think of the quiet days before the hole ripped through my program. I think about how I once believed I could be something more than the work.That belief cost me. They sent me back into fieldwork, reshaped me into something leaner, meaner, always behind the next assignment. I have not forgiven myself for that. I never will.

The cache finishes. I wipe the temp files, overwrite the traces, and shove an encrypted copy onto a dead drop I control. No crumbs. No surprise for anyone who might comb logs later.

I unplug the charger, close the laptop with the practiced care of someone who knows it can betray you as quickly as it can save you. There's work now that wants boots on concrete. A path I have to walk to see how tangled this really goes. I slide the encrypted drive into my pocket, shrug into my jacket, and head for the door.

Once everything is in place, I cross to the window. The glass is streaked from halfhearted cleaning, but the view below is crisp: Main

Street stretching out in brick and neon, the diner across the way spilling laughter into the evening, a pair of teenagers looping slow circles on battered bikes. Time here moves like molasses.

My hand lingers on the sill. For a beat I let myself imagine the quiet life I once thought would be enough — a storefront with my name on it, mornings of sweeping and stacking, no midnight reports. But my pedigree, my past, and the things I've lost won't let me stay. The work carves you; it sets a map into your hands you can never fold away. I let the curtain fall on that useless, small longing.

Tomorrow I make my first rounds. Tonight, my stomach wins the argument. I change out of my travel clothes into blue jeans and a plain black tee. I pull my hair into a low ponytail. Keep it simple. Best not to stand out. Still, in a town like this, I will. Clothes only do so much.

I lock the door behind me. The air is cool and thick; the town smells of frying oil and traffic. The diner across the street hums on. Two old men tip their hats as I pass, polite curiosity soft as moth wings. I walk steady, feeling the town press a little at the edges, familiar in ways that should be comforting and are not.

The Rusted Spur sits on the corner, its sign buzzing with a tired sympathy. Inside, the light is warm and the room smells of grease and beer. I touch the door handle, feel the grain under my palm, and push through.

The bar greets me with the heavy mix of fried food, beer, and old wood. Neon glows faint on the walls, buzzing just loud enough to remind me the sign outside barely clings to life. A jukebox hums in the corner, its lights blinking like it might sputter out at any second.

Locals crowd the bar, their laughter rolling louder than it needs to. Boots scuff against the floorboards, hats tipped back in a way that says they've been here long enough not to care how they look. A few eyes turn my way when the door closes, curious but not unfriendly. Just... watchful. I can feel them slotting me into whatever box strangers belong in.

I let them look. Then I move, slow and steady, cataloging out of habit—the mirror behind the bar, the fire exit in the corner, the two stools open near the end. I don't belong here, and I know it. The whole place feels lived-in, like every nail and scratch carries someone's story. I'm just passing through, a name they'll forget by morning.

I choose a table near the wall, one that gives me a clear view of the door without sitting dead center like a target. The place is dim, all wood paneling and neon beer signs that buzz faintly overhead. Country music hums low from the jukebox, nearly drowned out by the laughter and chatter of regulars who all seem to know each other's names.

The waitress arrives before I've had time to study the room fully. Blonde hair teased big, cutoffs clinging like a second skin, grin practiced but not unfriendly. She sets a cold bottle on the table.

"First one's easy," she says. "Clint'll keep you steady if you want another." She jerks her chin toward the bar, where a broad-shouldered man polishes glasses, knee braced as if it's been giving him grief for years. He catches my glance, offers a nod, then goes back to his work.

"Thanks," I murmur, lifting the bottle. The beer is sharp, cool, not half bad.

I've barely taken the first sip when movement shifts at the edge of my vision. A man swaggering over from a booth near the juke-box, baseball cap sweat-stained, grin crooked with the confidence of someone who's been told "yes" too many times. He drops into the chair across from me without asking, elbows wide on the table like he owns it.

"Well, hey there," he drawls. "Don't think I've seen you around before. You just passin' through, or we lucky enough you're stayin' awhile?"

I let the bottle rest against my lips, watching him over the rim. His words roll easy, but his eyes give him away—hungry, expectant. Waiting for me to bite.

I don't.

Instead, I take a slow drink, set the bottle down, and tilt my head just enough to make him wonder if I'm listening at all.

He leans in, the smell of cheap cologne and fryer grease clinging to him. "Name's Jimmy. Everybody knows me here. Play my cards right, maybe you'll know me too."

I arch a brow, silent. He mistakes the pause for interest.

"Tell you what," he says, tapping the table with two fingers, "I'll buy you another round, and you can tell me what brings a woman like you to Harrington."

Misty reappears before I have to answer, pen tucked behind her ear. "You hungry, sweetheart? Kitchen's still cookin'."

"Yes," I say simply. "Burger and fries. Mayo, tomato, extra onion. And another beer."

She scribbles, shooting Jimmy a knowing look, then winks at me. "Clint says holler if he gives you trouble." With that, she's gone, weaving back through the crowd.

Jimmy chuckles like the joke's his. "Don't mind her. Thinks she runs the place, but Clint's the real deal. Old rodeo man. Tough as nails."

I let him ramble, fingers brushing the condensation on my bottle. His shoulders square as he talks about knowing Clint, about Harrington owing him, about his job at Red Haven like it's a crown jewel.

That last bit I file away, face unreadable.

Laughter ripples from the booth near the jukebox before one of them stands. He's young—mid-twenties, deliberately tousled hair, the university type. Shirt pressed, sleeves rolled just enough to look casual, watch gleaming under the bar lights. He moves like the room already belongs to him, easy confidence in every step. His grin lands squarely on me.

"Evenin'," he says smoothly, sliding into the seat beside Jimmy like he's just been waiting his turn. "Didn't think I'd see someone like you here. I'm Chet."

Jimmy bristles, jaw tightening. "She's already got company."

"Looks like she's got options," Chet fires back without looking at him.

Misty returns, dropping the plate in front of me—a burger stacked with mayo, thick tomato slices, and extra onion, fries spilling over the basket. She sets the beer down last, foam slipping down the neck of the bottle.

"Thanks," I murmur, already reaching for the burger.

The two of them don't even notice. They're too busy circling each other, puffing out their chests. One bragging about touchdowns long past, the other about future plans that will never come.

I cut into the burger, chew slow, sip from my bottle. Silent. Unmoved.

Let them posture. Let them fight over air.

I'm not here for either of them. I'm here to watch.

I polish off the last bite of my burger, grease and onion clinging to my fingers, and chase it with the dregs of my beer. Jimmy's still crowing about the past, Chet smug about the future. Neither of them has noticed I haven't said more than five words since they sat down.

I wipe my hands on the napkin, lean back, and let my gaze drift. That's when I catch him.

My eyes flick past their puffed-up chests, their cheap claims, to the bar. Broad shoulders. Black Stetson tipped just enough to shadow his face. The way he leans with quiet confidence, like the room bends around him instead of the other way.

Heat coils low in my stomach, sharp and startling. I'd almost forgotten I could feel it.

I push back my chair, rising slow enough to make them notice. "Gentlemen," I say, voice cool as glass, "take notes. That at the bar—" my chin tilts toward him, "—is what a real man looks like."

Their faces redden, mouths opening, but I don't give them the satisfaction of an answer.

I cross the room, eyes fixed on him. The Stetson hides his face, but not the way that hunter-green flannel stretches across his shoulders, strong enough to hold me down without breaking a sweat. Hands broad, rough, capable—the kind that would know exactly how to pin and claim.

Heat stirs again, low and insistent, coiling through me with every step. I forgot what it felt like to want with this kind of urgency, to feel hunger sharpen into something almost dangerous.

I keep walking, pulse steady, breath even. But inside? My thoughts unravel, dirty and restless.

It's reckless. Stupid. Exactly the kind of bad decision I promised myself I wouldn't make.

And yet, I keep going.

He sits with his back to me, talking low to Clint and Misty, un-aware—or maybe uncaring—that I've chosen him. I step close, the air around him warm, steady.

My hand lifts before I can think better of it, fingers brushing the solid line of his arm.

"Excuse me," I murmur, my voice low, meant for him alone.

Chapter 5
Beau

The Rusted Spur is half-lit, the kind of place that smells like old wood, spilled beer, and fried grease that clings to the walls no matter how often they mop. Neon signs buzz above the back bar, their colors bleeding into the tin ceiling. A jukebox hums low with an old country song, pool balls crack in the corner, and laughter rolls out of the cluster of ranch hands hunched around a table near the door.

It's a familiar scene. Same faces, same routines. Old man Cooper holding court on his stool at the far end, talking about the weather like it might change if he says it enough times. A group of college kids packed into a booth, giggling into their plastic pitchers, trying too hard to look like they belong. Two women at the dartboard, one arguing about the rules while the other lines up her shot.

I take a slow pull from my beer, leaning back just enough to watch without standing out. Nights like this have a rhythm, a pulse I can count on. I know who's here, who isn't, who might matter if trouble starts.

Then the door opens, and the rhythm stumbles.

A stranger steps inside, and heads turn with that subtle shift only small towns can manage. Curiosity without invitation. And then recognition hits.

It's her. The woman from the diner in Dallas. The one who never flinched, never raised her voice, who shut a whole storm down with nothing more than a look. I hadn't expected to see her again, much less here, two hundred miles south in Harrington.

She moves through the doorway like she belongs, even if every eye in the place says otherwise. Not loud, not trying for attention, but carrying herself with a kind of quiet command that doesn't need it. Jeans, black tee, hair pulled back—simple. Practical. Yet she makes the whole bar feel like a backdrop.

I tip the bottle to my lips, buying myself a moment. There's something about the way she holds herself, calm but sharp, like she's already three steps ahead of the room. Most people wear their nerves when strangers stare. She doesn't.

Admiration isn't something I hand out easy, but damn if she doesn't make it hard not to. I turn back to the bar, draining the last drops of beer before setting the bottle down with a solid thunk. Fortune's got a sense of humor. Out of all the nights, out of all the towns, she walks into mine. Maybe I can get a read on her before I deal with the assignment tomorrow.

I glance toward Clint. "Eh, Clint, you know anything about that one?" I nod toward the woman, careful to keep my voice low.

Clint McGraw towers behind the bar, broad as ever, his bum knee keeping him stationed here instead of riding bulls like he used to. Permanent five o'clock shadow, eyes keen enough to catch everything.

He huffs, polishing a glass until it squeaks before sliding me a fresh bottle.

"Nah, Beau," he says, popping the top with a flick. "Only thing I heard was from Mary Ann down at the inn. Says she's here on business. Tight-lipped, that one. Best keep your eyes open, though. Feisty things usually come in plain packaging. And I've got a feeling that one'll give you a run for your money."

I take the bottle, tip it in his direction with a grin. "Then it's a good thing I don't back down from a little competition. Let's see who's running who."

I don't move from my spot at the bar. Instead, I watch and wait. "So, Clint, wanna wager? Five bucks says Jimmy swaggers his way over to her like a coyote sniffin' around a fresh meal. Or you got one of the Uni kids giving it a shot?" I pull a bill from my wallet and slap it on the counter.

Misty Lynn, all daisy dukes and big hair, sashays up with an order ticket before Clint can answer. She grins. "Placing bets on the chickadee over yonder?" A laugh slips out of her. "What we got—Jimmy or Chet from the Uni crowd?"

"Yup," Clint rumbles, setting a glass to polish. "And what's the call? Full-on rejection, a slap, or a drink in the face?"

"I say five for each one that happens," Misty teases, eyes bright. "Ten if it's your chosen horse."

"Fine," I say, grinning wide at the evening's entertainment. "My money's on Jimmy Ray Buckner. Man's never passed up fresh meat."

"I'll take Chet from the Uni crowd," Clint mutters, popping the cap off a bottle and sliding it to Misty.

"Both of y'all are gonna lose." Misty struts toward the woman's table, hips swaying. Just before she's out of earshot, she tosses back, "My horse is Beau." Then she winks.

I raise a brow at my newfound place in the bet. Nodding once, I accept it. "Fine. I'll bite."

I watch as Misty sets a cold beer in front of her. The woman lifts it without hesitation, the edges of the bottle brushing her lips before she tilts it back. The satisfied curl of her mouth lingers as she savors the drink.

As Misty makes her rounds, I catch sight of Jimmy over by the jukebox. Cocky son of a bitch. Captain of his high school football team before he barely scraped through graduation. Now he drives for Red Haven Foods, hat bent at the brim, sweat stains working through the fabric. Rumor has it he's the reason a cornfield went up in flames last summer—fireworks for some girl, went sideways fast. A whole damn crop lit up just to prove he was worth looking at.

He looks like he just crawled out of a barn, tattered jeans ripped at the knees, a muscle tee doing little more than showing off a trucker's tan. His buddy shoves him out of the booth with a laugh, and Jimmy smirks, rubbing at his goatee before licking his lips as he swaggers toward her table.

I catch the way she stiffens, just slightly, the moment before he rounds the corner and slides into the empty seat across from her.

I can't help but chuckle when she meets him with nothing more than a raised brow and a sip from her bottle. Cool indifference. She lets him ramble, head tilted as though humoring a child. No doubt he's dusting off the same tired story about the touchdown he *almost* threw to win the championship fifteen years back.

Jimmy waves Misty over and orders another round, puffed up like he's the king of the place. Misty's smile says she's more entertained than impressed, and when she leans against the bar, she flashes two fingers.

"Two more beers. Add them to Jimmy's tab."

Clint grunts, pops the tops, and sets them on her tray beside a greasy double cheeseburger and steak fries glistening under the lights.

"Eh, Clint, looks like it's Chet's turn." I take a sip of my beer, nodding toward the pretty boy in the booth with the university crowd. He's dressed neat, Harrington shirt tucked into dark jeans, posture just stiff enough to prove he thinks he's better than the rest. He's got that air—like the world's his oyster and everything in it's already promised. Brown hair deliberately mussed, green eyes lit like he's itching for a challenge.

He heads over to her table, ducking around Misty as she drops the burger and beers. The woman doesn't acknowledge him at first, though I notice Jimmy go rigid, a scowl curling as he takes a drink. She clinks her bottle against his in thanks, playing along, before finally meeting Chet's eyes. Annoyance flickers there, barely hidden.

The bar's noise swallows whatever lines the two of them throw her way. I can guess the kind—Jimmy bragging too loud about things that don't matter, Chet leaning in with that practiced charm that probably works on college girls. She doesn't give either of them much to work with.

Instead, she stays steady, cutting into her burger, chewing slow, drinking when she pleases. Indifference looks good on her. It's a quiet kind of power—letting them preen and posture while she refuses to play along. And from the way both of them keep pressing, it only makes them try harder.

Misty stops next to me, poking me in the shoulder teasingly. "When ya gonna get in there, Beau?" she says playfully. "Or are you scared they have the upper hand?" She laughs loud at her own joke, the sound carrying over the bar.

"Not just yet." I know that approaching her now won't do. I turn my back to the bar, motioning for another beer from Clint.

Then I feel a hand on my arm. "Misty Lynn, knock it off," I say gruffly before spinning around—only to find the woman standing in front of me.

Up close, I finally take her in. Her jawline is smooth and strong, the kind that speaks of quiet confidence. A few strands of hair have slipped from her ponytail, softening the deliberate line. Her eyes are a steady sage green, sharp but not unkind, watching me with the same cool assessment I'd seen back at the diner. She's precise, composed, every angle intentional, yet there's something about the way she holds herself that makes it hard to look away.

"Sorry. Not Misty," I say quickly, shifting my tone. "What can I do for you, miss?"

"About that." Her voice is calm, words coming fast. "I've got a problem—two local mosquitoes buzzing around, ruining my evening. I thought since you're sitting here all by your lonesome, you might consider humoring me with a game of eight-ball. Maybe they'll back off before I have to put a hurting on some egos."

I let the corner of my mouth lift into a grin. "Eight-ball, huh? You sure you're not just looking for backup against the mosquitoes?"

Her eyes narrow slightly, though there's humor there too. "If I wanted backup, I'd have asked the bartender. You looked bored enough to make useful company."

"Well now, that's flattering." I lean on the bar, studying her a moment longer. "Name's Beau."

"Clara." She says it simply, like it should be enough, then tips her head toward the pool tables. "So, we playing or not?"

I take a slow drink from my bottle before setting it down with a thud. "Not sure. Looks to me like the local boys just spotted a shiny new toy. And when they see something new, they all get riled up trying to be the first to claim it."

Her brows lift, unimpressed. "Toy? That's what you're going with?"

"Don't look at me, darlin'." I spread my hands. "That's them, not me. You're the one who came over here asking for my help, remember?"

She tilts her head, lips pressed together like she's weighing whether I'm worth her time. "So you're saying you won't play?"

I chuckle low, shaking my head. "Didn't say that. Just figured you oughta know what you walked into. Around here, a woman like you—confident, cool, outta their league—well, it rattles cages. And it's fun to watch."

Something flickers across her face, not quite a smile, not quite annoyance. "Then quit watching and rack the balls, cowboy."

For a second, I feel the urge to close the distance between us, the pull of her steady gaze hooking me more than I'd like to admit. I imagine brushing a strand of hair from her cheek, just to see if she'd let me. But I don't move. Not yet.

Instead, I push off from the bar. "Alright, Clara. Let's play."

The pool table is tucked into the far corner of The Rusted Spur, green felt worn smooth from years of games, chalk marks smudged across the rails. The overhead light casts everything in a soft golden cone, isolating us from the rest of the bar. Jimmy and Chet both track our movement, eyes narrowing when they realize she's chosen me over them. Jimmy mutters something to his buddy, jaw tight, while Chet leans back with forced nonchalance, like losing her attention doesn't sting.

Clara doesn't so much as glance their way. She steps up to the table, plucks a cue from the rack, and rolls the chalk between her fingers before applying it with practiced care. Her movements are smooth, deliberate, the kind that commands attention without asking for it.

"You rack or break?" she asks, looking at me sidelong.

"Ladies first," I say easily, spreading the balls across the felt.

She leans forward, setting the triangle, the line of her back catching the light. I force my gaze away, taking my beer to buy myself a second. When she pulls the rack away, she gives me a smile that doesn't quite reach her eyes. "Don't you dare go easy on me, Beau. Play like a man, or don't play at all."

My grin pulls wider. "Careful what you ask for, darlin'. I've been known to embarrass my fair share of challengers."

"Then it should be a good game," she shoots back, sliding into position for the break.

The crack of the cue ball echoes through the bar, scattering the racked balls. She sinks one on the break, then straightens, blowing a stray hair from her face. "Solid's mine."

I circle the table slow, sizing up my shot, but my attention keeps dragging back to her. Confident stance. Steady eyes. Something about the way she handles herself makes it hard to keep my thoughts on the game. I line up and sink one, the ball kissing the corner pocket.

"Not bad," she admits, sipping her beer. "Maybe you're not all talk."

"Trust me, Clara. I'm better at showing than talking."

She smirks, taking another shot, this time missing by an inch. Straightening, she leans her cue against the table. "You've got a smart mouth. Must be how you get by out here."

I chuckle, setting my sights on the next ball. "Funny, I was about to say the same about you. You don't strike me as the small-town type. More city slicker than country grit. Outta place in a joint like this."

"Is that supposed to be an insult?" she challenges, eyebrow arching.

"Just an observation." I make the shot, two balls clattering into opposite pockets. "Careful while you're here. Dirt's thicker than it looks. You might not wanna get those jeans dirty."

Her laugh is low, throaty, pulling at something in my chest I'd rather keep under control. "I'll manage. I'm tougher than I look."

I glance up at her, holding her gaze a second longer than I should. The urge to close the distance rides me hard. But I keep my hands steady on the cue, grounding myself in the game.

Across the bar, Jimmy's scowl deepens, his hand tightening on his glass until I think it might shatter. Chet's mask of indifference cracks, jealousy flickering plain across his face. Neither one likes the show unfolding in front of them.

But Clara doesn't seem to notice—or maybe she does and just doesn't care. She moves around the table with a confidence that draws every eye without trying.

And me? I already know this isn't just a game anymore.

The game stretches on, back and forth. Every time I sink a ball, she counters with one of her own, never rattled, never breaking stride. The air feels heavier under the pool table lights, humming with something neither of us names.

I lean on my cue, watching her line up her shot. "So, Clara," I say lightly, "what brings you to Harrington?"

She doesn't look up, just lets the cue slide through her fingers with practiced precision. The ball rolls, kisses the side pocket, and drops. Only then does she glance at me. "Business," she says simply, no explanation offered.

That single word lands harder than a whole speech. Cold, clipped, final. I nod like it's enough, but curiosity needles at me. I take another drink instead of asking more.

She misses her next shot by a hair, the ball rattling the lip of the corner pocket before rolling wide. My turn. I circle the table, slow, deliberate, studying the last two stripes still in play.

"Business, huh? Guess that explains why you didn't swat those mosquitoes yourself."

She smirks, leaning a hip against the table, watching me. "If I wanted them swatted, I'd have handled it. Sometimes it's more fun to see how the locals behave when they think they've got a chance."

The way she says it—steady, amused—sends a coil of heat low in my chest. I chalk my cue, line up, and drop the ball clean into the side. Only the eight left now.

I don't rush. I take my time, circling to where she stands. Close enough to feel the warmth coming off her. I line up, stroke smooth, and sink the eight in one clean shot. Game over.

Her lips part, just slightly, the barest flicker of surprise before she masks it. I step in, closing that last bit of distance. My voice drops, husky enough to carry only to her.

"It's been a pleasure, Clara," I murmur near her ear. "Maybe I'll be seeing you around town. And watch out for those mosquitoes."

I straighten, letting the words hang between us, and force myself to step back. Every instinct screams to linger, to reach out, to test just how much of that calm surface would crack if I touched her. But I don't. Can't.

Not with the work I do. Not with the stakes on the table.

I give her one last grin, tip my hat, and head back to the bar. Clint meets my eyes, no words needed, just that quiet knowing look he's carried for years. I slide a few bills across the counter. "Keep the change."

He nods once, tucking the money into the register without comment.

I push out of The Rusted Spur, the night air thick and heavy, stars faint above the orange wash of streetlights. Gravel crunches under my boots as I cross to my truck. I climb in, the familiar creak of the seat grounding me, though my thoughts are anything but steady.

Sage green eyes follow me, unyielding, refusing to let go. The pull of her lingers, sharp in my chest, far too easy to want.

I grip the wheel, force my mind back to the assignment waiting for me in the morning. Red Haven Foods. Warehouse twenty-seven. The reason I came here in the first place.

Focus, Beau. Stay sharp. Stay clean.

And yet, as I drive out into the night, I know I'll see Clara again.

Chapter 6
Clara

Morning comes too early. The curtains in the room let in a thin stripe of light that cuts across the bedspread, pulling me from restless sleep. I roll onto my back, staring at the ceiling for a long moment before forcing myself up. Another day, another assignment.

I dress methodically, the motions grounding me. A plain navy suit, pressed sharp, the jacket tailored just enough to fit but not enough to draw attention to curves I have no interest in showcasing here. Black ballet flats slip on easy, non-slip soles quiet on the carpet. From the inside pocket of my blazer, I check for the small items I always keep close—hair net folded neatly in its plastic sleeve, pen light clipped in place.

At the desk, I lay out my bag. Inspection forms stacked in order, clipboard polished with fresh sheets, evidence bags tucked into their pocket, gloves folded flat. Encrypted tablet, burner phone, credentials, all accounted for. I double-check every piece because order is what keeps mistakes from happening. And mistakes are not an option.

Since I am in the area, the college will serve as my first stop. Orion already holds the contract for food service there. A compliance sweep gives me cover, something concrete to build on before I approach Red Haven. No one will question a Lead Compliance Officer doing her job.

I zip the bag shut, but my thoughts don't follow. They drift back, unspooling against my will.

Travis. His name alone is enough to sour my mouth. The fight, the lies, the way it all collapsed. I thought distance would dull the sting, but it lingers, a bruise pressed every time I let myself remember.

Then the diner in Dallas. The chaos of voices, his arm flashing with fresh ink, and me holding steady when every eye waited for a reaction. Instead of cracking, I cataloged, measured, controlled. Because that's what I do.

And then there was the cowboy. The one who sent pancakes across the counter without asking, disappearing before I could decide what to make of it. Kindness or calculation—I still haven't chosen which.

Last night only added more questions. The Rusted Spur. Pool cues clacking, smoke in the air, laughter curling around me. And him again. Beau. That's what Misty Lynn had called him. He was amused, cocky, testing my edges with that easy grin. I should have ignored him, but when I needed an out, I asked anyway. He played his part. Better than I expected.

I pause, staring at my reflection in the mirror. Hazel-green eyes look back, steady as ever, though I feel less steady inside. He unsettled me, that cowboy. Left me wondering what it would be like to let someone in, if only for a night. Dangerous thoughts. Useless.

I shove them down and adjust the lapels of my jacket. The job comes first. Always.

Bag over my shoulder, I lock the door behind me. Time to see what Harrington's college has been hiding. The smell of coffee drifts under the door as I step into the hallway, bag over my shoulder. My stomach knots more from habit than hunger, but I know better than to skip food on a day like this. By the time I make it down to the lobby, the continental breakfast is already spread out—fruit in a wicker basket, a stack of bagels wrapped in plastic, small cartons of juice sweating in their bucket of ice.

Mary Ann is behind the counter, as bright-eyed as she was last night. "Good morning, Miss Hayes! Sleep alright?"

I school my features into a polite smile. "Fine, thank you." I keep moving, straight toward the buffet, choosing a plain bagel and a carton of orange juice. If I stop too long, she'll ask questions I don't plan to answer.

"Busy day ahead?" she presses, tilting her head like she's eager to trade gossip.

I nod without looking up from the toaster. "Something like that." The bagel drops, browned edges curling with steam, and I spread it with the thin foil packet of cream cheese.

But small towns thrive on conversation, and dodging every question makes you stand out more. I lean on the counter, bagel in hand, and give her one of my polite smiles. "Tell me something, Mary Ann. What can you tell me about Red Haven Foods?"

Her whole face lights up, glad to share something she knows. "Well, they're the biggest thing to happen to Harrington since the university, that's for sure. Red Haven's warehouse has kept this town from turning ghost. They supply schools, hospitals, restaurants—all sorts of places. Jobs in the warehouse, jobs driving the trucks, jobs in the office. Around here, if you don't work for the university, odds are you've got a paycheck tied to Red Haven somehow."

I take a small bite of bagel, listening as she warms up, words spilling faster.

"They do a lot for the town, too. Sponsor the football team, cover uniforms for the band, even helped with the new library wing at the elementary school. Their name's on banners at every charity run, bake sale, and church fundraiser. Folks might gripe about long shifts or missing weekends, but most say it's worth it. Without Red Haven, Harrington wouldn't have near as many families staying put. Place would've dried up years ago."

I nod thoughtfully, sipping the juice. On the surface, it's the perfect picture—community support, steady employment, polished goodwill. But I've learned polished fronts often hide the cracks underneath.

Mary Ann studies me curiously, like she's expecting praise or agreement. "Why do you ask?"

I offer her a practiced smile, folding the wrapper into my napkin. "Just curious. Always good to know what keeps a place running."

She seems satisfied enough with that answer, though her eyes linger on me as I shoulder my bag and head for the door.

Outside, the air is crisp under the early sun, the town waking slow. Red Haven's name echoes in my mind with every step toward the car. Too many donations. Too much polish. I'll find out what's real soon enough.

Main Street gives way to brick and wrought iron as I drive across town, the shift almost seamless. Storefronts thin, traffic lightens, and then the streets open into something altogether different. The road widens, framed by old oaks whose branches arch overhead, filtering the morning sun into mottled patches. Sidewalks are broader here, cleaner, lined with black lampposts capped in glass globes.

The campus rises ahead of me, stately and proud, the kind of place designed to impress. Harrington University, founded nearly a century ago by the Harrington family themselves. Their name is etched into the very bones of the town, stamped on plaques, carved into cornerstones. The first building I pass is red brick, its white columns sweeping two stories high, windows trimmed in dark green shutters. Another looms beyond it, a tall clocktower that anchors the quad, bells chiming on the hour.

The place feels curated, preserved. Grass is clipped short, flowerbeds spill with seasonal color, and benches sit in precise intervals along the walkways. Students cross the green in pairs, arms full of books, coffee cups in hand, the chatter of their conversations lifting into the air. Professors in jackets and ties walk with the kind of unhurried purpose that only comes from tenure and routine.

It reminds me of another university I once inspected—old enough to command respect, updated enough to function smoothly. The kind of campus where donors write big checks, where alumni send their kids back generation after generation.

I ease into a visitor's lot near the student center, sliding into a space between a dusty sedan and a gleaming SUV with a faculty decal.

From the outside, Harrington University is everything the brochures promise: history, prestige, permanence.

But I know better. Campuses like this, for all their polish, rely on what goes unseen. Food service tucked into basements, kitchens that never stop, vendors making deliveries before dawn. And here, that vendor is Red Haven Foods.

I shut off the engine and sit a moment, letting my eyes trace the quad. Students lounging on the grass, a girl tossing crumbs to a squirrel, a group gathering near the steps of the library. Picturesque, wholesome. Exactly the kind of image a place like this wants stamped into every pamphlet and alumni letter.

My bag rests in the passenger seat, heavy with forms, gloves, and the tools of the job. I zip it open, check again for the inspection paperwork, and slide my tablet into the side pocket. Nothing left but to get to work.

I step out of the Jeep, straighten my jacket, and join the stream of students heading toward the brick archway that marks the main entrance. Harrington may want me to see polish, but I'll be looking for cracks.

The security office sits just inside the main archway, a small brick building with glass doors and the seal of the university painted across them. Inside, the air smells faintly of burnt coffee and old paper. A pair of officers sit behind the desk, one older, half-occupied with paperwork, and the other younger, eager in a way only small-town campus police can manage.

I step forward, sliding my credentials across the counter. "Clara Hayes, Lead Compliance Officer, Orion Group. Here to conduct a scheduled inspection of Dining Services."

The older officer glances up, gives the briefest nod, and goes back to his forms. The younger one, though, leans in with a smile that's meant to be charming. "Well, Miss Hayes, welcome to Harrington University. Don't see many suits around here. What brings you all the way down to our corner of the world?"

I keep my expression polite, measured. "Work."

"Work," he repeats, as though turning the word over might give him more. "Well, I gotta say, it's nice seeing someone new around here. Bet the students will be on their best behavior knowing you're on campus."

The clock on the wall ticks loud in the pause that follows. 10:45 a.m. Lunch service will be gearing up in fifteen minutes, and the last thing I want is to waste time playing twenty questions.

"Since lunch is about to start," I say, cutting the edge off my tone with a practiced smile, "I'll need directions to the Dining Services Director's office."

That puts him back on track. He clears his throat, opens a drawer, and pulls out a laminated guest badge on a blue lanyard. "Of course. You'll want to head through the quad, past the library, and down the main stairwell in the Student Union. Director's office is right beside the main dining hall. Can't miss it."

I take the badge, slip it over my neck. "Thank you."

"Anytime, Miss Hayes," he says, still trying with that smile. "If you need anything else, you know where to find me."

I nod, already turning away. Small talk has never been my weakness—it's the other way around. People think they're learning something about you in the pauses, in the smiles, but I've learned to give them nothing. Not here. Not anywhere.

Outside again, the late morning sun filters through the trees, striking the brick in a way that almost makes it look golden. Students pass by, arms full of books, heading to early lunch. I adjust the strap of my bag and start across the quad, badge catching the light against my blazer.

I watch them for a moment as I walk—laughing, unhurried, sprawling on the grass with no more responsibility than a class paper or midterm. For a second, I let myself wonder what it would have been like to have that. To move through life with that kind of freedom, to test mistakes without the world crashing down on you. I never had that.

My upbringing was measured in rules and expectations. Responsibility wasn't something I grew into; it was handed to me like a chain, each link added until the weight of it was normal. My life became about order, duty, control. Looking at these students, I feel the distance between what was and what could have been. But wondering is wasted time. The work in front of me is what matters.

The Student Union rises ahead, a wide brick building trimmed in white, glass doors opening to a lobby buzzing with chatter. I follow the directions through the hall and down a stairwell, the sound of clattering trays and voices swelling with every step. The Dining Services office sits tucked just off the main corridor, a plaque on the door polished to a shine.

I knock once before stepping in.

A woman in her late forties looks up from her desk, posture already half-tense, though she greets me with a practiced smile. "You must be Ms. Hayes. From Orion, right?"

"That's right." I offer my badge, then take the chair she gestures toward.

"You'll have to forgive the timing," she says with a dry chuckle, hands folded neatly on the desk. "It's a bit of a circus today. Lunch service is starting, Red Haven just showed up late with their delivery, and the produce truck from the local market pulled in at the same time. To top it off, I'm down two staff members."

Her smile is polite, but the edge of it is tight. Defensive.

I nod, setting my bag across my lap. "I understand. It's never convenient, is it?"

"Never," she agrees, exhaling through her nose with the sound of someone who's repeated the same line a hundred times. "But you're here now, so let's get through it."

Her words are professional enough, but I can feel the tension humming under them—the silent wish that I'd chosen another day, another hour.

I click my pen, pull out the forms, and give her the kind of steady smile I've perfected. "Let's begin."

She rises from behind the desk, smoothing her blazer as though bracing herself, and motions for me to follow. Through the open doorway, I catch the clatter of trays, the sharp call of orders, the rattle of delivery carts in the hall. It's the sound of organized chaos, the heartbeat of a campus trying to keep pace while stretched thin.

I slip my bag over my shoulder, checking once more that every paper is in place. The Director is already waiting at the door, her expression polite but tight. I nod for her to lead on.

The smell of food—frying oil, baking bread, fresh produce—hits stronger with each step as we head toward the kitchen. It mixes with the sharper tang of disinfectant, the kind of scent that masks more than it reveals.

Whatever waits for me beyond those double doors, I'll see it with my own eyes.

For now, I fall in step beside her, ready to watch, listen, and take note.

The inspection begins.

Chapter 7
Beau

Morning breaks hot and bright, the kind that burns off the mist before it can settle on the pasture. I push open the back door, boots sinking into dew-damp grass, and breathe in the mix of hay, earth, and manure that always reminds me I'm home.

The horses nicker from the fence line, waiting for feed, and cattle low in the distance. Routine settles me—the kind of rhythm city folk will never understand. I check the troughs, run my hand down a flank, and pitch a few bales into the pasture.

"Boss," a voice calls, easy and familiar.

Caleb rounds the corner, a sack of feed slung over his shoulder like it weighs nothing. He's been my right hand since he was barely out of high school, all rangy limbs back then. Time and work filled him out, made him steady. His hat's pushed back on his head, sweat already running down his temple even this early.

"Heard you rolled in late last night," he says, grinning wide. "Rusted Spur?"

I grunt, not offering much, but he catches the twitch at the corner of my mouth.

"Knew it," he says, dropping the feed with a heavy thud. "Bar's been buzzing all morning. Some lady walks in, makes Jimmy Ray look like a fool, then shuts down Chet from the Uni without saying much of anything. Had half the place talking."

My brows lift. "That right?"

"Mm-hm," Caleb says, his grin sharpening. "Funny thing though. Word is, you ended up shooting pool with her. Thought you didn't bother with strangers."

I stop at the fence, arms folded, and watch the horses jostle for position at the hay. "Her name's Clara."

Caleb whistles low. "Clara. So she's got a name." He tilts his head. "Pretty?"

I give him a look, and he laughs. "Alright, alright. Don't get your spurs in a twist. Just not every day someone new shows up around here and gets *you* to play along."

"She's not from around here," I say simply.

"No kidding. Word is she handled Jimmy and Chet like she'd been dealing with fools her whole life." Caleb chuckles, tugging at his gloves. "Can't say I don't respect that."

I let the corner of my mouth twitch into a smirk. "She's got steel in her, I'll give her that."

"Steel, huh?" Caleb eyes me like he's weighing whether to press further, then shrugs. "Just don't forget—steel cuts both ways, boss. Try not to let her hustle you too hard next time, huh?"

"She wasn't hustling," I say, smirking faintly. "Ain't a hustle if I won the game."

Caleb barks a laugh, shaking his head. "You sure about that? Maybe she just let you win. Might've been her way of reeling you in."

I grunt, not dignifying that with an answer, though my jaw tightens. Clara didn't strike me as the type to hand out wins for free. Still, the thought lingers longer than I like.

I shake my head at Caleb's grin, brushing dirt from my hands. "Speaking of, I've got another gig coming up. Won't be around much. Gonna need you to keep things running here."

Caleb straightens, his easy smile fading into something steadier. "Another one of *those* jobs?"

I nod once.

He sighs, shifting the feed sack higher on his shoulder. "Alright, boss. You know I've got it. Just don't go getting yourself killed. Can't run this place on my own."

"Wouldn't dream of it," I say, though my tone carries more dry humor than promise.

Caleb narrows his eyes at me but lets it go, heading toward the barn. "I'll handle things here. Just remember who fixes the mess when you disappear."

I grunt, half a laugh, and turn back toward the house.

Inside, the air is cooler, the hum of the ceiling fan spinning lazy circles above the kitchen. I pour a mug of coffee—black, no sugar, no cream—and carry it down the hall to my office.

The space is plain, walls lined with old maps, shelves stacked with ledgers and binders that look more like ranch business than what I actually do. The only real giveaway sits on the desk: a manila envelope stamped with Marcus's hand.

I drop into the chair, boots propped on the edge of the desk, and take a long swallow of coffee. Bitter. Strong. Exactly the way I like it. Flipping the envelope open, I slide the papers out, scanning the top sheet again. *Red Haven Foods.* My next assignment, close to home. Too close. My eyes linger on the name, but my mind drifts anyway. Clara. Hazel-green eyes steady as a drawn gun, the way she called me out without a word across that pool table.

I rub my jaw, irritated at myself. Can't afford distractions. Not with this work.The briefing is straightforward on the surface, but the language between the lines tells me otherwise. Protection detail. Extraction if needed. Chatter of a threat—nothing concrete yet, just smoke without fire, but enough to put the whole thing on my plate. And not just for anyone.

Victor Leclair.

His name is bold at the top of the page, the kind of client who doesn't get shuffled down the chain. High-level, international ties, business interests that stretch far beyond Harrington. If Leclair is flying in, it means something worth guarding is about to happen. Something worth silencing, if the chatter proves right.

According to the file, he'll be arriving by private jet into Dallas, then transferred under cover to Harrington. A quiet entry, no fanfare, no press. He'll be in town for a week—meetings, site visits, dinners. No details listed, but enough for me to know every move will need eyes on it. My eyes.

I flip the page, scanning the security notes. Known associates. Places of interest. Contingency plans. It's all there in clean lines and clinical language, but my mind keeps slipping back to last night. Clara. That was the name she gave me. A stranger who played pool like she had nothing to prove, who looked me dead in the eye like she'd been sizing me up from the start.

I drag my attention back to the folder. Focus, Beau. Marcus wouldn't have handed this to me if it was simple. Red Haven's tied in somewhere—has to be, or else why bury it in their paperwork? Leclair, Harrington, Red Haven. Three pieces of a puzzle I've got a week to fit together.

I take another long swallow of coffee, the burn clearing the fog from my head. Distractions are dangerous. Clara may have left her mark, but she's not the job.

The job is keeping Victor Leclair breathing for the next seven days. And if that means cutting through whatever Red Haven's tangled in, then that's exactly what I'll do.

I close the file, tap it twice against the desk, and lean back in my chair. Time to put the cowboy away and step into the role Marcus expects. Protector. Enforcer. Cleaner, if it comes to it. I push up from the chair, the file still spread across the desk. Sitting and staring at words won't get me what I need. Not with Red Haven in my backyard.

By the time I hit the front porch, the sun is high enough to burn the dew off the grass. Heat presses down, thick and unforgiving. I climb into my truck, the engine rumbling to life, and point it toward Harrington.

The road winds past open fields before narrowing into two-lane blacktop. I roll the window down, let the hot wind whip through, and keep my thoughts fixed on the job. Marcus wants answers. Leclair needs protection. And if Red Haven's tied to the chatter, I'll find out quick enough.

The closer I get to the warehouse, the more the landscape shifts. Pasture gives way to gravel lots, chain-link fences, and the low sprawl of industrial space. The Red Haven logo catches the sun from a sign bolted high above the loading docks, bold and clean, like it's daring anyone to question them.

I ease into a spot across the street, dirt-caked truck looking out of place beside the polished semis lined in a neat row. From here, I've got a clean line of sight.

Activity hums on the dock. Drivers haul dollies stacked high with cases, warehouse staff in red polos check clipboards, scanners chirp with every pass. A supervisor in a white hardhat paces the line, barking at two men who struggle with a pallet jack.

Sweat runs down my back, the cab stifling even with the window cracked. Still, I don't leave. I watch, and I wait. Because Marcus is right—if something's brewing, Red Haven will show it in the smallest cracks.

And I've always been good at spotting cracks.

I take a slow sip from the lukewarm thermos of coffee on the dash, eyes still on the warehouse.

Time to see what Harrington's golden employer is really hiding.

I settle deeper into the seat, hat brim pulled low, making myself part of the background. From here it looks like any other warehouse—trucks in, trucks out, staff moving cargo with the same tired rhythm I've seen a hundred times before.

At first glance, it's all by the book. Scanners chirp, clipboards shuffle, pallets roll. Workers laugh between themselves, the kind of banter that keeps long shifts from grinding you down.

But then, something snags my attention.

One of the Red Haven rigs eases back into the dock, same as the rest. Logo's there, bright and bold across the side, polished enough to look legitimate. To anyone else, it's just another delivery. But then I see it. Low near the bumper, half-hidden in road grime, a small flower etched in faint paint. Too neat to be wear, too intentional to be an accident. Looks like nothing if you aren't looking for it. If you are, it sticks out like a brand.

The driver climbs down, dark jacket zipped tight despite the heat. His stride's deliberate, clipped. He hands off paperwork to the floor supervisor. Too quick. No scan, no match against the manifest, just a nod before two workers wheel the pallets off the truck.

The load's wrapped plain—brown paper, no stamps, no labels—and heavier than the rest. They don't route it to the staging area either. Straight through a side entrance I haven't seen used once today. The door shuts fast behind them.

Everything else on the floor keeps humming like nothing's off. No questions. No second looks. Which tells me all I need to know. This isn't an accident. This is how they operate.

I shift my weight, eyes lingering on that faint flower mark near the bumper. Subtle. Deliberate. And worth remembering.

I drum my fingers against the steering wheel, the itch between my shoulders familiar. Something about that delivery isn't right. Too casual, too quick. If it were just a one-off mistake, the supervisor would've barked someone's ear off. But no one blinked. Which means it's not a mistake at all.

My eyes track back to the truck, the driver leaning against the cab with his arms crossed. Jacket still zipped, posture tight. He scans the lot, not the way a tired man would, but with precision—like he's waiting for something. Or someone.

I jot the time, plate number, and description into my notebook, committing the rest to memory. Details matter. They always do. The truck pulls out minutes later, rolling down the road like it was never here. The hum of the dock settles back to normal, efficient and polished once more.

I lean back, finishing the last swig of bitter coffee, and let the unease settle in my chest. Red Haven runs too tight a ship for slipups like that. Which leaves one possibility. Whatever came in on that trailer wasn't meant to be seen. And now I can't shake the thought that I was supposed to notice.

The truck eases down the road, blending into traffic like it was born for it. I start my truck slow, easing out of the gravel lot a few car lengths back. Nothing suspicious about a beat-up pickup rolling down the highway. Around here, it's half the vehicles on the road.

I keep my distance, let the heat shimmer between us. For ten minutes it's nothing but blacktop, fences, and scrub trees flashing past. The truck holds steady at the limit, never swerves, never hesitates. Too steady. Like a man reading off a script.

I flick a glance at the cab. The driver's still in that zipped jacket, one hand fixed on the wheel, the other resting stiff on the door. He doesn't fidget. Doesn't check mirrors more than once. No radio, no smoke, no sign of the small habits long-haul drivers live on.

My fingers tap the steering wheel, restless. Most folks wouldn't notice. But I've lived too long on the edges of things to mistake discipline for comfort. That driver isn't hauling groceries.

We pass out of Harrington's sprawl into open county road, dust curling up behind the tires. The truck slows just enough to take a turn down an old service road that doesn't see much use. No signage.

No clear destination. Just gravel disappearing under the weight of eighteen wheels.

I follow at a distance, engine rumbling low, the crunch of gravel under my tires drowned by his. The road narrows, trees closing in on both sides, sunlight fractured into patches across the hood.

Up ahead, the truck makes a wide turn into a gated property. Chain link, topped with barbed wire. The gate rolls back at the driver's approach without him lifting a hand. Automatic. Someone expected him.

I roll to a stop at the bend, far enough not to be seen, but close enough to catch the tail end as the gate clatters shut.

Through the trees I glimpse the yard—small warehouse, prefab metal, no markings on the building. A couple of men in work boots unload the brown-wrapped boxes, moving with the same sharp hurry I saw back at Red Haven. The driver stands by, jacket still zipped, watchful.

My gut knots tight. Whatever this place is, it isn't on any of the paperwork Marcus handed me. And that means Red Haven's got more than food moving through its channels.

I scribble the coordinates into my notebook, careful with every detail. Plain warehouse. Barbed wire. Automatic gate. Unmarked load. Then I turn the truck around, gravel spitting under my tires. Pushing too far now would burn the cover. I need more eyes, more time, more angles.

Still, one thing's clear.

Red Haven isn't just delivering groceries. And I've just stepped into something a hell of a lot bigger than the job description.

Chapter 8
Clara

The hallway narrows as we move away from the offices, the hum of voices and clatter of trays growing louder with every step. My heels click in rhythm with the Director's, the laminated guest badge swinging against my blazer. The smell of food intensifies—baked bread, frying oil, and the earthy tang of produce—layered over the sterile bite of disinfectant.

The Director glances at me with a tight smile that doesn't quite reach her eyes. "As I said earlier, it's a bit of a circus today. Red Haven rolled in late, the local farm truck pulled up at the same time, and I'm missing two of my line staff. Not our smoothest morning."

I offer her the same calm expression I give everyone. "That's why I'm here. To see the smooth mornings and the rough ones."

She exhales through her nose, nodding once, and pushes open the double doors.

The kitchen explodes into sound. Pots clatter, knives hit cutting boards in rapid rhythm, voices call orders back and forth. Delivery boxes line one wall, some stamped with Red Haven's logo, others marked from local farms. Staff weave between each other in tight patterns, practiced but strained, the pace just short of frantic.

I slip my pen from my pocket, clipboard balanced against my arm. My job isn't to soothe or sympathize. My job is to see.

The Director leads me past the noise of the kitchen to a small office tucked off the main corridor. The plaque on the door reads *Executive Chef,* the wood worn from years of use. Inside, the space is cramped but orderly: a desk with a calendar tacked above it, binders stacked along one wall, and a row of hooks meant for coats and aprons.

"This is Chef Russo's office," the Director explains. "You're welcome to leave your things here while you work."

"Appreciate it." I set my bag neatly against the wall, unzipping the side to pull free my clipboard and pen before tucking the rest out of sight. From my blazer pocket, I remove the hair net, unfolding it with a practiced snap before slipping it into place.

When I step back into the kitchen, the noise wraps around me again. My gaze sweeps the room automatically, mapping exits first. One at the far end, marked with a glowing red sign. Another set of double doors near the dish pit. Clear, accessible, no obvious obstructions.

Coolers and fridges line the back wall, stainless steel doors streaked with handprints. I count three walk-ins, two reach-ins, and a smaller beverage cooler tucked near the line. The equipment is standard for a university kitchen—flat tops, fryers, a tilt skillet, prep stations crowded with cutting boards.

I keep my eyes moving, checking the details that matter. Temperature logs clipped beside the coolers, though one looks days out of date. A red sani bucket under the prep table, water murky, rag draped across the rim. My gaze narrows when I spot a chef's knife blade-down in another sani bucket, handle poking up like an after-thought.

Uniforms are mixed—some crisp whites, others stained and fraying. Most staff wear hair nets or hats, but one young man at the grill has nothing covering his head, blond hair damp with sweat. Another worker hurries past me in sneakers, the kind better suited for jogging than standing on tile slick with grease.

It's all small, easy-to-miss things. But small things tell me more than clean surfaces and polite smiles ever will.

I jot quick notes on my clipboard, pen scratching against paper, and continue scanning the line. The Director trails me, her posture stiff, a hint of defensiveness in the way she explains, "Like I said earlier, it's not our smoothest day. We're short-handed, and deliveries hit all at once."

"I understand," I reply smoothly, though I don't look up from my notes. Understanding doesn't mean excusing.

I pause near the dish station, watching steam rise from the industrial washer, plates rattling in endless cycles. Staff weave around me, careful but rushed, the kind of hurry where mistakes multiply.

I move down the line, pen tapping lightly against the clipboard as I watch each station. A young woman portions pasta with mechanical precision, her gloves dusted in flour. Another ladles soup into pans, steam fogging her glasses. The fryer hisses at the far end, baskets lifting golden curls of fries.

I stop at a chafer filled with chicken, slipping my thermometer from my pocket in one smooth motion. The lid clatters as I tilt it back, the aroma sharp with seasoning. I slide the probe into the thickest piece, waiting for the numbers to climb. Not high enough. My tongue clicks against the roof of my mouth as I write a note, expression neutral. One careless temp can turn a meal into a liability.

Staff shift nervously in their places as I pass. A few meet my eyes before dropping them again. I keep my pace steady, letting the silence of my notes say more than words would.

At the back of the kitchen, the double doors swing open with the rush of air, carrying in the scent of diesel and produce. I follow it out to the dock, clipboard tucked close. The concrete bay is alive with motion—boxes stacked on dollies, voices calling numbers, hand trucks rattling down the ramp.

Two deliveries side by side. On the left, crates stamped with the name of a local farm, vibrant green leaves poking from one box still damp with morning dew. On the right, the bold logo of Red Haven

Foods, stamped across cardboard in corporate blue. Their boxes are uniform, efficient, stacked with military precision.

The truck looms in the dock, its chrome catching the light, trailer yawning open like a mouth ready to swallow the whole operation.

The driver is easy to pick out. Mid-thirties, lean but wiry, sweat soaking through his cap. He checks each case with quick efficiency, barking a number back to the receiving clerk who scribbles it down. His uniform polo bears the Red Haven emblem, though the collar is frayed. A barcode scanner hangs from his belt, clicking with each box he tallies.

I stand just inside the threshold, making quiet notes. Red Haven arrived late, she'd said. And here they are, unloading as if they own the place, their timing setting the whole operation off balance.

The driver glances up once, eyes skimming over me with the detached awareness of someone who's been watched before. He goes back to his work without a word.

I note that too.

Every detail matters.

I step fully onto the dock, clipboard balanced against my arm, and angle toward the produce delivery first. The air smells fresher here, earthy, the kind of scent you only get when something came out of the ground that morning. The farm's driver is a heavyset man in his fifties, sun-weathered skin, cap pulled low. He straightens when he sees me approach, wiping his hands on his jeans.

"Morning," I say evenly. "Ms. Hayes, Orion Group. I'll need to see your manifest."

He nods quickly, no fuss, and pulls a clipboard from his truck's side pocket. "Right here, ma'am. Thirty crates—lettuce, tomatoes, cucumbers, onions, all from Henderson Farms."

I scan the sheet, numbers neat, no discrepancies at a glance. I click my pen, jotting a brief note before handing it back. "Thank you. You can continue unloading."

He tips his cap, grateful I didn't linger, and goes back to moving boxes.

Then I turn to the Red Haven truck. The difference is immediate—the air sharper, colder, freight stacked with corporate precision. Their driver is younger, maybe mid-thirties, lean muscle under his uniform polo. Sweat darkens the fabric between his shoulders, and the frayed collar tells me he's been in it longer than most.

"Manifest," I say, voice calm but firm.

He doesn't meet my eyes at first, just pulls a folded paper from the cab and hands it over, his scanner still in the other hand. "There you go. On time and in full."

I arch a brow at the wording, noting the emphasis. "On time?" I echo, flipping through the sheet.

His jaw tightens almost imperceptibly. "Truck was loaded late out of Dallas. Not on me."

Defensive. But polite enough. His tone carries the edge of someone who's been blamed for things before and refuses to take it now.

As he shifts his weight, his watch slides up just slightly, and I catch the faintest mark peeking from beneath it—dark ink, small, pressed against the thin skin of his inner wrist. It disappears again when he adjusts his scanner. I jot a note without looking up, as if it's about the manifest.

"Everything checks out on paper," I say, handing it back, "but I'll still need to verify counts against the invoices inside."

"Standard procedure," he replies quickly, too quickly, as if reciting something drilled into him. His lips twitch like he wants to add more, but he doesn't. Instead, he nods toward the boxes. "You'll find it all matches."

I pause a moment longer than necessary, letting the silence stretch. His eyes finally meet mine, steady but guarded, waiting for me to press harder.

I don't. Not yet.

Clicking my pen closed, I tuck the clipboard against my side. "Thank you. You can continue."

He exhales through his nose, almost relieved, and turns back to his work, barking another number to the receiving clerk.

I don't linger, only step back inside where the kitchen noise swells around me again. My clipboard is already crowded with notes—timing, defensiveness, ink on the driver's wrist. Small tells, but telling all the same. The Director waits by the office door, the Executive Chef beside her with his arms crossed tight. Both wear the strained expressions of people who already know the list won't be flattering.

I don't waste their time. "Temperature logs aren't consistently updated. At least one entry is missing. Food on the line ran below safe holding temperature. Staff uniforms are inconsistent—one individual not wearing a hair covering, another not in proper footwear. Knife found submerged in a sani bucket. Delivery timing created unnecessary congestion and risk."

The Director exhales slowly, lips pressed tight. The Chef mutters something under his breath but keeps his arms folded. I don't comment. My job is to observe, not soothe.

"I'll file the full report," I continue, voice steady, "but I recommend a follow-up inspection. End of next week, same time. That should give you enough runway to correct the issues."

The Director nods, resigned. "We'll be ready."

"Good." I tuck my pen into the clipboard and meet her gaze. "One more thing. While I'm in Harrington, I'll be conducting further business with Red Haven Foods. Do they have an office on campus I can use temporarily?"

That earns me a sharper look. She hesitates, exchanging a glance with the Chef before answering. "Red Haven has a liaison office tucked behind the dining hall. Mostly used for delivery coordination and invoices. It's small, but you're welcome to set up there. I'll let their rep know to expect you."

"Appreciated," I say with a faint smile, already jotting the note at the margin of my form.

The Chef grumbles something again, quieter this time, but the Director cuts him a look sharp enough to silence it. She turns back to me, posture smoothing into polite professionalism. "Will that be all for today, Ms. Hayes?"

"For today," I confirm, sliding the clipboard under my arm. "I'll see you next week."

I collect my bag from the office, adjusting the strap across my shoulder as I step back into the sunlight. The quad is alive with students headed to lunch, laughter carrying on the breeze. I keep walking, mind already shifting from kitchens and compliance logs to Red Haven. Their office is my next step.

The directions are easy enough to follow—down a side corridor off the dining hall, where the noise fades and the hall narrows. A small sign with the Red Haven logo marks a plain wooden door, its brass knob dull with use. It's tucked away, unobtrusive, like an afterthought. Perfect.

I let myself in.

The office is exactly what I expected: practical, stripped of charm. A desk with a terminal set to the side, filing cabinets scuffed from years of use, a corkboard peppered with invoices and delivery slips. There's a faint smell of coffee that's gone stale, and the hum of a small refrigerator in the corner.

I set my bag down, pulling out my tablet and notes, arranging them in clean lines across the desk. The space is temporary, but it will do. It gives me a foothold inside Harrington University without raising questions.

Sinking into the chair, I let my eyes roam the corkboard again. Delivery schedules, signed invoices, notes from staff about substitutions and shortages. Red Haven's fingerprints are all over the operation here. Too neat. Too visible. The kind of presence small towns grow comfortable with until they stop questioning it.

I open my tablet, logging the first notes of the day. Inspection findings. Delivery details. A brief entry on the driver—defensive tone, late arrival, ink on his wrist. Small details, but they matter when patterns begin to form.

The office hums around me, quiet except for the muffled sounds of lunch service on the other side of the wall. I pull my hair net from my blazer pocket and tuck it back into its sleeve, setting it carefully in the bag beside me. Everything in its place. Always.

For now, this office will be my anchor. A temporary base while I peel back Red Haven's polished layers, one by one, and trace the threads that lead back to Victor Leclair. I close my notebook, letting the silence settle, and reach for the terminal on the desk. If I'm going to be here, I might as well see what doors it can open.

Chapter 9
Beau

The gravel road fades behind me, dust trailing the rearview, but the image of that unmarked warehouse sticks like a burr under the skin. Plain metal walls, barbed wire, men unloading boxes too carefully to be anything ordinary. Red Haven's fingerprints are all over it, but not the kind they'd ever put on a billboard.

I drive in silence, the hum of the engine my only company. Marcus's file sits back on the desk, neat and clean, but nowhere in those pages did it mention anything about hidden depots tucked down service roads. Which means either Marcus doesn't know, or he doesn't want me to.

Neither sits right.

By the time I hit the county road, the sun's starting to slip west, turning the horizon into a smear of heat and gold. My stomach growls, but I ignore it. Food can wait. Answers can't.

I roll into town slow, eyes on the familiar storefronts, the slow shuffle of locals going about their business. Harrington looks the same as it always has—small, steady, harmless. But underneath, I know better now. There's rot hiding under the brick.

I pull into the lot outside a diner on the edge of town, one with strong coffee and no questions asked. A place where I can sit, spread my notes, and think. Because tonight I need a plan. Marcus wants Leclair protected. Red Haven's got something to hide.

The Fork and Fiddle's neon sign flickers in the dusk, half the bulbs burnt out, but the smell of fried food still cuts strong through the air. I park the truck out front, engine idling for a second before I kill it. My gut tells me to keep moving, but coffee and a bite will keep my head clear.

Inside, the place hums with the easy rhythm of small-town evenings. Locals fill the booths—old men hunched over pie and coffee, a pair of teenagers splitting fries, a family corralling kids with promises of milkshakes if they sit still. The clatter of plates and low twang of country on the jukebox fill the rest.

"Beau," a voice calls, easy and familiar.

Tommy Ray wipes his hands on his apron as he ambles over, his limp just noticeable if you're looking. He's been working here since high school, never quite left Harrington behind. "Ain't seen you in here for a bit. You want the usual?"

"Coffee, black. Burger and fries, to go," I say, sliding into a stool at the counter.

Tommy scribbles on his pad, then leans his elbows on the counter, dropping his voice like he's letting me in on something. "Heard you been down at the Spur last night, stirring up talk." His grin is wide, nosy. "Some lady, right? Don't worry, I won't tell the others you actually smiled."

I shake my head, lips twitching despite myself. "You hear a lot, Tommy. Question is, you hear anything useful lately?"

His grin fades, replaced by something sharper. "Depends what you mean by useful. Folks been whisperin' about Red Haven. Couple of late-night deliveries rollin' through, unmarked. And the kind of folks drivin' those trucks? Not the usual crew. Heard one fella say they saw a rig pulling into a side road outside of town, place that don't belong to no one official."

I feel my jaw tick, but I keep my tone even. "That so?"

Tommy nods, glancing over his shoulder before leaning closer. "And there's talk of outsiders—suits—asking questions up at the college. That's the kind of thing folks around here notice."

Suits. Clara.

I shift, resting my forearms on the counter. "Anything else?"

He shrugs, straightening. "Nothing that'd make sense. Just folks saying Harrington's gettin' too much attention for a town that small. But you didn't hear that from me."

The cook hollers from the back, and Tommy turns, grabbing the brown paper bag and sliding it across the counter. "Burger, fries, coffee. On the house this time. Just don't go sayin' I never gave you anything."

I nod, picking up the bag, the heat of it pressing into my palm. "Appreciate it."

As I head for the door, Tommy calls after me, voice carrying over the clatter of dishes. "Careful out there, Beau. Place feels different lately. Like the quiet before a storm."

I push out into the night, the neon buzzing overhead, and climb back into my truck.

Different. He's not wrong.

And I've got the feeling whatever's coming has already started.

The bag warms my hand as I step out into the night, steam seeping through the paper. I'm halfway across the lot when the crunch of hurried footsteps draws my attention.

Too late.

She rounds the corner fast, eyes fixed somewhere else entirely, and collides with me hard enough to jolt the bag out of my grip. I catch it before it spills, though the coffee inside sloshes dangerously close to the rim.

"Easy there," I mutter, steadying the bag.

Her head snaps up, hazel-green eyes wide, a flicker of recognition sparking before she schools her expression into something cooler. Clara. Same as last night, though this time she looks less like the woman who'd held her ground at the pool table and more like someone lost in thought, fighting battles in her head I can't see.

"I—" she starts, then cuts herself off, straightening her blazer like the collision never happened. "Sorry. Wasn't looking."

I tilt my head, smirk tugging at my mouth. "I'll say. Nearly made me wear dinner home."

Her lips twitch, the closest thing to a smile. "Guess I owe you a new bag, then."

"Nah." I shift the bag in my hand. "Burger's still intact. Fries too. Crisis averted."

For a moment, the lot is just the two of us—her caught between distraction and composure, me wondering why the hell fate keeps tossing her in my path.

"You always barrel through parking lots like that?" I ask, tone light but probing.

"Only when I've got too much on my mind," she says, almost too quick, as though admitting it surprises even her.

Her eyes flick past me, scanning the diner's neon sign like she suddenly remembered where she is. Whatever's on her mind, it's heavy enough to keep her anchored there a second longer than she wants.

I catch myself studying her again, the way that blazer fits sharp across her shoulders, the faint shadow of tiredness under her eyes. Not the kind of tired you get from work alone—deeper, heavier.

"Well," I say finally, shifting my weight toward the truck, "maybe next time, try not to take me out with you."

Her gaze snaps back to mine, sharper this time, like she doesn't appreciate the jab but won't give me the satisfaction of saying so. "I'll keep that in mind."

We stand there a beat too long, the air thick with something that feels like unfinished business.

"Clara," I say, her name low, testing it again.

She inclines her head in acknowledgment, but she doesn't offer anything else. No explanation, no reason for why she's here of all places.

I nod once, slow. "Take care now."

With that, I move past her, climb into my truck, and set the bag on the seat beside me. Through the windshield, I see her pause, drawing in a breath before walking toward the inn down the street. My hand lingers on the wheel longer than it should. Harrington's too small for coincidences like this.

For a second I think that's it—she'll disappear inside and we'll go our separate ways. But then her gaze drifts, landing on my truck. Something flickers across her face, subtle but sharp. Recognition.

Her eyes narrow, anger flashing there before she smooths it away, too late for me not to notice. I ease the truck into gear, rolling out of the lot, but my grip on the wheel tightens. What the hell was that?

It wasn't just surprise. It was knowing.

And if Clara recognizes my truck, that means she's been paying closer attention than she lets on. Curiosity gnaws at me as the diner fades in the rearview. I shouldn't care, not with Victor Leclair on the horizon and Red Haven already stinking of trouble. But I can't shake the way her expression changed in an instant—from calm to fire, like I'd just stepped across a line I didn't even know was there.

I keep the truck steady on the highway, the paper bag sliding on the seat with every curve. The smell of grease and coffee fills the cab, but my appetite's gone flat. All I can see is Clara's face when she looked at my truck—calm one second, fire the next. It wasn't the kind of look you give a stranger. It was recognition, and not the good kind.

I replay it in my head, the shift so quick most folks would've missed it. Not me. I've built my life on catching the tells other people try to hide. That flare of anger was real, and it was aimed straight at me.

The question is why. She gave me her name, played pool like she had nothing to lose, kept cool under pressure. But anger like that? That's personal. That meant she'd seen something—or some-one—before.

The road stretches ahead, dark fields broken by the glow of scat-tered farmhouses. My thoughts circle back to Marcus's file—Red Haven, the chatter of a threat, Victor Leclair's arrival. Clara doesn't appear in any of it, but that doesn't mean she isn't tied in. Could be coincidence, but I stopped believing in coincidence a long time ago.

I take the turnoff back toward the ranch, the truck rattling over the old wooden bridge that's seen better days. Gravel spits under my tires as I climb the long drive, headlights cutting across pasture where the cattle bed down for the night. When I step into the house, the quiet feels heavy, too heavy after the noise of Harrington. I drop the bag on the counter, peel back the paper, and stare at the burger without really seeing it. My appetite's gone.

Instead, I carry the coffee into my office, setting it beside Marcus's folder. Leclair's arrival. Red Haven's polished front with rot under-neath. And Clara—colliding into me twice in as many days, sharp enough to leave an impression, and now angry enough to make me wonder what she really knows.

I lean back in the chair, boots propped against the desk, and fish a joint from the breast pocket of my shirt. Silver Zippo flicks, flame catching, and I draw in deep until the burn settles low in my chest. Smoke curls upward, twining with the lazy spin of the ceiling fan. Nights like this remind me of the years I spent overseas—long stretches of waiting broken by sudden bursts of violence. You learn to read the air, to feel the shift in people before it happens.

Harrington doesn't look like a war zone, but the same rules apply. Trouble hides in plain sight, and if you miss the signs, it'll eat you alive. The job is clear: protect Leclair, handle the extraction if it comes to it, keep the threat from ever reaching him. But something tells me Clara's not done crossing my path.

If she's tied to Red Haven, she's more than a distraction. She's a variable. And variables get people killed if you don't account for them.

I drag a hand down my face, take another slow hit, and stare at the fan above me. Clara's anger, the unmarked trailer, the hidden warehouse—all threads in a web pulling tighter by the day. I can feel it.

Looks like Harrington's about to get a whole lot messier.

Chapter 10
Clara

I don't move right away after Beau's taillights disappear. My fists clench at my sides, nails pressing into my palms until I force myself to breathe. That truck. The same red pickup that nearly sideswiped me in Dallas. I hadn't thought twice about the idiot behind the wheel then, but now? Twice in two days is no coincidence.

Back in my room at the inn, I lock the door and lean against it, the faint smell of carpet cleaner doing little to mask the decades-old mustiness. My pulse still hums from the collision outside, though anger has replaced surprise. Recognition like that isn't chance. Either he's following me, or he's tangled in the same web I've been sent to cut apart.

I drop my bag on the desk and pull out my laptop, the screen casting pale light over the peeling wallpaper. Notes and inspection forms scatter the surface, but I shove them aside. Those are for the cover. The real assignment—the one no one here in Harrington would ever suspect—waits behind the encrypted message I received two days ago.

Red Haven Foods. On paper, it's just another distribution hub feeding half the region, supplying cafeterias, hospitals, even Harrington University. The warehouse looks clean enough, organized to a fault, all smiles and slogans about community. But I know better. That polish hides something rotten. I'm not here to nitpick about hairnets or temp logs. I'm here to confirm what Red Haven is really moving through those unmarked deliveries.

And then there's Victor Leclair.

I click open the dossier. His face stares back from a grainy surveillance still—clean-cut, polite smile gone flat in black and white. French national, and not a distant investor—he's listed as an executive with Red Haven Foods. The name tightens something in my chest; this isn't just another audit or acquisition inspection. There's scale and reach behind it, and there's history.

On paper, Leclair's connection to the Harrington warehouse looks routine. But it's his son that matters. Three years ago, an Orion operative turned traitor—Leclair's own son—stole the Black Bible hard drive right out from under my division. My program. My security protocols. That breach gutted everything I had built, and I still taste the anger when I think about it.

This assignment is supposed to be redemption. If I can trace any contact that leads back to Leclair's son, I might finally recover the hard drive and close the wound he left.

The dossier offers only hints: import-export fronts with messy ledgers, whispers of arms deals, quiet disappearances in places no one talks about. Orders are clear. Establish the operational link, find a way to reach the son, recover the Black Bible hard drive. No mistakes this time.

Assassination. Cold, clean. No questions, no fallout that can be traced back.

The room feels smaller as I stare at the screen, suffocating with the weight of it. I've done this before. Missions that never make the news, targets no one will mourn. But something about Harrington unsettles me—the way the town clings to Red Haven like it's their salvation. The way they smile too easily when they should be asking harder questions. And then there's Beau, dropping into my path again and again like a ghost I didn't summon.

I push back from the desk and pace the narrow space, avoiding the sagging quilt on the bed, the yellowed lampshade. My upbringing taught me to keep control, to bury hesitation under precision. My father's voice echoes even now: *Discipline over doubt. Always.* It kept me alive through training, through missions that broke softer recruits. But tonight, that discipline feels thinner than it should.

Beau's smirk when he caught me off guard at the bar. The way he played pool without posturing, without flinching when I pushed him. And tonight, that damn truck pulling away while recognition burned in my chest. If he's tied to Red Haven, then he's more than just a distraction. He's a problem.

I sit back down at the narrow desk and open the folders again. The liaison office gives you the bones of a supply chain — invoices, delivery manifests, packing slips, routing codes — the kind of paper trail most people never bother to follow. That's where you find the truth, tucked between neat columns and stamped signatures. At first glance, the paperwork looks as polished as the rest of Red Haven's face: neat printouts, corporate headers, neat initials in the approval boxes. But the more I read, the more tiny things begin to irritate the edges of the picture.

An invoice dated the twelfth, stamped and signed, but the manifest timestamps show the load scanned at 02:14 a.m., a time when the receiving dock is supposed to be locked down. There are duplicate serial numbers on two separate pallets listed as different SKUs. One delivery slip shows a routing code that points to a "local transfer" — but the supposed receiving depot on that transfer doesn't exist in the county registry. Several manifests have blank lines where weights should be; others list weights that don't match the packing lists taped to the boxes in the photos on the corkboard. A handful of vendor codes map back to shell accounts when I run them through the database on the terminal. Someone is masking movement by changing the labels that matter most.

I lean forward and run my finger down a page until my nail catches on a scrawled note in the margin. "Late arrival — moved to side entry." Same phrasing I saw at the dock today. Too many of these little notes point to the same pattern: official deliveries that loop off the record for a while, returned to the chain once they reach their "final" destination.

There is also the human element. Signatures that don't quite match, initials that look hurried, stamps pressed at odd angles like the person was distracted. One delivery manifest bears a dispatch stamp from a depot I've never seen on any of Red Haven's supplier maps. Another file shows an "internal transfer" code used repeatedly at 02:00–03:00 hours. A clerk could blame sloppy nights, but sloppy across multiple files and weeks looks deliberate.

I open the binder labeled "College Accounts" and find contracts listing Red Haven as the official vendor for most campus dining. Everything is ticked, insured, in good standing. But beneath the contract addendums someone has appended small change-orders marked "special handling" with routing notes that route through Dallas, then back to a code that reads like an internal transfer. Why route through a major distribution hub and then back to the local campus? Questions fold into more questions.

Beau's truck flashes through my mind — that flare of red in Dallas, the same truck in the Fork and Fiddle's lot. I should be neutral about that. My cover is cold and clinical. Still, the image of the truck, the man who drove it, the near-miss in Dallas—all of it pricks at the back of my neck. He called me Clara at the bar; he played pool with me. He probably has no idea who I answer to. I make a note: *Local contact — Beau. Watch.* I don't write more than the name. Records are for eyes that don't know how to read between lines; I'll keep the meaning to myself.

I close folders and re-open files, cross-check timestamps with the emailed manifests and the hand-scribbled notes pinned on the corkboard. The pattern tightens: odd routing codes, blank weights, duplicate serials, "internal transfer" designations during overnight hours, and one repeated depot stamp that points to a property not listed on any public register. Whoever set this up knows enough about logistics to hide movement in plain sight.

Tomorrow I'll be at the docks. I'll watch the drivers when they arrive. I'll cross-match manifests with what actually comes off the trailers and I'll see where those unmarked pallets really go before anyone re-tags them. I'll talk to the drivers if I have to — get a name, a time, a plate number. If Red Haven's moving more than food, if

Victor Leclair's network is using distribution to mask something else, I'll find the trail.

I shut the laptop and fold my hands over the desk. The room is small, the hum of the fridge loud in the silence. The job is clean in its instructions and ugly in its implications. Verify the connection, confirm the pattern, neutralize the threat.

I breathe out and let the plan settle. Tomorrow, I'll go where the paperwork points. I'll watch. I'll follow the boxes. And when Leclair comes, I'll be where I need to be.

Chapter 11
Beau

The next morning starts the way most do—coffee strong enough to scrape the back of my throat, boots pulled on before the sun's all the way up. The name Leclair still hangs there, a splinter in the back of my mind. Familiar, but blurred, like a face seen through smoke. I can't place it, and the not knowing grates worse than if I had.

Before the day gets away from me, I spread blueprints across the kitchen table. The warehouse schematics are clean, too clean. Wide bays, rows of storage, clear corridors marked in neat blue lines. But I know better—walls shift, doors get locked, shadows cut corners the plans don't show. I trace the outline with my finger, memorizing choke points, entries, and exits. If something goes bad, paper maps won't save me, but knowing where the bones of the place are will.

By the time the light slants in through the window, the chores are calling. Horses fed, stalls mucked, water troughs filled until the surface ripples clean. There's something grounding in it, the rhythm of sweat and hay dust, the steady breath of the animals. Work I can see and finish with my own two hands, unlike the questions chewing at me about Leclair.

When the clock pushes past ten, I wash the grit off, trade my worn jeans for cleaner ones, and grab my hat from the peg. The red truck rumbles to life, coughing once before it settles into its steady growl.

Today's the official walk-through at the warehouse. I've played the game enough times to know it'll all look polished on the sur-face—guards at their posts, visitor logs neat and up to date, security checks logged right on schedule. But paper doesn't hide everything. Protocols bend. Corners get cut. And if Leclair's name means what I think it might, those cracks will show. All I have to do is be watching when they do.The warehouse squats at the edge of Harrington like it grew out of the concrete itself, big block walls and a chain-link fence that sags in places. A flag snaps lazy in the breeze above the guard shack. To most people, it probably looks ordinary. To me, every detail's a tell.

The guard at the gate straightens when he sees the truck, his eyes flicking to my badge before he even asks. That earns him a point. His uniform's crisp, though his boots are worn down to the stitching. His partner leans against the wall, bored, one hand wrapped around a cup that smells more like bourbon than coffee. That one I file away.

I roll the window down, hand over my credentials, let the silence stretch until the guard actually checks the hologram instead of just waving me through. Another point. When he passes it back, I lean over the clipboard and sign the visitor log. That's when I see it.

Clara Hayes. Signed in this morning. Independent inspector, neat handwriting, badge number logged.

I let my finger rest against the entry a second too long. So she's here now. Not coincidence.

"Morning, Beau," the Head of Security greets me at the entrance, a thickset man with a clipboard tucked under his arm. His handshake is firm, his eyes watchful. "Appreciate you coming out early. We'll do a full walk-through—show you the lay of the land before Mr. Leclair gets here."

"That's the idea," I say, adjusting my hat as I fall in step beside him.

We move down a narrow corridor, the windows along the office wing opening out to the floor below. I glance through every set of blinds we pass. A woman in accounts keeps her head bent low over a calculator. Another office is too neat, files squared off in impossible stacks. No wasted motion, no easy tells.

The air shifts as we step into the dock bay, the sharp smell of diesel mixing with cardboard and dust. That's when I see her.

Clara.

She stands near the receiving desk, notebook in hand, head tilted just so as she watches a worker tally pallets. Her posture is precise, her notes neat, but there's a weight behind her eyes that isn't just professional. Serious, yes. Focused. But something else too. Something I need to put a name to before it catches me off guard.

"Inspection's got everybody sharp today," the Head of Security mutters beside me, oblivious to the way my attention's fixed on her.

"Looks that way," I answer, eyes narrowing as I watch her scribble another line.

She doesn't look up, not yet. But the way she occupies the space tells me she's not here to play dress-up as some clipboard warrior. She's here for something that matters. And if I'm right, it's something that runs a whole lot deeper than compliance checklists.

"Conference room," I say as we move past the dock, my tone casual but deliberate. "Figure I ought to know where Leclair's meeting is set. No sense guarding a door I haven't seen."

The Head of Security nods. "Back wing, near the offices. Tucked away to keep things quiet."

Figures. Out of the way, controlled, no traffic unless you want it. We cut back through a narrow hall, blinds tilted just enough to give me glimpses into offices—desks too tidy, computers locked, files squared in neat stacks. Everything staged.

He stops halfway down, raps lightly on a doorframe. "Ms. Hayes," he says, stepping in. "Thought it best to make an introduction. This is Beau Maddox. He's been brought in to oversee security for Mr. Leclair's visit."

The woman inside looks up, steady and unflinching. Clara Hayes. I'd marked her earlier on the dock, but seeing her here, seated behind a stack of notes like she belongs, drives the point deeper. She isn't skimming the surface—she's dug in. And judging by the bristle in her stare, she doesn't plan on moving.

"Ma'am," I say, dipping my head, hat in hand.

Her eyes narrow a fraction, though her tone stays cool. "Beau, is it? And you'll be responsible for...?"

"Security," I answer, leaning on the back of a chair just enough to look casual. "My job's to keep things running safe while Mr. Leclair's in town."

"Of course." She sets her pen across the top of her notes, posture precise. "Clara Hayes. Independent inspection. I'll be reviewing compliance and procedures ahead of his arrival. We all have our roles."

I let a faint grin tug at my mouth, holding her gaze a moment longer than polite. "Looks like yours is making sure the rest of us don't cut corners."

She doesn't return the grin. Instead, her head tilts just slightly, like she's measuring the weight of my words. "And which firm do you work for, Beau? Harrington's not exactly known for its private security talent."

I shrug, slow and easy. "Plenty of firms out there."

"That wasn't an answer." Her voice stays calm, but her pen taps once against the clipboard, steady as a metronome.

I match her silence for a beat too long, then let the corner of my mouth twitch. "You always this nosy on an inspection?"

"Only when the details matter."

The amusement fades from my grin, leaving something steadier in its place. I straighten off the chair, meeting her eyes head-on. "Orion," I say at last, the word landing between us like a stone dropped in water.

Her pen stills. For a heartbeat, nothing moves in her expression—just the faint flicker in her eyes, too quick for anyone but me to catch.

"Then I suppose," she says lightly, almost too lightly, "we'll be seeing a lot more of each other."

"Looks that way," I answer, tipping my hat.

The walk-through runs its course. I keep my pace easy, my questions simple, but I don't miss a thing. Fire exits propped with wedges. Cameras angled a hair too high, leaving blind spots along the south corridor. A guard signing a checklist without looking at it. On the surface it all shines, but the seams are right there if you know where to press.

By the time I climb back into the truck, the sun's sliding low, staining Harrington in shades of copper and rust. I roll the window down, let the evening air cut through the lingering warehouse grit. The drive stretches open, two-lane blacktop running straight as a rifle barrel toward the ranch.

Halfway back, my phone buzzes on the dash. I glance at the screen and answer, letting the corner of my mouth lift. "Hey, Quinnie."

"Don't call me that," she says immediately, though the laugh in her voice gives her away. "You know I hate it."

"Yeah, I know. That's why I do it." I settle back in the seat, one arm hooked over the wheel. "So how's Driftwood? Running that bookstore keeping you out of trouble?"

"Mostly. Though you'd laugh—last week I had to break up a shouting match over Romantasy versus Dark Romance. Two women nearly came to blows in the fantasy aisle."

A grin tugs at me. "Figures. You swap knives for novels and still end up refereeing fights."

"Hey, don't knock it. Wings and fangs bring out the worst in people. I've seen cartel bosses with less passion."

That pulls a laugh out of me, low and genuine. "Sounds vicious."

"Occupational hazard," she fires back, tone playful. Then, after a beat: "You could use one of those. An actual hazard that doesn't involve saving the world. Might knock some of that all-work, no-fun attitude out of you."

"Somebody's gotta keep the wolves from the door," I mutter, though the corner of my mouth betrays me with a grin.

"And somebody's gotta remind you you're still human."

I shake my head, warmth slipping in under the banter. "You've been bossy since the day you could walk."

"Please. You loved it," she shoots back. "You'd be lost without me keeping you in line."

"Maybe," I admit, the ranch gates coming into view. "But you're still my little sister."

"And you're still my favorite pain in the ass," she says without missing a beat.

The line goes quiet for a moment, not awkward but comfortable, the kind of silence that only belongs to family. Gravel crunches under my tires as I turn down the drive.

"Get some rest, Quinnie," I say finally.

"You too, big brother. Try not to do anything stupid."

Her laugh lingers in my ear even after I end the call, warmer than the fading light spilling over the fields. For a moment, the mess of Harrington feels far away.

Chapter 12
Clara

Morning comes hard and bright as I drive toward the Red Haven warehouse, the sky a flat, merciless blue that makes everything look sharper than it ought to. The building sits back off the county road like a stern promise—steel siding, concrete apron, loading docks numbered in faded paint. A chain-link fence runs the perimeter, topped with barbed wire; cameras perch on poles like silent gulls.

At the front entrance, two receptionists sit behind a low counter under a bank of security monitors. I step forward, badge in hand—not the Orion lanyard this time but the temporary Red Haven visitor pass the dining director arranged. My credentials meet their screen and a clerk keys my name in, eyes flicking up to me as if checking that I look the part. "Ms. Hayes, escort will meet you at the dock," she says, handing over a laminated badge and a clipboard to sign. Her tone is professional, practiced. No surprise here; they expect inspections.

A young man in a neon vest appears within minutes—short, efficient, polite enough, introducing himself as Marco from Receiving. He clips a radio to his belt and leads me across the lot. The dock is a hive of motion: forklifts lift and set, pallet jacks squeak, men in red polos shout counts and nod to drivers as trailers tilt down. Heat rises from the concrete in waves, and diesel fumes braid with the iron scent of the warehouse. Marco keeps his pace steady, glancing back at me every so often as if to confirm I'm still there.

"Someone from campus put you up to this?" he asks conversationally, voice pitched low over the din. I keep my reply short. "Routine inspection." That's all I give.

The first thing I do once I'm positioned at the edge of the dock is clock exits. Two main loading bays face the apron, numbered one and two, with roller doors that lift on command. A side door on the north end opens onto a gated service alley; a smaller pedestrian door with keypad access sits near office windows. Cameras focus on the bays, but their blind spots are obvious if you know where to look—angles that miss the shadowed corridor leading to a secondary loading area. My pen is already moving.

Manifests are checked openly at the receiving desk—truck plate, driver name, SKUs. The scanner beeps, steady and rhythmic, meant to be comforting in its predictability. Most drivers follow the drill without hesitation.

Another Red Haven trailer backs into the dock, logo stamped bold across the side like the rest. On the surface, it blends in. Routine. But when the sun shifts, I catch it—low near the bumper, half-hidden under grime. A flower, faint but deliberate. Familiar, though I can't place why.

The driver moves with a practiced economy, handing Marco a printed manifest. Clean enough on the surface, but the margins are crowded with pencil scribbles—alterations disguised as notes, the kind meant to slip past a casual eye. Marco doesn't blink. He scans, nods, and signals for two men to move the load.

Instead of the staging area, the pallets veer straight for the shadowed corridor. A secondary door groans shut behind them, cutting the shipment from sight. The floor keeps moving like nothing's happened. But my gut knows better.

A supervisor in a hardhat notices my attention and moves closer—too close to be casual. He's all measured smiles and clipped responses when I catch him looking: "We run late loads sometimes, Ms. Hayes. Preference of the client." I make a neutral note about client preference and watch him walk away. His shoulders are tight, his eyes roam to the cameras as if checking who's watching who. That small nervous motion is a detail I file away.

I count the coolers and walk-ins set into the back wall—three full-size walk-ins, two reach-ins, and a refrigerated staging room. Temperature log clipboards hang at each door. I glance down: daily entries, signatures, times—mostly tidy. One log has a gap in the early hours and a hurried signature stamped later, written in different ink. I copy the times into my notebook.

Uniforms are mostly compliant—reflective vests, steel-toe boots, high-visibility gear—but there are cracks. A man slips by in worn sneakers, another peels his vest off once he's past the desk. Forklifts cut corners, loads roll without proper straps, manifests are stacked carelessly, some even signed in pencil. Small violations on their own, but they add up fast when you move this much product.

So I watch. I track the rhythm of trucks pulling in, the way manifests overlap with pallets, the flow of work that's supposed to look seamless. Hours later, the crew from the trailer with the faint flower marking finally emerges from the side door. The plain boxes they carried in are no longer plain—now they wear fresh Red Haven barcodes, labels slapped over the brown wrap. A stamp, a date, a new SKU.

Suddenly legitimate.

Re-tagging shipments in a hidden corridor. Exactly the kind of irregularity my cover story told me to watch for.

When Marco checks in with me, he keeps his tone guarded but professional. "Everything's normal now. Anything you need?" I hand him back his radio with a smile that doesn't soften the inquiry.

"I'll need copies of the manifests for the last three nights, and access to the secondary transit logs. Also the driver roster for the past month."

He hesitates fractionally, then nods. "I'll get those for you."

I sign the clipboard, badge clipped back on, my notebook thicker than when I arrived. The warehouse runs like a well-oiled machine when someone is watching, but I've marked the seams where the oil leaks.

In the office, the shift is immediate. The air smells of stale coffee and toner, binders lined up too neatly on the shelves. A supervisor in a navy polo meets me with a stiff smile.

"You'll see our reports are current," he says, sliding a folder across the desk. "Variance logs were corrected last week."

I flip through, noting the pristine headers, the pages too fresh to have been handled much. "Corrected," I repeat. "Yet these substitutions don't match the pallet counts I observed this morning."

"That's a clerical error," another manager cuts in, voice sharper. "We're moving volume here, things slip."

"Clerical errors don't reappear month after month." I jot a note without looking up. "I'll need the original manifests, not reprints."

The two men exchange a glance, one shrugging, the other pressing his lips tight.

"This inspection," I continue evenly, "was scheduled in light of Mr. Leclair's upcoming visit. I'll be reviewing my findings with him directly."

That gets them. Their composure flickers, the easy smiles tightening. One finally mutters, "If that's necessary, of course."

"It is," I say, snapping the folder shut. The managers scatter once I've closed my notebook. I take a steadying breath, letting the silence of the office settle, when a knock sounds at the open door.

"Ms. Hayes," the security manager says, stepping in. "Thought it best to make an introduction. This is Beau Maddox. He's been brought in to oversee security for Mr. Leclair's visit."

The man who follows him makes my stomach tighten. Broad-shouldered, dark hair brushing his collar, hat in his hand. Recognition snaps into place—the red truck, the diner, the bar.

"Ma'am," he says, dipping his head, hat in hand.

I don't blink, though every instinct tells me to watch him closer. "Beau, is it? And you'll be responsible for...?"

"Security," he answers, leaning on the back of a chair just enough to look casual. "My job's to keep things running safe while Mr. Leclair's in town."

"Of course." I set my pen across the top of my notes, posture precise, everything controlled. "Clara Hayes. Independent inspection. I'll be reviewing compliance and procedures ahead of his arrival. We all have our roles."

He grins faintly, holding my gaze longer than necessary. "Looks like yours is making sure the rest of us don't cut corners."

I don't give him the satisfaction of a smile. Instead, I tilt my head, cool, measuring. "And which firm do you work for, Beau? Harrington's not exactly known for its private security talent."

He shrugs, slow and easy. "Plenty of firms out there."

"That wasn't an answer." My voice stays calm, clipped. Steady. Deliberate. A warning to myself as much as to him.

He lets the silence stretch, playing the game. Then the corner of his mouth twitches. "You always this nosy on an inspection?"

"Only when the details matter."

The grin fades, replaced by something steadier. He straightens, eyes fixed on mine. "Orion."

The word lands like a gut punch. My hand stills mid-tap, but I keep my face neutral, the mask intact. Inside, I'm cursing hard enough to taste it. Orion. Not just me. They've doubled the net, and they didn't tell me. Which means I'm not trusted. Which means I'm being measured. Again.

"Then I suppose," I say lightly, almost too lightly, forcing a small curve into my lips, "we'll be seeing a lot more of each other."

"Looks that way," he answers, tipping his hat.

I mark something down on the clipboard without looking at the page, just to keep my hands moving. The script is clean, the posture precise, but my pulse hasn't settled. Orion thinks shadowing me will keep me sharp. What they don't realize is it makes me reckless.

The rest of the walk-through passes in a blur. I keep my expression professional, though Beau's grin lingers at the edge of my thoughts. By the time I make it back to the front desk, the building feels cooler, quieter, as if it's holding its breath.

The receptionist glances up with a quick smile. "Ms. Hayes, everything satisfactory today?"

I return the smile, setting my notebook on the counter. "Productive. I'll be finalizing my notes this evening. Mr. Leclair is due tomorrow?"

She checks her screen and nods. "Yes, ma'am. His arrival's confirmed for the morning. You're on the schedule to meet with him here at ten."

"Perfect." I sign the visitor log, neat and precise. "I'll be ready."

She turns back to her screen, already distracted by another message pinging through. While her attention flickers, I let my pen slide across the counter, nudging the lanyard draped over its edge. A badge, generic, worn smooth from use. My hand closes over it casually, as if I were only gathering my things. The receptionist doesn't notice; her typing fills the silence.

The badge is warm in my palm by the time I slip it into my jacket pocket. A small key to a larger door.

I thank her, polite as ever, and make my way out. The hum of the building fades behind me, replaced by the heavy heat of Harrington's evening air. Tomorrow, I'll sit across from Victor Leclair himself. But tonight, I'll be back—alone, with time to pull apart the seams they worked so hard to hide.

Chapter 13
Beau

Sleep never comes easy. Tonight it doesn't come at all. I drift for maybe an hour before the sweat hits, cold and sharp, clinging to my shirt like a second skin. The joint barely dulls it.

The dream takes its time, creeping in slow. At first it's quiet, just the hum of desert wind and the crunch of boots on sand. Then the smell hits—oil, blood, gunpowder baked into the heat. I know this place. I've walked it a hundred times, both in daylight and in memory.

I see my unit ahead, silhouettes moving through the shimmer, all shoulders and shadows. Their laughter carries over the comms, warped by static, half there and half gone. I call out, but the words never reach them. They keep moving forward. Then the sound cuts. A blast follows. The world folds in on itself, noise and light swallowing everything.

When it clears, I'm the only one left standing. The ground is blackened. The air tastes like ash. I look down and realize my hands are clean. Too clean. That's always what gets me. The part where I'm untouched and they're gone.

I wake choking on it, heart pounding like I've been running instead of lying flat in bed. The sheets are twisted, damp, a noose around my legs. I sit there breathing hard, waiting for the world to steady. It doesn't.

The house is too quiet. Out here, every creak carries, every shift of wind against the siding sounds bigger than it is. The silence presses harder because of it. I brew coffee strong enough to strip paint, sit with it on the porch, and let the smoke curl into the dark. It fogs my head but doesn't settle me. Doesn't touch whatever gnaws under my ribs.

It's been years since I left the service, but the guilt never made the trip home. It stayed behind, buried with them. Every night I tell myself I came back to take care of the farm, to keep what's left of my family from falling apart. Still feels like I traded one battlefield for another.

The clock blinks two-thirty. Victor's jet is due just after sunrise, and Dallas is a four-hour haul. No point lying back down.

Jeans, boots, hat. Routine in the dark. My hands move on their own, the kind of muscle memory built from years of leaving in the dead of night.

The truck coughs awake, headlights carving through the gravel drive. I ease onto the road, the ranch vanishing behind me in the rearview.

The highway stretches long and empty, blacktop shining under the beams, mile markers ticking past like clock hands. Out here it's nothing but dark fields and the occasional pair of glowing eyes on the roadside. Four hours of asphalt and my own thoughts before I hit Dallas.

My muscles stay coiled tight, anticipation for the job riding under my skin. I tick the information I know in my head, piece by piece, reviewing the plan like a litany. Security checks. Arrival schedule. Chain of command. Backup exit if things sour. Over and over, until the rhythm settles in, steady as the hum of tires on the asphalt.

But no matter how many times I cycle through it, Clara keeps edging in. The set of her shoulders on the dock, the sharp look in her eyes when we were introduced. She's too precise to be ordinary, too controlled to be just an inspector with a clipboard. Every move she made told me she was there for more than compliance.

I shift in my seat, jaw tight, the wheel steady under my hands. The job's supposed to be simple: protect Leclair, make sure the visit runs clean. Variables complicate things. And Clara Hayes feels like a variable with teeth.

The glow of Dallas creeps up over the horizon by the time I hit the edge of the city. I take the turnoff for the private airstrip, headlights sweeping over chain-link and razor wire. Security waves me through the gate, my badge flashing in the light, and I roll into the hangar as the first gray streaks of dawn cut across the sky.

The air reeks of jet fuel and oil, the kind of mix that settles into your clothes and stays there. I park near the hangar, kill the engine, and step out into the heat. The hum of turbines vibrates through the pavement. Across the tarmac, an SUV idles in the corner, headlights off, windows tinted dark.

I cross to it, boots echoing against the concrete, and rest a hand on the hood—warm from sitting too long. The driver gives a short nod but says nothing. We both watch as the jet rounds the bend, its lights cutting through the haze like a blade.

The engines wind down to a low growl. Everything in me tightens, a muscle memory I can't shake. The smell, the sound, the waiting—it all feels too familiar. Another arrival. Another operation about to turn.

The jet door lowers with a hiss, engines winding down as Victor Leclair steps into the hangar lights. Mid-fifties, trim build, suit tailored to perfection. Silver hair combed back sharp, every line deliberate. But it's the eyes that pin me—cold gray, restless, cataloging everything in sight like the hangar's just another chessboard.

I move forward, hat in hand. "Mr. Leclair. Beau Maddox. I'll be overseeing your security while you're in town."

His gaze brushes over me like I'm another uniform, not worth a second thought. No handshake. No word. Just the faintest sneer curls at the corner of his mouth before he looks past me.

The woman at his side steps in, tablet already open. "Mr. Leclair's schedule is full today. You'll coordinate through me." Her voice is clipped, efficient, used to filling the silence he leaves behind.

I let a beat pass before answering. "Then make sure he knows the warehouse has been checked. I'll walk him through protocols myself."

She doesn't look down, doesn't type a note. "That visit will be rescheduled. Another meeting takes precedence. Tomorrow, perhaps."

My jaw tightens, but I tip my hat anyway. "Tomorrow, then."

Victor keeps moving toward the waiting SUV, never sparing me more than that first flick of his eyes. The assistant gestures toward the waiting SUV. "You'll ride with us."

I climb in, sliding into the back opposite Leclair. He sits angled toward the window, posture loose but controlled, like he's not wasting an ounce of energy on me. His assistant claims the seat beside him, tablet balanced on her knees, voice low as she scrolls through his schedule.

The first stop is a glossy office tower in downtown. No mention of it in the brief Marcus gave me. I get thirty seconds to sweep the lobby before Leclair is whisked inside, already surrounded by men in suits.

Another stop follows, different building, same treatment. I'm kept close enough to look official, not close enough to overhear.

Back in the SUV, the real conversations happen in hushed French. Names of companies I don't recognize. Numbers, contracts, shipment dates—all spoken like code meant to pass unnoticed. They don't bother hiding it, assuming I can't follow. My expression stays schooled, gaze fixed out the window, but every word clicks into place. I keep count, file details away for later.

We roll south, miles eating under the tires. Killeen. Austin. Each time, another office, another closed door. I'm given just enough access to do a cursory sweep, not enough to dig. It grates—half measures never kept anyone alive.

From Austin, we turn west, the sun dropping low over the hills as the road bends toward Harrington. The assistant keeps talking in low French, Leclair answering with the ease of a man giving orders he expects to be followed. I keep my expression blank, but every word filters through clean. They don't know I understand, and I plan to keep it that way.

When the SUV finally slows, it isn't at a hotel or even a private estate—it's the Harrington University campus. We roll past manicured lawns and iron gates until the vehicle eases up in front of the presidential housing, a stately brick residence that looks more like a donor's prize than school property.

Of course. They keep him here when he visits—close to the board, close to the president, close to the checkbooks. Safer to flatter him with prestige than risk him wandering too far.

The assistant slips out first, smoothing her jacket as she circles back to open his door. Leclair doesn't rush. He adjusts his cuff, steps out like the whole place was built to impress him personally, and takes in the grounds with the faintest nod.

I climb out opposite, scanning the perimeter. Two of his guards fall into step like they own the place. They're competent, but they're not reading the angles I am.

"This place gets cleared before he steps foot inside," I say flat, catching both men's eyes. "I want the upstairs swept, basement too. Windows locked, doors checked."

They hesitate, glancing toward the assistant like they need her permission. I don't give them the chance. "Now."

One peels off without a word, the other a beat later. I turn back to her. "If he's staying here, it's under my eyes. I'll run the sweep myself."

Her lips press thin, but she nods. "Very well. Just don't delay the schedule."

I don't answer, already moving through the front door. The place smells of polish and old money, halls lined with portraits of men who built their reputations on tuition and donations. Perfect stage for Leclair.

The sweep runs quiet at first. Upstairs, rooms are set for show—beds turned down, towels folded crisp, not a hair out of place. Downstairs, the study reeks of furniture wax, shelves stacked with volumes no one's touched in years.

But in the back hall, I catch it. A latch left loose on a side window, just wide enough someone with patience could slip it. Nothing obvious, but enough.

I slide it shut, twist until the lock clicks firm. One of the guards trails me, and I make sure he sees it. "This is the kind of thing that gets men killed. Next time, it doesn't wait for me to find it."

His face hardens, a flicker of embarrassment there, and he nods once. Good. The rest of the sweep turns up clean—no unlocked doors, no hidden company. When I circle back to the front, the assistant's waiting, tablet in hand, eyes sharp with impatience.

"All clear," I tell her. "He can stay here tonight. Safely."

She inclines her head like it's nothing more than a box ticked, then turns to usher Leclair inside.

I watch them step through the polished doorway, my gut telling me the unlocked latch wasn't carelessness. It was an invitation.

Chapter 14
Beau

The assistant starts to follow him inside, but I cut her off.

"Schedule for tomorrow," I say. My tone leaves no room for argument.

She blinks, clutching her folder tighter. "Mr. Leclair's itinerary is managed internally. You'll be updated when necessary."

I take a step closer, slow enough to press the point. "No. I don't play catch-up. If I'm covering him, I get every detail. Hour by hour. Where he's going, who he's meeting, how long he's there. Otherwise, you're asking me to protect him blind."

Her lips press thin. "He doesn't appreciate interference."

"Then he'll just have to appreciate being alive."

That lands. She exhales, opens the folder, and smooths the page with reluctant fingers. "Breakfast with the university president at ten. Meeting with the Board of Regents. Lunch with donors. Afternoon tour of Red Haven's Harrington warehouse. Dinner—private. Not specified." She flips to another note tucked in the file. "And a compliance briefing, rescheduled for tomorrow morning at the presidential house. Eight o'clock sharp. With the independent inspector."

Clara Hayes.

I keep my expression steady, but the name scratches in the back of my mind. Her again.

"Private dinner's a hole in your plan," I say evenly. "I want the name, the place, and the time before sunrise."

She hesitates, eyes flashing irritation before she nods. "Very well."

"Good." I step back, giving her space to retreat. She slips inside, the door shutting soft behind her.

I stand in the quiet, letting the weight of the schedule settle. Leclair's movements are dressed up as business, but every polished stop is another stage, another mask. Tomorrow, I'll find out which ones crack.

I don't head off campus. Not yet. My truck's still sitting at the Dallas airstrip, and hitching a ride back with Leclair's entourage isn't my style. Besides, men like him draw shadows after dark, and I'd rather see them coming than wake up to the fallout.

The presidential house glows soft against the manicured lawns, all warm lamps and polished brick, like the university's own crown jewel. Too neat. Too exposed.

I find a quiet spot across the quad, where the oaks hang heavy and the security lights don't quite reach. Close enough to keep eyes on the comings and goings. Far enough to stay overlooked.

From here, the place looks like what it's meant to be—safe, prestigious, untouchable. My gut says otherwise.

So I wait, leaning into the shadows, watching the doors, the windows, the pattern of lights switching off one by one. Every detail logged, every movement filed away.

Tomorrow the schedule plays out. But tonight, I'll be the one keeping watch.

The guards move in predictable loops—two at the front walk, another circling the perimeter in staggered passes. They're competent enough, but not alert. Not like men who know trouble when it's close.

Through an upstairs window, muffled voices drift down. French. I catch enough to piece it together. Orders. Caution. And then, clear as a bell: *Elle est ici.* She's here.

I keep my pulse steady. They don't know I planted the bug in Victor's suite before the sweep ended—slid under the lip of his desk, a sliver no thicker than a fingernail. Every word feeds into my receiver, his voice calm and measured, the assistant's tone clipped and deferential.

Headlights cut across the quad, and a car rolls up the drive. Too late for a donor, too early for morning staff. The driver's side door opens, and a woman steps out, tall coat cinched tight, blonde hair catching a shard of light before she dips her head. Her stride is sharp, deliberate, confident enough to be dangerous.

Recognition prickles the back of my neck, though the angle and the dark keep her face hidden. I can't place her clean. But something about the way she moves tells me I should.

She doesn't knock. One of the guards peels the door open for her, and she slips inside without a word.

I lean back deeper into the shadows, jaw tight. Whoever she is, she isn't here for charity. And if Victor's muttering about "she's here" connects to her, then tomorrow's going to bleed complications.

I slip the earpiece deeper, the tiny receiver warm against my skin. The bug I planted under the desk is doing its job—the room is a thin, bright line of sound in my head, voices layered and low, the clink of glass, the whisper of coats. I've never heard the woman's voice before, but something in it hits like shrapnel—precise, cold, and aimed to wound.

Through the static come fragments—French, then English, then French again—phrases that make the hairs on my arms rise.

"Livraison spéciale," a man says—special delivery.

"Treize femmes," the woman answers, deliberate. Thirteen women.

"Projet spécial," another voice. Special project.

"Côte du Maine," the assistant murmurs flatly. Coastal Maine.

A pause, then: "Pour lui." For him.

My stomach knots. Coastal Maine. For him. The words stitch into something I don't want to see.

More details thread through, softer but no less lethal. "Cache candy pour distribution Upper East Coast," the woman says—code, maybe, or something meant to sound harmless. A shuffle of paper. "Armes en transit," another voice adds—arms in transit, weapons shipment.

They argue timing, windows, routes. Names flicker. A freight broker. A number. "Dans la semaine. Avant la pleine lune." Within the week. Before the full moon. Scheduling like they're booking freight, not consigning people and weapons. The casualness is worse than any shout.

The assistant presses about manifests. The reply is clipped: "Étiquettes changées. Nouveau SKU. Pas de trace." Labels changed, new SKU. No trace.

I sit back against the oak, receiver hissing faint in my ear. Thirteen women. A "special project" bound for some coastal town in Maine. Weapons shipment. Cache candy for the Upper East. All of it tied to him. Whoever that is.

My jaw tightens. This isn't Leclair playing international businessman. This is infrastructure. And if tomorrow's schedule is cover for it, then I'm walking into something far worse than dirty contracts.

I ease the earpiece out, the voices fading to a hiss before I cut the receiver dead. Silence presses in, heavy after what I just heard. My pulse hasn't slowed, not really. Thirteen women. Coastal Maine. Weapons, candy, a special project for him. It runs in a loop I can't shut off.

When my watch is up, I make the slow walk across the courtyard. The presidential house glows warm behind me, all polished windows and false calm. My assigned quarters are nothing like it—a spare room in the adjacent staff building, meant for traveling detail. Cot, desk, single lamp. Barely a step above a storage closet, but four walls and a lock are all I need.

I close the door behind me, lean against it for a beat, then drop onto the cot. The springs complain, thin mattress sagging, but I don't bother undressing. My eyes fix on the ceiling, but it's not blank up there. It never is.

The words from tonight keep circling—*treize femmes... pour lui.* But what claws deeper is the way it stirs old ghosts.

A job from years back. Border town, cartel safehouse. We were supposed to secure the intel, extract the hostages, get out clean. But clean didn't happen. One wrong sound, one nervous guard with his finger too tight on the trigger, and the room turned red.

I remember the rush of it—adrenaline burning white through my veins, the clarity sharper than any drug. Every shot placed, every body dropping exactly where I put them. I stopped counting after six. Stopped thinking, too. Justice, kill, justice, kill—it all blurred until I wasn't sure which I was chasing anymore.

When it was over, I stood in the wreckage, chest heaving, pistol warm in my grip. And for a second—just a second—I wanted more. Another fight. Another body. Anything to keep that clarity burning.

That's the part that haunts me. Not the blood. Not the screams. The way it almost felt *good*.

I force a slow breath, fists clenching against the thin blanket. That was the night I promised myself I'd never go back full time. Not unless I had to. Because once you start enjoying it, the line between hunter and monster gets too damn thin.

The ceiling hums faint with the building's old wiring, steady as a heartbeat. I hold on to it, anchor myself in the silence.

But sleep won't come. Not with ghosts at my shoulder and a fresh list of horrors waiting in the morning.

Chapter 15
Clara

Sleep never comes easy in places like this. The walls are too thin, the carpets too old, the air heavy with someone else's years. I lie awake in the motel bed, staring at the ceiling fan creaking overhead, and know I'm not going to rest until I see what's behind that secondary corridor.

I roll out quietly, pulling on dark clothes, gloves snug, hair tied back. The badge I lifted earlier presses cool against my palm as I slip it into my pocket. One card, one chance to move without alarms.

The clerk at the desk barely stirs when I cross the lobby. I take the side exit anyway, the one that doesn't groan. Outside, the air is damp, carrying the hum of insects and the faint tang of diesel drifting from the highway. Harrington sleeps. I don't. Tonight, I go back to the warehouse.

The badge flashes green at the gate. Inside, the night shift is thin—forklifts idle, operators leaning back with thermoses, more interested in killing time than watching corners. Good. I move slow, shadows my cover, small flashlight dimmed to the lowest beam.

Voices cut across the bay. Two men. Their boots scuff the concrete as they head my way. I flatten against a stack of pallets, heart steady but sharp in my chest. One hums under his breath, the other taps a cigarette against his palm, grip loose with boredom. They wheel a pallet straight past me, close enough I catch the tang of smoke on his jacket. Neither so much as glances my way. Careless. Too confident no one's watching.

When their footsteps fade, I slip to the side door. The metal groans faintly as I ease it open just wide enough to slide through. The corridor smells of oil and dust. Pallets loom in the dark, boxes stacked neat and wrong. Labels crooked, ink too fresh.

I crouch, slide my knife under a sticker, and peel it back. Beneath is a faded barcode, brown and old. Not replaced. Covered. Photos taken, fragment bagged, label smoothed flat. Enough to raise suspicion. Not enough to close the loop. I sweep my light further, tracing the concrete wall. That's when I see it—metal seams, faint, a door disguised as part of the wall. No handle. No label. And definitely not on the building plans I reviewed.

I run my fingers along the seam until I find the catch, a recessed panel no bigger than a coin. The multitool fits clean, and with a firm twist, the door unlatches.

It swings open on hydraulics, smooth and silent. Not a side room. A passage. Wide, reinforced concrete, sloping down at a gradual angle. Just enough pitch to keep you moving forward, but broad enough for pallets, carts, even a small vehicle if needed.

The air hits different the moment I step through—cooler, filtered, the faint tang of ozone and chemical cleaners. A low hum rolls up the corridor, mechanical and steady, undercut by something sharper. Voices. Distant, layered.

I stand still, letting my ears adjust. The sound isn't storage silence. It's industry. Activity. Movement.

I ease a few steps inside, staying tight to the wall. Overhead, strip lights glow faint behind wire cages, enough to mark the path but not bright enough to be welcoming. My pulse hammers as I take in what this means. This isn't an add-on or a maintenance tunnel. It's infrastructure. Built for traffic. Built to stay hidden.

I press along the service corridor until a plain steel door stands half-ajar, its hinge whispering from a previous shove. No keypad, no guard. I slip inside on the hush of corridor noise, shoulder checking it closed behind me. The room opens into low light and quiet power—rows of cabinets and open crates stacked high along the walls. The air smells of oil and gunmetal. Rifles, sidearms, and blades gleam under the caged lights, all tagged, cataloged, ready for transport. Enough firepower to arm a small battalion. My stomach knots. Whatever Red Haven's moving through here isn't protection—it's preparation.

I pick something small. A pistol would be heavy and awkward to jam under a jacket; a dagger fits the need better—silent, easy to sheath, no trigger to clink. Fingers slide along the foam until my hand closes on cold metal: a compact combat dagger, tanto point, full tang, scale grips worn smooth. It fits in my palm like it was made for me.

There's a tiny mark near the hilt, pressed into the metal as if stamped before heat treated: a simple flower, five petals, the center a dot. Same motif I saw on the trailer, only cleaner here, forged not painted. Familiar enough to hitch my throat but not clear enough to name.

Someone laughs out in the corridor, the sound too close. I freeze, then move slow. The dagger slides into the small sheath at my waist and rides flat against my hip. No bulk. No clatter. My jacket settles over it like nothing is there.

I wait until the footsteps pass, close enough I can feel the floor vibrate under me, then edge back to the doorway. The corridor yawns on; the hum pulls like a promise. I take two more steps and tuck myself against the concrete, breath shallow, listening. Voices cross the space—men swapping coordinates, someone swearing softly. They never come down this far. They assume the secondary corridor is safe.

The dagger rides snug against my ribs as I press forward, deeper into the tunnel. The hum grows sharper, layered now with voices that rise and fall in uneven rhythm. One cuts through, clear even at a distance.

Female. Confident. Familiar enough that my stomach knots. I slow, steps feather-light, and edge toward the glow bleeding under a doorframe. A slit in the metal lets me peer inside. The air hits me first—stale, sour with sweat and fear. Rows of cages line the walls, women packed inside, some huddled, some clutching one another, tears streaking their faces.

The sight slams into me hard, colder than any steel in this place. A woman paces in front of them, phone pressed to her ear. Her heels click against the concrete, each turn sharp and precise. "Yes," she says, voice smooth, detached. "The order's confirmed. A special request. Coastal Maine. Driftwood." She pauses, listening. A faint smile curves her lips. "Delivery within the month. Consider it handled."

The women in the cages flinch at her words, though she doesn't spare them a glance. She turns on her heel again, long coat swaying, the cadence of her stride one I know too well. The sound crawls into my chest, scraping old memories raw. I retreat half a step, breath locked tight in my lungs, forcing my pulse steady. Whoever she's speaking to, whatever they're arranging—it isn't random. And the fact that Driftwood is in her mouth means this isn't just business. It's personal.

I shift my angle, careful not to let the light catch me. From here, all I see is the sweep of a dark coat as the woman turns, the hem snapping sharp with each pivot. Her voice carries, crisp and commanding.

"Thirteen. Prepare them for transport. The preference request is already filed. No mistakes."

A pause. Another turn. "Yes. Within the week. Make sure they're ready."

The words cut through the room like a blade. The women in the cages flinch, some curling tighter against the bars, others stifling sobs. My fingers tighten around the dagger at my hip, the flower's edge pressing into my palm.

I stay just long enough to etch the image into memory—the cages, the voices, the smell of fear baked into the concrete. Proof, but not something I can fight here. Not now.

Time to move.

I slip back into the shadows of the corridor, retracing each step in silence. Every footfall measured, every breath pressed thin.

The first guard rounds the corner too fast to avoid. His eyes widen, hand going for his weapon. I'm faster. My elbow drives up under his ribs, a sharp exhale leaving his lungs before he can call it in. He folds halfway, and I catch his wrist, twist, and bring the edge of my knife to his throat. A warning, not a kill. He goes still. I ease him down against the wall, unconscious before he hits the floor.

The second one isn't so easy. Boots scuff behind me. I spin as he lunges, catching his forearm before the strike lands. Momentum does the work—I pivot, hook his leg, and drive him sideways into the crate stack. Metal clangs, echo sharp in the narrow space. He swings wild, fist grazing my shoulder. I duck, ram my knee into his stomach, and the sound he makes is a broken wheeze.

I pull the knife free but hold it low, ready if he tries again. He doesn't. I leave him gasping and step over his boot, pulse still hard in my ears.

The badge flashes green at the gate, and the cool night air washes over me like a reprieve I didn't earn.

By the time I reach my Jeep, the dagger rides steady against my ribs, but my pulse hasn't slowed. My fingers feel every inch of its weight, the metal warm from my skin.

Thirteen women. A special request. Driftwood.

The words loop like static in my head, louder than the hum of the engine. Victor's name used to be the target—simple, clean, another operation in a long list of necessary evils. But that was before the numbers, before the crates, before the proof of what Red Haven was really moving through those hidden corridors.

I grip the wheel tighter than I mean to, jaw locked until my teeth ache. The mission isn't just about Victor anymore. It's about who he answers to. What he's protecting. What I've ignored too many times because it wasn't my job to look deeper.

Headlights cut through the dark as I pull out onto the road. My reflection flashes across the windshield—calm, composed, lying. I tell myself this is still a job, that I'll hand the evidence off and let the suits decide what comes next. But the truth slides colder than the dagger's edge.

This stopped being about orders the moment I saw what they were really hiding.

I press harder on the gas, the road unfolding ahead in ribbons of shadow and light, and try not to think about how it always comes down to the same choice: follow orders, or follow what's left of my conscience.

Chapter 16
Clara

Morning comes too soon. Sleep never finds me, not after what I saw in that corridor, but I still dress sharp and precise. Dark slacks, pressed blouse, hair pulled tight. Professional armor. Whatever storm waits for me inside Red Haven, I won't face it looking shaken.

The sun climbs hot over Harrington as I park outside Warehouse #Twenty-Seven. Workers filter in through side entrances, yawning over coffee, oblivious to the rot under their feet. I straighten my jacket, badge clipped where it belongs, and step through the front doors.

The receptionist glances up as I approach, her smile thin and practiced. "Ms. Hayes. You're here for your meeting with Mr. Leclair?"

"I am," I reply, voice cool.

She hesitates, fingers tapping across the keyboard before she looks back at me. "It's been rescheduled. Mr. Leclair had other pressing matters to attend to. Your briefing will now take place tomorrow morning, same time."

The words land like a stone. My expression doesn't flicker. "I see."

"If you'd like, I can arrange space for you to continue your inspection today."

"That won't be necessary," I say evenly. "I'll manage."

I pause just long enough to press my point. "Make a note for his team—tomorrow morning, breakfast at the presidential house. Eight o'clock sharp. We'll cover the Red Haven paperwork then."

The receptionist hesitates, as if weighing whether she has the authority. I slide a single page across the desk, the header stamped with

Orion's acquisition logo. "This meeting is mandatory. I'll be here on time. All he needs to do is sit."

Her shoulders ease. She nods, tucking the page into the folder marked for Leclair's assistant. "I'll be sure it's passed along."

"Good." I offer a smile that doesn't touch my eyes. "That way we won't have to waste another day."

When I step out into the sunlight, the arrangement is already set. Tomorrow morning, Leclair won't sidestep me again—not with Red Haven's future tied to the signature I intend to put across his desk.

My heels click against the polished tile, measured, controlled. Frustration burns underneath—he's here, in Harrington, and already dictating the tempo. But on the surface I remain composed, every inch the inspector making her rounds, filing notes, biding time.

I turn from Warehouse Twenty-Seven and its polite evasions. If Leclair shifts the schedule, I'll set it myself. The university lies on the far side of town, kept deliberately apart from the industrial strip—donors and their gifts polished clean of grit. If he's being housed in the presidential residence, that's where the seams will show: the donations, the favors, the carefully protected image. All the things men like Leclair rely on. All the things I intend to uncover.

I slip into my Jeep and cross town, the streets thinning as I move away from the warehouses and into tree-lined avenues. At the university gate I flash the forged visitor badge I assembled last night, the procurement logo and copied signature doing the work. The guard studies it for a beat, then waves me through. Small-town security trusts credentials more than curiosity. I use that as currency.

The presidential house sits on a low rise, manicured lawn and stone steps meant to impress. It looks like a donor's prize, all brick and columns, with heavy doors and lanterns that throw warm pools of light on the walkway. Inside, a receptionist in a blazer greets me with practiced cordiality. I introduce myself as the compliance inspector sent to verify accommodations for a visiting donor. The smile she returns is the one trained faces give when they believe their world is in order.

They give me a tour. I move with them, gaze soft, mind sharp. Public rooms first: foyer, study, dining room grand enough to seat visiting trustees, reception parlor with portraits of past presidents. Plush carpets hide hardwood that creaks if you know where to listen. She shows me the guest suite he will use—wide windows, private bath, small service kitchenette off the hall. It is designed to flatter, to keep the guest comfortable and visible to the right people.

I ask about staff rotations and cleaning schedules under the pretense of ensuring privacy and service. Which doors staff use, how late contractors are allowed, when the kitchen locks. The house manager answers in schedules and nods. I press on sight lines, camera coverage, and maintenance access. I watch her fumble on the map for any true vulnerabilities and I file that away.

Outside, I walk the perimeter under the soft sun, noting the service entrance, the HVAC intake on the north side, a basement egress half-hidden by shrubbery, a delivery lane that feeds directly to a covered entry. I mark windows that open to the ground, the lantern posts with blind spots, the hedges that would hide a body from casual view.

It all looks tidy and deliberate. Leclair being kept here is convenient to his supporters and to the PR machine. It is also convenient to anyone who wants him close and exposed.

Tomorrow I will be on my feet at first light. Tonight I make a plan. I will sweep it myself, quietly and clean, and I will map the routes that matter. If his removal is going to pull a son out of hiding, I make certain the stage is set.

I step back inside the house manager's office and keep my tone flat, professional. "I need the dining room set for breakfast tomorrow at eight. Mr. Leclair's compliance review will take place there. I'll need a table cleared for documents and space to lay out acquisition memos."

She taps the tablet, obliging. "We'll have coffee and a light spread. I'll alert the kitchen staff."

"And security." I press the point. "Please make sure someone from Mr. Leclair's detail is present for the briefing. I will need the lead to confirm sight lines and staff rotations. Also leave a hard copy of the notice in the guest file and send the calendar invite to his assistant." I slide a single sheet across the desk headed with Orion's acquisition logo, folded so it sits where a human will touch it first.

Her fingers pause, then she nods. "Consider it done. I'll put it on the house calendar and notify his team."

Good. The meeting is now a human thing they cannot ignore. Paper in a hand. A ping on a phone. Tomorrow morning they will have to answer for the rooms, the staff, and the routes I plan to walk.

The Fork & Fiddle smells like fried catfish and biscuits, the kind of scent that settles in the booths and clings to your clothes. A jukebox in the corner wheezes through an old country tune, skipping just enough to grate.

I slide into the first open booth, patched vinyl sighing under my weight. Before I've settled, a young man in an apron hustles over, coffee pot in hand.

"Uh—coffee?" he asks, voice caught between polite and uncertain.

"Not yet." I line up three sugar packets from the caddy, tear them open, then peel the foil tops off three creamers. Only once they're stacked neatly to the side do I slide the cup toward him. "Now you can pour."

He blinks, then obeys, filling it almost to the rim. I stir slowly, set the spoon aside, and take the first sip. Sweet. Precise. The way it has to be.

Before he can hover, a sharp voice cuts from behind the counter. "Tommy Ray, don't make her nervous with that puppy-dog routine. Go top off table three."

The man—Tommy Ray, apparently—flushes pink, mutters something under his breath, and moves off with the coffee pot. The woman who sent him looks to be in her sixties, silver curls pinned in a bun, red lipstick bright as the neon OPEN sign. Her apron is embroidered with a single name over the pocket: MABEL. She grins as she ambles over, spatula in hand like it's an extension of her arm.

"You keep frowning like that, sweetheart, you'll curdle your eggs before I get 'em to you," she says, eyeing me with a shrewdness that makes it clear nothing in here escapes her notice.

"I'll take eggs," I reply evenly. "And a burger. Mayo, tomato, extra onion. Fries on the side."

Her pencil scratches against her notepad. "Now that's an order." Then her gaze lingers, one brow lifting. "Not from around here, are you?"

"No." I sip my coffee. "Passing through."

She hums, lips quirking. "Figured. Folks here don't doctor their coffee like that. Three-and-three before you pour? That's city habits, sweetheart. Around here, we drink it black and call it good."

"I prefer precision," I answer.

Mabel's laugh rattles the cups stacked on the counter. "Well, you'll stand out whether you want to or not. Harrington notices things. Remember that."

She leaves me with my coffee, and I let the sounds of the diner wash over—locals talking weather, crops, and, under it all, whispers about "the university house." No one says Leclair's name, but the hush in their voices says enough.

When Mabel brings my plate, she sets it down firm, hand briefly on my shoulder. "Eat. And keep your ears open. Quiet's never as quiet as it looks."

I cut the burger clean down the middle, blade scraping faint against the diner plate. Juice pools, mixing with the sheen of melted cheese, and I spear half with my fork, bringing it up slow. The first bite hits heavy—grease and onion sharp against my tongue—before I chase it with a fry, its edges crisp, snapping between my teeth.

Around me, the diner hums with the usual noise—weather complaints, a tractor that won't start, someone bragging about their boy making the basketball team. Easy to tune out. What matters are the softer threads, the ones spoken just low enough most folks won't catch them.

"...ain't right, all those girls up and gone," a man mutters two booths back. His voice is gravel, the kind that carries even when he tries to keep it low.

"Runaways," another answers, though not with conviction. "Kids get restless. They light out."

"Not this many. Not all at once." A fork clatters against a plate. "And you've heard the talk. That group, what do they call themselves—Black Bloom? They've been sniffing around. Always comes to trouble when outsiders plant roots."

The first man snorts, uneasy. "Bloom, weeds—it's all the same. Sheriff'll look the other way if the university's happy."

Mabel swoops past their booth, topping off mugs without missing a beat, but her glance flickers sharp. She's heard it too.

I chew slowly, keeping my eyes on my plate. Missing girls. Black Bloom. Connections that don't belong in a small town but fit too well with what I saw last night in that corridor.

I take another sip of coffee, steady, and file it away. No questions here. Not yet.

Chapter 17
Beau

I wake before dawn, not from rest but from running in circles all night. Sleep never stuck, not really. I drifted in and out, the line between dream and memory blurring until I couldn't tell which ghosts were mine and which belonged to last night's whispers. Thirteen women. Coastal Maine. Weapons in transit. They threaded themselves into the old scenes—bodies on concrete floors, my pistol too steady in my hand. Different places. Same weight.

In the dream, the air smells like cordite and seawater. The floor's slick, echoing under boots I don't remember putting on. My old unit moves ahead, faces half-lit by emergency strobes, names I can't make myself say. Every corridor ends the same—doors locked, voices behind them, a countdown I can't stop.

Then she's there. A woman I don't know, but something in me reacts before I think—dark hair, sharp eyes, blood on her sleeve. She moves through the smoke like she's been here before, like she belongs to the place. Her voice cuts through the din, low and certain. *"You were supposed to save them."*

It hits harder than the gunfire. I turn to answer, but the room shifts. She's gone. My team's gone. All that's left are the bodies, lined like markers in the sand.

I wake with my pulse in my throat, sheets damp, breath jagged. The clock reads five-forty, and dawn hasn't broken yet. I sit there a while, staring at my hands, half expecting to see blood.

Clara. The name sits in my head, wrong and right at the same time. Maybe it was her face, maybe not. But she was there—in the dream, in the smoke, in the guilt that won't quit.

Outside, the sky's the color of gunmetal, the world holding its breath before the light hits. Another day starting the same way all the others do—with ghosts that don't know when to leave.

The cot groans when I swing my legs over the edge. My shirt sticks with the damp of sweat, the stale kind you can't wash out with one night's sleep. I strip it off, toss it into the corner, and pull a clean one from the bag I keep half-packed. This one's slate blue instead of green. Doesn't matter much, but it feels like something new between me and the night.

I splash water over my face at the small basin, stare at the reflection that looks older than it should. Grey eyes, lines carved deeper by things I won't name out loud. I towel off, drag a hand through my hair, and let the silence stretch.

Half-slept or not, today's already heavy. The dream still sits at the edges of me—Leclair's name tangled with cages in the dark, the faceless woman's voice giving orders, the memory of another time when I let the job pull me too far.

I shrug into my jacket, slide the pistol into place, and step out into the morning chill. The air is thin, damp with dew, the kind of quiet that makes every sound carry. Harrington's just starting to stir. For me, the day never stopped.

The grounds are already alive with motion—groundskeepers raking, early staff slipping in through side doors—but I skirt the paths until I find a strip of trees past the tennis courts. Secluded enough. Out of sight, but close enough to keep ears on the house if needed.

The grass is wet under my boots as I cut away from the main walk, into a stand of trees that hasn't seen a rake in months. Quiet enough. Private enough.

I pull the burner from my jacket and let it buzz once before the line clicks alive. No greeting. Just a breath, steady.

"Benny."

A soft chuckle rolls back, amused. «Cuidado, hermano.» *Careful, brother.* «Even whispers grow legs.»

"Then let it walk," I murmur, voice low. "I caught chatter. Thirteen women, deadline before the full moon. And they called it a project—for him. And there's more. Weapons. Candy. Upper East distribution."

The silence stretches long enough I picture him lighting a cigarette, leaning back like the world's just confirmed what he already knew. When he speaks, it's a whisper laced in steel. «Siempre mezclan miel con pólvora.» *They always mix honey with gunpowder.* "Bodies with product. Always both."

I press my palm against the trunk of a tree, bark rough under my hand. "That's the line they fed. You know as well as I do, if it's dressed up that neat, it's dirtier than it looks."

That draws a hiss, sharp through the line. «Eso es red grande.» *A big net.* Drift nets, he means. Something wide enough to catch more than what's listed. "You want me on ports?"

"Casco Bay. Rockland. Anywhere they can land quiet. And see who's suddenly renting cold storage on the coast."

He exhales, a sound like smoke curling against the receiver. «Entendido.» *Understood.* Then, in English, his tone cuts sharp: "But Beau—don't lose yourself again. You remember Bogotá. You chase this for justice, you'll confuse the rush for the mission."

Bogotá. The name alone cracks open the memory. Blood wet on tile. My hands steady, too steady, when they shouldn't have been. That thin line between ending a threat and enjoying it.

"I remember," I say, voice clipped.

I hesitate, then add the thought gnawing at me. "And Benny—dig on Clara Hayes. Orion sent her in clean, clipboard in hand, all procedure. But she's too calculated, too precise. Doesn't read like someone just ticking boxes. Reads like someone already playing three moves ahead."

A pause, then his chuckle, low and dangerous. «Así que no es solo el trabajo que te inquieta.» *So it isn't just the job making you restless.*

"Don't start," I mutter.

«Relax, hermano. I'll find her shadow. Every mask leaves a seam. But be sure you want to see what's underneath before I pull the thread.»

The call ends, leaving only the rustle of branches overhead. I slide the burner back into my jacket. Thirteen women. Weapons. Candy. All tangled in Leclair's visit. And Clara Hayes—too clean to trust.

The morning sun breaks through the canopy, sharp and gold. Too clean for what I've just heard. The line goes dead, leaving only the rustle of leaves overhead and the wet earth under my boots.

A flicker pulls my eye. Movement, faint, at the edge of the trees. A shadow slipping between the trunks, quick enough it could be nothing—grounds crew, early staff cutting corners. But it lingers in my mind, the way the shape held still too long before it vanished. Watching.

I step forward, slow, scanning the brush. Nothing but the drip of dew, the sway of branches in the morning breeze. Whoever it was is gone, if they were ever there.

Still, my gut knots the way it always does when someone's listening who shouldn't be.

I head back toward the main path, jaw tight, eyes sweeping the grounds like I'm just another guard on routine patrol. But I know better. The bug in Leclair's room isn't the only thing feeding ears.

I shake the thought off and cut back across the lawn, boots damp, shirt collar sticking against my neck. The house is already humming—staff moving in and out with trays, folders, voices low and clipped in half a dozen accents.

The assistant is exactly where I expect her: perched at a side table, tablet in hand, glasses low on her nose. Efficient. Sharp. Cold as polished steel.

"Schedule," I say flat, no room for negotiation.

She looks up, lips parting like she wants to remind me she sets the order here. Then she sees my face. Thinks better of it. With a tight swipe across her screen, she rattles it off. "Breakfast. Presidential house dining room. Mr. Leclair, yourself, Ms. Hayes. Eight sharp."

I nod once. "After that?"

"Private calls until ten. Campus tour with university president. Lunch with board members. Afternoon reserved for... flexible business." Her pause on that last part says enough. Business that doesn't make the official calendar.

I don't press. Not yet. "Fine. I'll walk him through every change myself."

She inclines her head, already retreating behind the glow of her screen.

By the time I cut through the hallway toward the dining room, the smell of coffee and bacon is already curling through the air, heavy enough to almost feel normal. Almost.

Leclair sits at the head of the table, silver hair combed back, smile practiced for photographs but hollow in person. He doesn't stand when we enter—he never does.

And then there's her. Clara Hayes.

She's already seated, notebook open, pen lined parallel to the margin. Professional. Precise. Exactly as she was in Dallas, only sharper in the daylight.

Her gaze flicks up, brushing over me once before locking on Leclair. Nothing given away. Nothing wasted.

I take my place against the wall, not bothering with the food. My job's not to eat. My job's to watch.

And as the two of them sit under that high ceiling, sunlight glinting across the polished table, I know this isn't just breakfast. It's a test.

For all of us.

The room holds itself too still, like everyone's waiting for a cue. China clinks faintly as coffee is poured, steam curling upward and fading into the morning light spilling through the tall windows. The smell of eggs, butter, and smoked bacon hangs heavy, rich enough to cover the tension but not enough to cut it.

Leclair takes his time. He doesn't rush to fill the silence, doesn't fidget, doesn't even look at the food set neatly before him. Instead, he folds his napkin with deliberate care, aligning the corners until they're perfect. When he finally settles it across his lap, it feels less like table manners and more like a man staking claim to the pace of the room.

Only then does he lift his gaze to Clara.

"Miss Hayes," he says smoothly, voice carrying that practiced warmth that fools most but reaches no deeper than the surface. "I must apologize for yesterday. Urgent matters pulled me away." A faint smile touches his mouth, careful, rehearsed. His eyes remain cold, sharp, unblinking. "I trust you understand."

The words are polite. They hang in the air like a gauntlet.

Chapter 18
Clara

The air in the presidential house still smells faintly of polish and wood smoke, a setting crafted to flatter men like Leclair. He sits at the head of the table now, the picture of contrition wrapped in silk and silver hair. His smile is smooth, his apology smoother. I let it wash past me, my own expression warm, forgiving.

"Of course, Mr. Leclair," I say, tone honeyed. "Schedules are impossible things. Why don't we enjoy breakfast first? Work always goes better when no one's running on an empty stomach."

I gesture lightly toward the plates already laid out—eggs steaming, biscuits soft enough to collapse at the touch of a fork, fruit arranged too neatly to be casual. Beau lingers near the window, arms folded, silent as a wall. Let him glower. My job isn't to spar. It's to extract.

I sip my coffee and give Leclair a smile that could pass for gracious interest. "Tell me, how long has it been since you were last in Harrington? I imagine you have family ties that keep you moving between places."

His gray eyes flick toward me, then down to his plate. Calculating. I keep my smile in place, tilting my head just enough to soften the question, to make it sound like curiosity instead of what it is.

"I always admire men who can balance family and business," I add gently, as though confiding. "My father used to say that if you lose one, the other always follows. Sons, especially, can be such an anchor in a life like yours."

His fork pauses mid-air, just for a beat. Subtle, but enough.

I laugh lightly, as if I've said nothing more than a polite pleasantry. "But forgive me, I digress. Harrington must be a relief after the constant pressure of your other ventures."

The coffee is the right shade of cream when I lift it again, spoon resting at the edge of the saucer. I don't waste words; too many and he'll hear the pressure, too few and he'll smell the trap. The balance is in the pauses, the polite laugh, the hint of admiration that strokes his ego while sliding the hook deeper.

"It must be difficult," I murmur, dabbing my lips with a napkin as though the thought is an aftertaste, "carrying so much of a legacy alone. To build, to preserve, while ensuring there's someone ready to inherit the weight. Especially in a world that changes faster than most men are willing to admit."

Victor's smile doesn't falter, but it freezes. His fork clicks softly against porcelain before he lays it down, too carefully.

Across the room, Beau shifts just enough that I notice. His weight leans forward, the kind of motion that says he's watching the exchange as closely as I am. Protective, suspicious, calculating in his own right. I don't look at him. I don't give him that satisfaction. But I feel the way his attention sharpens, the way he registers the pause I coaxed out of Victor.

"Men like you," I continue, softer now, sweet enough to pass for admiration, "don't simply build businesses. They build legacies. Families. Futures. That's what makes Harrington such a fitting stage. The university, the donations, the way the community speaks your name like it's woven into their own survival."

Victor's gaze lifts, gray eyes unreadable. He studies me for a long moment, as if deciding whether I'm sharp enough to be a threat or just another woman playing at professionalism. His assistant clears her throat, pouring water, shifting papers, trying to ease the silence—but it doesn't break.

I smile, gentle and patient, as though I'm perfectly content to wait him out. Every second he chooses silence over deflection is its own answer.

Inside, I catalog it. A pause at family. A flicker at the word "son." A mask that fits a little too tight when pressed.

Beau takes a slow step from the window, boots clicking faint against the polished floor. His presence is meant to anchor Victor, to steady him, but I catch the glance he throws me from the corner of his eye. Measuring whether I'm baiting too openly—or already drawing blood.

I set my cup down with a soft clink and lace my fingers over my notes. "Shall we begin, Mr. Leclair?"

My tone is calm, compliant. But inside, I know the game has already started.

I smooth the first page of my notes, posture exact, tone brisk but unthreatening. "Red Haven's warehouse operations appear compliant at a surface level. Manifests are logged. Safety measures in place. Vendor lists clean enough for an acquisition brief."

Victor nods once, reaching for his water. He looks relaxed, but the stillness in his shoulders says he's bracing.

"Still," I continue lightly, "there are inconsistencies. Subcontractors tied to the same post office box in Billings. Multiple vendor names, all with overlapping contacts. It could be clerical. It could also be deliberate. My role is to separate the two."

He sets the glass down a fraction too hard. A ring of condensation blooms on the table. "Clerical," he says smoothly, "nothing more. The paperwork is... curated. Necessary, when certain assets cannot be tied directly to Red Haven's name."

My pen stills on the page. Assets. Not products. Not shipments. Assets.

I glance up, the smile never wavering. "Of course. That's why we review. To ensure nothing vital slips through."

He inclines his head, recovering the mask, but the word hangs between us like smoke.

Assets.

I jot a single, neat note in the margin and move on, voice pleasant. "Temperature logs, equipment certifications, and personnel files were all current as of my last review. Tomorrow, I'll need access to your procurement chain—clean copies, so we can finalize the brief."

Victor gestures with his fork as if dismissing the formality. "You'll have what you need. I want this acquisition to appear seamless."

I let the phrase sink in, smiling as though reassured. Inside, the knot pulls tighter. Assets. Seamless. Slips that tell me more than he meant to.

I keep my face easy as the meeting winds down, pen tapping the margin in polite rhythm. He lets the air settle like a man who knows he's won the pause. When I move into the practical—follow-ups, documents to sign, exact times—he answers like a banker counting change.

"Tomorrow, then," I say, sliding the final page toward him. "I'll need the procurement chain, vendor contracts, and the signed manifests. After that, the signatures." My voice is business; my smile is neutral.

Leclair watches the paper glide. He lifts a spoon to his coffee, sets it down without stirring, then leans back, palms open in the smallest, most theatrical sign of concession. "Perfect. And —" he inclines his head toward his assistant, voice smoothing into something casual, "—please arrange a private walkthrough for Ms. Hayes after her inspection. I'd like her to see the storage area without interruptions. Have Facilities escort her through the west service entrance. And make sure the van is available. Discretion, please."

To anyone listening it sounds ordinary: an executive avoiding curious eyes, a man who prefers discretion for proprietary areas. The assistant nods, fingers already moving. She taps a line into her tablet, then slides off a short message to someone in security: "Private escort + van for inspector after inspection — west service entrance. Proceed per protocol." She hits send.

It takes her three seconds to make it look like logistics. Three seconds for words to become an order.

I fold my notes, close the folder with the practiced motion of someone who signs things for a living. "Then we'll reconvene tomorrow at eight for final signatures," I say, calm. "Thank you for your time, Mr. Leclair. I'll see you in the morning."

He stands, offering the smile that photographers teach men to use. "We'll be ready," he says. The assistant rises with the soft efficiency of someone who moves the world one spreadsheet at a time. She presses a printed confirmation into my hand—time, place, initials—exactly the sort of breadcrumb that makes the hour feel official.

I nod, lift my cup, murmur another pleasantry, and leave the table as if I'm stepping out of a soundstage. Smooth. Polite. Nothing to see.

Outside the dining room, Beau catches my shoulder for a moment—a light brush of fingers, nothing more. "You ready?" he asks, low.

"Always," I say, and let my smile be exactly what it should: unflappable, routine. We walk the short distance to the main hall together. He falls into his perimeter, eyes sweeping as he always does. I move back into my method—notes, angles, people. Every detail filing itself into the small, steady cabinet in my head.

Still, there's a flicker I store away, the kind that nags later: when the assistant's thumb hovered over the send key, the almost-imperceptible tightening at the corner of her mouth as she typed that note.

Nothing overt. No alarm bells. Just... an angle. A way something felt rehearsed, not incidental. I tuck it under the others—useful, but not urgent.

I walk the corridor alone, the hush of the presidential house settling behind me. The receptionist's desk is empty, only the faint tick of a clock keeping time. My heels strike the polished tile in even rhythm. On the surface, I look like any other inspector wrapping up her morning. Inside, the angles keep filing themselves away.

At the front doors, a man in a gray security uniform is waiting. Broad, clean-shaven, radio clipped at his shoulder. His badge catches the light when he inclines his head. "Ms. Hayes? I've been asked to escort you. Facilities wants to show you the west entrance—smoother for tomorrow's walkthrough."

I offer a polite nod, nothing more. His badge looks right. His voice is steady. Still, the itch between my shoulders stirs. "Very well," I say, tone cool but agreeable.

We walk together through the side halls, his stride unhurried, professional. Sunlight filters through tall windows, warm against the polished wood, and each step pulls me further from the main entrance.

The west service door looms ahead, metal framed, glass narrow and tinted. He holds it open, his smile faint but practiced. Outside, the air is sharper, colder. A van idles at the curb, white paint glinting beneath the morning sun.

My pulse slows, heavy. The hair on my arms rises. The van door slides back, quick and quiet.

Three men step out. Black gloves. Hard eyes.

I pivot instinctively, but the first guard blocks my arm before I can draw breath. Fingers clamp down tight on my wrist, the practiced pressure of someone who's done this before.

The van's engine hums low, steady as a heartbeat.

I keep my face smooth, even as my mind sharpens into angles. I catalog every detail—the license plate half-smeared with mud, the scar along one man's jaw, the smell of engine oil clinging to their jackets. All of it is evidence. All of it is memory.

Still, the fact remains: I am surrounded.

And this time, there is no easy way out.

Chapter 19
Clara

The sun is already climbing, sharp light bouncing off the presidential house's brick and glass as I step out through the west entrance. The guard at my side keeps his tone polite, practiced, as though this is nothing more than a courtesy escort. My gut knows better.

The van waits at the curb, engine idling. Too convenient. Too clean.

The second guard appears from the blind side, and that's all the confirmation I need. I twist hard, snapping my elbow into the first man's ribs. He grunts, staggered, and I drive my heel down onto the instep of the other. His curse tears through the quiet morning as I wrench free, knife sliding from my sleeve into my palm.

"Not today," I hiss, slashing low. The blade rips a line across the first guard's forearm and red blooms quick. He doubles over, cursing in French, and for a second I see the street, sunlight, the door I just walked out of.

Another man comes at me fast. I pivot, shoulder in, and his jaw caves with a clean crack. He staggers, more surprised than hurt. For a breath I think I can run.

The fourth man is already on me. He drives a shoulder into my ribs and the wind leaves me. I swing; my blade tears through cloth and finds skin, but a hot sting punches through my side. A syringe, buried in the crook of my ribs. Chemical heat lances through me, sharp and immediate. Muscles threaten to go leaden.

"No—" I try to say it but a hand clamps over my mouth, nails digging into my cheek. The world narrows to breath and the scrape of boots.

Panic wants to take over. I let it be the noise and not the motion. I bite down on knuckles, teeth breaking skin, and the man curses, loosening his hold a fraction. I kick, heel smashing into a knee, twist, and land a hard elbow into a throat. One of them staggers back, coughing and swearing, which gives me a second to shove against the alley wall and push.

They close on me like animals. One hooks an arm under my armpit and lifts, jerking me off my feet. The drug is a burning rope coiling through my veins; my limbs feel like someone tied weights to them. I flail, catch another sleeve with the tip of the blade, and the resistance sends a shock up through my wrist. My forearms burn; the blade is buried to the hilt in a sleeve and then ripped free.

They don't let me finish. A boot catches my stomach and the air explodes out of me. I fold, breathless, and the alley tilts. Voices blur into a single harsh line. Hands on my shoulders, hands on my wrists. They press me up against the brick, the cold digging through my shirt. The knife skitters from my fingers and hits the gravel with a sound that feels like surrender.

They bind my wrists with a length of coarse rope, tight enough to sting. A strip of fabric is shoved into my mouth and taped at the corners. The tape is rough; my tongue tastes of adhesive and iron. My vision swims. I spit against the gag but the tape holds. Someone drags my chin up; the light catches on a face I don't want to see.

A boot heels my ribs and I gasp, sound muffled against the gag. I wrench my shoulders and try to brace, to make them work for it, to sell fear and pain without letting them suspect I'm anything else. They want me broken, not broken open. I give them the bruises and the screams they expect. My breaths come short and quick. Every movement hurts, but I shape it into the story I need them to read.

They haul me farther into shadow, where a van waits with the door cracked. One of them checks my pockets and tosses the unmarked key and anything else into a small bag. A guard mutters in French, sharp and efficient. They move with the practiced cruelty of men who have done this before.

As they lift me into the van, my shoulders scrape the metal frame and the world tilts sideways. My cheek presses to the cool interior and the tape pulls at the corner of my mouth when I try to speak. I clamp my jaw against the sting.

The van door slams and the engine coughs to life. The van pulls away, tires whispering over wet pavement, and the alley shrinks fast. My hands are stinging, my side burning where the syringe did its work, my lungs tight. I stop fighting for a breath, because the fight won't win me anything alone.

Darkness licks at the edges of my vision, but fragments stick.

The van rocks hard as it takes a corner, my shoulder slamming against the wall. I bite down on the cry that wants to escape, forcing my eyes open. The world swims, but one detail cuts through the blur.

The man braced beside me grips the rail above, sleeve tugged back just far enough to expose ink across his forearm. Not just a flower—though the bloom sits stark and black at the center. Around it coils a ring of thorns, each barb hooked and deliberate. A narrow shield frames the design, etched in hard lines, with a sword driven clean through the stem. The style is old, purposeful. Not street art. Not casual. A mark of allegiance.

The van jolts again. My head snaps forward, then back. Through the haze I catch more—the scuffed steel-toed boots of the man across from me, mud dried in the treads. The faint clink of metal when he shifts, like keys—or shackles.

A low murmur of French threads through the cabin. Clipped, efficient.

"Les portes seront prêtes." The doors will be ready.
"Pas de témoins." No witnesses.

I force my breathing even, as though I've gone slack. Their focus slips away, conversation flowing over me like static.

The van slows. Gravel grinds under the tires. A gate creaks, then slams shut behind us.

When the doors swing open, daylight cuts in—harsh, white, blinding. I squint, disoriented, as they haul me down by the arms.

The smell hits first. Oil. Metal. Damp concrete. Different from the clean polish of Red Haven's main floor. This place isn't meant to be seen.

I stumble as they drag me across the threshold, boots scraping over uneven flooring. Overhead, a single strip light buzzes, half-dead, throwing more shadow than clarity. Stacks of crates loom like walls, stamped with numbers too blurred for me to focus on.

Somewhere deeper, a door slams. A woman's voice cuts sharp, carrying authority I've heard before. My gut coils even as my vision wavers, dark edges creeping closer.

The tattoo flashes in my mind again. A sigil. A warning. And maybe the last thing I'll remember before the dark takes me.

Darkness crawls back slow, leaving me strapped upright in a chair. Wrists cinched tight. Ankles bound. A single bulb swings overhead, throwing long shadows against concrete walls that sweat damp in the corners. The air stinks of bleach and oil.

One of the guards shifts close, bored enough to lean on routine, but his forearm catches my eye. The tattoo sprawls from wrist to elbow—black ink lines twisting into a thorned shield, a sword piercing through its center, a flower blooming at the hilt. Different from Travis's, but close enough that my stomach knots. Related. Connected. I keep my eyes steady, as if I never noticed.

The chair has learned the shape of my body. Metal against spine, ropes biting wrists until every shift scrapes fire along raw skin. The boots never change—circling behind me, deliberate, measured—but the voice does. It seeps from a speaker mounted high in the corner, clipped French turned to precise English, cold as a scalpel. She never steps into view.

"Regular office workers don't fight back like you did," the speaker says on the first day, voice almost curious.

I don't look up. I keep my voice even, bored. "They do when they're a woman traveling alone. Most of us take self-defense courses. Comes with the job if you don't want to end up a headline." Flat. Practical. The kind of answer that dies in paperwork. Boots scrape, a lamp snaps on, heat blasting my skin, then off again, leaving me shivering in the sudden cold. Testing. Prodding. No marks.

Meals mark the time—gray meat, soggy bread, water flat as tap. Always the same tray, always the same boot steps. By the second meal on the second day, my hands tremble when I reach for the bread. The speaker clicks on again. "Why this facility?"

I swallow slowly, push the tray away. "Because it's where the client sent me. Procurement and Compliance Division doesn't pick sites. We follow paper trails. Red Haven Foods is part of a federal supply chain. That's why." My tone is bureaucratic, lifeless, exactly what they'd expect from an Orion suit punching clocks.

Later, the game shifts. Ice water poured slow over my wrists, soaking the rope until it burns deeper. A thumb grinding nerves until white sparks scatter behind my eyes. "You are lying," the voice hisses from the speaker.

"If I were lying," I rasp, "I'd have written better paperwork."

Sleep becomes a flicker, not a state. Light through the high vent shifts from pale gray to black to gray again. By the third round of the same meal, I know it's been three days. My ribs are a drumbeat under bruises, every knot alive beneath the surface. They're waiting for the slip. The hesitation. The moment I lose the shape of Clara Hayes.

"Who else knows you are here?" the speaker asks at last, calm and cutting.

I let the question breathe before I answer. "Client liaison in Mid-Atlantic office. Standard protocol." My tone doesn't waver. A half-truth, wrapped tight in procedure.

Silence. Then the command: "Tighter." The ropes cinch until my ribs scream. A thumb digs under my collarbone, not enough to break, just enough to grind bone against nerve. Still no marks. Still deliberate. My breath hitches, but my voice stays level. "If you want to confirm, call Orion. You'll find exactly what you expect. Routine inspection. Nothing else."

The lie tastes metallic, but it holds. And as long as it holds, so do I.

The voice comes through the speaker, clipped French folding into the room like a blade. "Je pensais qu'il y avait plus à elle." I catch the words like loose coins. I thought there was more to her. The accent cuts the consonants clean; there is a familiarity in the cadence that feels private, like naming an old bruise. I never see who speaks. The sound bounces off metal and concrete, anonymous and intimate at once.

One of the men snorts nearby. "She's clean. Minimal risk. No markers. No ties we can trace." He pats a tablet, thumbs flicking through images I do not get to see. Another voice, flat and practical, says, "Make her look like she belongs in public. Return her to campus. Quiet. No leave-behind."

The French voice lowers until the words land in my chest. "Vous savez quoi faire." You know what to do. It is casual as breaking a twig, the tone of someone issuing orders to an old partner. My skin prickles. A name slides through me like a sharpened thought but I clamp my teeth on it. I will not give air to recognition. I will not let my mouth betray the fact that, even taken by Red Haven and their men, the rhythm of that voice fits into the hollow places in me.

They free my hands with practiced care, checking the marks at my wrists as if deciding whether the scars tell a story. One of them runs a damp cloth across my face and neck, wiping away the sweat and the oil and whatever else their questions scraped loose. A brush passes through my hair. They fuss with my collar until I look like the kind of woman who gets into sedans and goes home to spreadsheets. The charade is precise. My bra is shifted, button straightened, lipstick wiped to the faintest sheen.

When they blindfold me for the drive back, the fabric is cool against my eyes; the world snaps to black and the warehouse shrinks to the scent of motor oil and wet cardboard. The blindfold is not a gag—my throat remains free, my voice still mine. They seat me in the back of a van, hands steady on either side as they lift me in. The floor buzzes under my soles. Someone hums a half-tune, as if to fill the silence.

The ride is a study in small, meaningless motions: the click of a belt, the whisper of jacket fabric, the drone of the engine on the highway. I keep my breathing shallow. Through the blindfold I can still catalog—left-hand turns, a long stretch of open road, the muted hiss of rain beginning against metal. They keep conversation clipped, all business. Every so often the woman's laugh—soft, private—floats through the cabin and pins me with recognition I refuse to name.

At the campus drop-off they take more care. One man guides me to the curb; another steadies my shoulders and straightens my blouse. They loosen the blindfold long enough for me to blink at the night sky, but not long enough to make anything out. Students pass by in small clusters, phones glowing, oblivious. The men position themselves like statues behind me as if they could rewrite what I just was. One leans close, voice a dry sandpaper whisper.

"If anyone finds out about this," he says, eyes on some point behind my head I cannot see, "you won't make it back next time. Keep your mouth shut. Keep your job. We watched your answers. We watched your face. This was mercy."

Mercy. The word lands in my mouth like iron.

I nod because it's part of the script. Out loud I am Clara Hayes—the procurement rep who filed the paperwork and took the briefing and drove home. Inside, my blood is a hammer, beating a rhythm I don't let show. They leave me at the curb with a last, almost tender straightening of my collar, then vanish into the night like ghosts with a plan.

I climb into my car, fingers numb, and drive away. The campus lights blur past. Every shadow looks like a face I half-remember. Every turn brings me farther from the warehouse and, for now, closer to my cover. But the woman's words—soft, intimate, familiar—burn along the back of my skull. The voice tugs at something buried, a thread of recognition that makes my skin prickle. For a heartbeat I think I know it—then dismiss the thought as impossible. Whoever I'm remembering is all gloss and empty chatter, someone who plays at being shallow, not someone who commands a room like that. I shove the notion down, sharp as a pinprick, and drive on.

By the time I reach the inn in Harrington, every muscle throbs from the hours in that chair, rope-burn ridging my wrists, my ribs sore from the blows no one will ever see. I drop my bag on the narrow bed and sit on the edge, breathing until the world narrows down to the clock on the wall and the ache in my ribs. Pain is a fact, not an excuse. It tells me I survived. It tells me what I need to do next.

The plan is not complicated. Nobody knows where the Black Bible is. It's been in the wind since the theft, a ghost in the margins of ledgers and a rumor in men's drink. That's why killing Victor is useful. He is a mark big enough to pull his son out from whatever hole he's hiding in. Kill the father. The son shows his face. The son leads me to the drive.

I bind off two things in my head, like closing knots. One: make Victor look like an accident, something that can be blamed on him and his own choices. Public blood would complicate the clean lines we need, so no spectacle. Quiet, surgical. Two: leave a breadcrumb the right people will read. Not a confession, not a calling card. Just something that draws the son, nothing else. No explosions. No crowds. No sloppy evidence. Clean entry, clean exit. That is how you get a boy to come looking for answers and a file to come along with him.

I fold the plan into the small dark space between my ribs and let it sit there, heavy and honest. Reckless is a word I use for other people's mistakes. Tonight I own it.

I strip down to the black base layers I keep for nights like this. The fabric breathes and moves with me the way armor should. Jeans over them, a lightweight tactical vest that looks like a fitted jacket from the right angle, pockets stuffed with what I need and nothing I do not. I slide my Glock into its holster, thumb the safety without thinking, and tuck a pair of spare magazines into the inner flap where my hand will find them blind. A thin silencer goes in the duffel. A pen camera finds the buttonhole of my hoodie. A single burner phone, charger wrapped small, goes in the front pocket. Cash in a strip against the lining. A passport with a name that will not be missed until it is too late sits folded in the back.

I pull the hood up and cinch the drawstrings low. The mirror catches the edge of my face and nothing more. No softness. No apology. Just focus. I check the sky. No moon. Good. Less to cast shadows and show shapes.

There is a small thrill in the risk. Not the kind that tastes like victory. The kind that tastes like cold metal on your tongue and the bitter tang of old wounds. I breathe that in and let it settle. Tonight might be the moment that closes things. It might be the moment that opens a new kind of hell. Either way, I will not be the one who backs away.

Outside the inn, the night feels thinner somehow, like someone has pulled the veil back and left the mechanics bare. Main Street lies quiet. A couple of porch lights burn like watchful eyes. I move with the purpose of someone practiced in leaving without notice. The key turns silent in the lock. The stairs hold my footsteps the same way they always do. Habit comforts when the rest of you wants to fray.

I slide into the driver's seat and don't start the engine right away. I count the plan through one last time in my head: arrival, placement, the small controlled scene that implicates a man and not the town, breadcrumb left light enough for a son to see and heavy enough to pull a reaction. Ten minutes. Maybe eight. Enough time to get in and get out before the house staff notices. Enough time to make them think it was chance.

When I finally start the jeep, the sound is small and civilized. I drive the route I scouted earlier, keeping to back streets, the kind of path that eats time and leaves no obvious trail. My hands are steady on the wheel. My jaw is set. I am moving through the town I have only ever observed from the margins, walking right toward the heart of what I have to break open.

Tonight is a single clean strike. Tonight I make them move. Tonight I finish it.

Chapter 20
Beau

I take my place against the wall, same as always — quiet, still, watching. The dining room smells like polish and wood smoke, a backdrop designed to make Leclair look carved out of power. He plays the role well. Silver hair, smooth apologies, a smile trained for photographs.

I've never worked with him before. Don't need to. You learn a lot just standing still in a room like this. Who talks too much. Who listens too little. Who's pretending not to notice the cracks.

Clara sits across from him, precise as cut glass — notebook squared, pen lined neat, her voice pitched soft and warm. She doesn't push, not where anyone else would notice. But I catch the flicker when she steers him toward family, toward legacy. For a second, his fork stops mid-air. Most people would miss it. I don't.

The rest of the meeting hums along, business as usual, until Leclair shifts gears. Casual on the surface, but too deliberate underneath. He tells his assistant to arrange a private walkthrough for Ms. Hayes. West service entrance. Escort. Van. He might as well have stamped the word *off-book* across the table.

The assistant types fast, thumb hovering half a second too long before hitting send. Her face stays neutral, but there's a tightening at the corner of her mouth I don't like. Rehearsed, not routine.

Clara stays smooth. Folds her notes. Smiles like the request is nothing more than courtesy. To anyone else, that's all it looks like. To me, it sets the air a degree colder.

I shift my weight forward, boots clicking once on the floor, but keep my mouth shut. It's not my place to step in — not yet. Still, the knot in my gut doesn't fade. I don't know Leclair, not well enough to judge his tells. But I know when something doesn't sit right.

By the time the meeting breaks, the others filter out with coffee cups and small talk. I stay where I am, arms folded, eyes on the door Clara walked through.

Whatever that "private tour" really meant, I'll be watching.

It's been several nights since I last saw Clara, and the absence gnaws at me more than it should. She's not mine to keep track of, not mine to lose sleep over, but the quiet feels wrong without her shadow in it. I tell myself it doesn't matter—just two more nights and this assignment is over. Leclair gone, Orion satisfied. Then I get six months, maybe a year, where I can ignore their calls and stay tucked out here on the edge of Harrington. Back to ranch dirt, back to silence.

The campus at night is still enough to hear my own breathing. I like it that way. Every step is deliberate, heel then toe, leaving space for the kind of sounds that don't belong. Lamp posts throw weak yellow circles across the walkways, shadows bending long beneath the trees. The ocean wind pulls hard at my coat, sharp with salt, like it wants to drag me off the path entirely.

It should feel routine. Just another patrol, another night closer to being free again. But the gap of those missing days presses at the edges of my thoughts. People who vanish in this world don't always come back, and if they do, it's never whole. I don't know which thought unsettles me more—that Clara's gone, or that she isn't.

That's when I catch it — a scrape that's not wind, not gravel. Someone moving where they shouldn't be.

I hold still, listening. The rhythm is wrong: deliberate, but uneven, like every step costs more than it should. I ease out from behind the sycamore, eyes tracking the figure under the glow. Hood up, shoulders tight, cutting across the quad like she owns it.

Clara.

It's not her face that gives her away but the shape of her walk. She's trying to be invisible, but anger has weight, and she's carrying it. When she finally turns, the lamplight catches her hazel eyes — green and gold at once, bright enough to scorch if I let them.

"You lost?" I keep my tone easy. "Or just looking for trouble?"

She doesn't flinch, but the pause before she answers is a tell. "Neither," she says, clipped. "I needed air."

"At midnight?" I step closer, studying the way she's holding herself. Shoulders hunched, arms too still. Not her usual smooth cover. More like someone fighting to stay upright. "Most people pick a coffee or a run for that."

Her mouth ticks up, humorless. "Most people aren't me."

"Lucky them," I say.

Her eyes narrow, hood shadowing everything but that burn of color, like a blade catching light. "You gonna give me a lecture, Beau? Because I don't have the patience tonight."

"No lecture." I lean against the tree, hands loose at my sides. "Just pointing out you look like you got dragged through hell and decided to keep walking."

For a heartbeat, her jaw works — tight, stubborn. She doesn't answer, just shifts her weight, and even that small move pulls a wince through her. She tries to mask it, but I catch it.

"You're hurt."

"I'm fine." Too fast, too sharp.

I shake my head, a low chuckle slipping out. "Funny, because fine usually walks straighter than that."

That earns me a glare. "You don't know me well enough to judge."

"Maybe not," I admit, "but I know the look of someone about to do something reckless."

Her shoulders square, defiance bristling through the pain. "Then stay out of my way."

I step in, closing the space just enough to make her meet my eyes. "That's the problem. You come sneaking around at night, sore as hell, looking like you're ready to start a fight — it's my job to get in your way."

She laughs once, brittle. "Your job? Since when?"

"Since the moment you lied to my face," I fire back, voice low but steady. "You said you work for Orion. What do you really do for them, Clara? Because reps with clipboards don't limp across quads at midnight."

Her hazel eyes flare — not with fear, but with something hotter, angrier. She doesn't answer, not directly. Instead, she tips her chin up, pain and defiance braided tight. "If you can't tell," she says, "then maybe you're not as good as you think you are."

The words sting sharper than they should. For a second, I almost let her walk. Almost. But there's a pull under my ribs I can't shake — the need to know what's got her out here, the instinct to shield her from it even as she throws barbs in my face. I'm not supposed to care. I'm supposed to guard the perimeter, follow the assignment, nothing more.

Yet here I am, watching her limp into shadows she has no business carrying alone.

I curse under my breath and push off the tree, ears chasing the scrape of her shoes, the ragged sound of someone too furious to rest. That itch in my gut from Leclair's little "private tour" doesn't feel like coincidence anymore.

Whatever she's planning tonight, it isn't random. And it sure as hell isn't safe.

So I follow.

Clara moves fast, faster than someone that sore should be able to. I shadow her from a distance, boots finding the same silent rhythm I've lived by for years. She doesn't look back. Doesn't hesitate. Whatever she's chasing, it's already lit in her veins.

We cross the quad and cut toward the edge of campus, where the lamplight thins and the presidential house rises against the dark — all polished windows and brick meant to look historic. From here, it's quiet, deceptively so. Too quiet for someone like her to be prowling.

I hiss under my breath. "Clara—stop."

She does, but only long enough to glance over her shoulder. Her hood shadows most of her face, but the set of her mouth is pure defiance. "Go back, Beau. This isn't your fight."

My jaw tightens. "It is if you end up on the wrong side of it."

For a second, we're frozen in the dark — me wanting answers, her refusing to give them. Then the night answers for us.

An explosion rips through the stillness, a blinding bloom of fire and shrapnel that tears out from the second floor of the Presidential House. For half a heartbeat, the world holds its breath—then everything moves at once.

Glass erupts outward in a glittering storm, each shard catching the orange light like falling stars. The shockwave punches across the courtyard, flattening the hedges and shoving the air clean out of my lungs. I hit the ground hard, arms thrown over my head as heat rolls over me in waves.

The night fills with noise—alarms shrieking, car horns wailing, the metallic ring of debris raining down. Smoke curls upward, thick and black, swallowing the pale marble of the facade. The upper balcony collapses in on itself, wood and plaster crumbling into the inferno.

Leclair's room—the corner suite with the gilded windows—is gone. In its place, a yawning wound of flame devours what used to be velvet drapes and polished floors. Embers drift through the air like fireflies, landing on the lawn and blooming into tiny pockets of flame.

Somewhere beyond the ringing in my ears, someone screams. Others are running—guards, staff, bystanders—shadows crossing through the smoke, shouting orders drowned out by the crackle of burning timber. The air tastes of iron and fuel. My vision swims from the force of it, but I can't look away.

Leclair's room is gone. Erased in a single breath.

Clara stumbles, then straightens, firelight burning in her hazel eyes. She looks back at me, hood slipping just enough to show the grim curve of her mouth.

"Looks like you've got your hands full," she says, voice steady in a way it shouldn't be.

Before I can close the gap, she pivots, melting into the dark.

The alarms start screaming, red lights strobing across the lawn. Emergency squads swarm the drive — radios crackling, boots pounding, shouts cutting the night. Students spill out of dorms, half-dressed and wide-eyed, craning for a view of the flames.

I lunge forward, scanning for her, but she's gone.

"Goddammit."

By the time I reach the house, the fire crews are already dragging hoses across the lawn. I push through smoke and bodies, giving my name, flashing my clearance. An officer thrusts a clipboard at me, rattling off headcounts.

"Accounting for staff, sir. East wing made it out. Kitchen staff too. But—" He hesitates, eyes flicking back to the blaze. "Couple of Leclair's people were on the second floor. We've got at least two confirmed injured, maybe worse."

My stomach knots. I scan the names scribbled down, the empty spaces where others should be.

The fire roars louder, chewing through timber and glass like it was always meant to burn.

Clara's words echo in my head — *Looks like you've got your hands full.*

She wasn't wrong.

But if she had anything to do with this, I'll find out.

And if she didn't... then someone just declared open season on all of us.

Chapter 21
Clara

The sirens wail behind me, but I don't slow down. I slip between buildings, hugging the dark where the lamplight doesn't reach, lungs burning with each breath. My legs ache, my ribs throb from every step, but I don't give the pain a voice. Pain means I'm still moving.

I duck into a narrow alley that smells of wet brick and old grease, pressing my back to the wall long enough to steal a look at the fire tearing through the presidential house. Glass shatters in a rain of sparks, students crowd the quad, emergency lights paint the night red and white.

Victor Leclair's wing is gone.

For a moment I just stand there, chest tight, tasting smoke on the back of my tongue. I wanted him gone — but not like this. Not in a way that throws questions I can't afford to answer.

And Beau. His face flashes in my mind, the way he caught me in the quad, the way he looked at me like he could see the truth if I let him. He'll be buried in that chaos now, answering to every uniform and authority who thinks they're in charge. Which means he won't be looking for me. Not tonight.

I draw my hood lower, force my body back into motion. Every muscle protests, but stopping isn't an option. I need distance. I need cover. And more than that, I need answers.

Because if Victor wasn't mine to take off the board, then someone else just moved first.

And that makes them either an ally I can't see or an enemy I haven't met yet.

Harrington isn't safe anymore. Not for me. Not with Beau prowling the same ground, his eyes too sharp, his questions too close.

By the time the last echo of sirens fades, I'm already slipping through back streets with my hood low. The inn's wooden sign creaks in the wind when I reach it, a sound too normal after the fire and chaos I left behind. I slip inside, climb the narrow staircase, every groan of the boards a reminder of the bruises blooming under my clothes.

My room smells faintly of lavender cleaner and pine. I don't bother with the light. I move straight for the suitcase, tossing clothes inside in tight, practiced folds. Laptop. Charger. Notes. Every scrap of evidence packed before anyone can think to knock on my door and ask where I was when Leclair's world went up in flames.

Beau will. If not tonight, then tomorrow. He'll keep circling until he corners me with questions I can't answer. And I can't let him be the one to unravel this.

Dallas is the only play now. Too many shadows here, too many variables I don't control. In Dallas, I can get distance. In Dallas, I can keep hunting without Orion breathing down my neck or Beau standing in my way.

The zipper bites shut. I sling the bag over my shoulder, teeth clenched against the ache that runs from my ribs into my spine. Pain can wait. Distance can't.

One last look at the room—clean sheets, folded blankets, the kind of false comfort that never belonged to me anyway.

The bag is heavy on my shoulder, but I don't stop moving until I reach the back lot where my Jeep waits. I left it here for a reason—unremarkable, reliable, the kind of vehicle no one looks twice at. The engine turns over with a steady growl, and just like that, I leave Harrington behind.

I don't bother checking out of the inn. I paid for the week, left the key in the drawer. Let them think I'm still there, tucked beneath lavender sheets. The illusion will hold long enough to keep questions pointed in the wrong direction.

The highway stretches north, long and empty. Three hours of asphalt and night air, headlights carving a path toward Dallas. My body protests the whole way—ribs aching, wrists tender, muscles tight from the ropes—but the hum of the road drowns it out. Sirens and fire fade behind me, and with them, the weight of Harrington.

By the time the skyline rises ahead, steel and glass catching the faint glow of the horizon, I've already built the wall back in my mind.

The night has burned itself down to embers, every mile of highway chewing through what little strength I had left. My ribs ache with every breath, wrists raw beneath the sleeves I keep tugging down. The city doesn't care. Dallas never does.

The horizon smears pink over the glass towers as if the world is pretending at softness. I know better. Daylight doesn't change what waits for me here—it just means I'll have to move faster, quieter, sharper, before anyone notices I'm still standing when I shouldn't be.

Victory Park. My safe house. A high-rise built for people who need to be seen but not touched. Secure elevators, reinforced locks, guards who don't ask questions. Here, I can vanish above the noise of the city, watch without being watched.

I'm grateful I kept the Fort Worth cover home intact. To anyone looking, that's still where Clara Hayes lives—commuter address, utility bills, a trail of receipts to keep the story alive. It's enough to keep shadows guessing while I disappear into the clouds.

Inside the high-rise, the air is clean, filtered, sterile. I drop the bag by the door and finally let myself stand still. Dallas sprawls beneath the windows, glittering with the kind of indifference only a city can hold.

I peel out of my jacket, wincing when the motion pulls at my ribs. The bruises burn hot beneath my skin, spreading like fire every time I move. The shower hisses to life, steam curling up the mirror as I strip down. Hot water scalds across my shoulders, and I let it, standing still as if the heat alone can wash away Harrington—the ropes, the blows, the fire. For ten minutes, I breathe. Nothing more.

When the water runs lukewarm, I kill it, towel off quick, and drag the kit from the cabinet. Antiseptic, bandages, painkillers, elastic wrap. My ribs ache as I wind the fabric tight, breath shallow but steady. Better. Contained. The marks on my wrists and ankles sting under the ointment, angry reminders I can't afford to ignore. By the time I pull on clean clothes, the ache hasn't gone, but it's controlled. Managed.

By the time I'm dressed—loose sweats, a tank that won't dig into the bruises—the apartment feels too quiet. Too clean. The kind of silence that presses until you fill it with purpose. I strip the towel off my damp hair and force my body into the rhythm I know best: movement, control, precision. Pain can wait. Answers can't.

I clear a corner of the kitchen counter, slide my laptop into place, and fan out the folder I smuggled back. Notes stack in neat piles, manifests, names half-scribbled in margins. Every inconsistency I logged on Victor Leclair. Every word I didn't like.

I flip through them with deliberate precision, highlighter steady in my hand. *Assets. Private walkthrough. Seamless.* Each word a thread. Threads mean patterns, and patterns lead to answers.

But it's the tattoo that needles me. The ink I glimpsed once, faint beneath a cuff, then again in Harrington's shadowed corridors. I dig through my files, searching for reference points, anything that might explain the mark. Cross-check, rerun searches, sift.

And then it surfaces—buried in an old intelligence brief. **The Black Bloom.** A sigil tied to shipments that never appeared on record, a whisper of a faction that cloaks itself in shadows even Orion never quite pinned down. The symbol is a marker. A warning. Maybe a claim.

Someone else cut Leclair off the board before I could. Which means they're inside the same game. And I still don't know if they're competition or collateral.

The Black Bloom. The words pulse on the page like they've been waiting for me to find them, old ink burning fresh in my veins. My grip on the highlighter tightens until the plastic creaks. Whoever carries that mark isn't just another player—they're the kind you don't survive brushing up against unless you already know the rules.

I push back from the counter, needing air, movement, anything to shake the coil winding tighter in my chest. That's when my gaze drifts—unplanned, instinctual—toward the window.

The plant sits there, a fern in a matte black pot. A detail for cover, nothing more. I bought it three months ago so neighbors would look in and see "home" instead of an operative waiting to burn down their empire. I haven't watered it in weeks.

And yet the soil is damp.

My pulse tightens.

I scan the room, details snapping into focus: the stack of mail on the table isn't aligned the way I left it. A coaster is out of place by two inches. The faint smell of smoke clings to the air, too sharp to be from my own clothes. Someone's been here.

I close the laptop in one smooth motion and slide the notes back into the folder, every movement controlled, measured. Whoever walked through this apartment wanted me to know it. To feel it.

I move through the space slow, deliberate. The rug near the door is rotated, its corner tucked under instead of lying flat. A chair is angled half a degree off from the line of the table. The small details no ordinary intruder would care about. This wasn't a burglary. This was a message.

It's when I circle back toward the window that I see it.

Nestled at the base of the fern, half-hidden by the fronds, is a single white lily. Its petals glow faintly in the slant of evening light, too delicate, too deliberate to be anything I missed before.

A card rests beneath the bloom, neat script across its face:

Mistakes are the only legacy that lingers. Even yours.

My stomach knots. White lilies. Orion's quiet signature for burned assets. The flower is as final as a headstone, left behind when someone's time is up.

I touch nothing. Not the card. Not the bloom. Not even the fern that's been watered by someone else's hand.

Legacy or not, they've marked me finished.

The air feels thinner. Every shadow in the apartment stretches long, predatory. I don't sit. I don't breathe too loud. I gather only what I can carry, leaving everything else behind.

Because if Orion has drawn the lily on me, it means two things: They know exactly where I am. And they don't plan on giving me another chance.

I straighten, bruises screaming in protest, eyes fixed on the Dallas skyline beyond the glass. Whoever made this move is already watching.

And if they think leaving fingerprints in my life will scare me off, they don't know me well enough.

"Shit." The word snaps out of me before I can swallow it.

I move fast, bruises protesting but my training taking over. Lights off. Shades drawn. Every blind spot checked. My Glock clears its holster with a familiar weight, low and steady. I sweep the apartment room by room — bedroom, bathroom, kitchen — heart ticking a steady metronome in my ears. No one here now. Just the ghost of someone's presence and the tiny shifts they left for me to find.

The kit under the bed comes out next: second set of clothes, burner phones, cash, passports. I start packing in precise motions, folding only what I can carry, erasing fingerprints of myself as I go. Laptop wiped. Drives pulled. SIM card snapped in half and dropped into a glass of water. By the time I'm done, the high-rise looks like a hotel room waiting for its next guest.

I thumb open my encrypted app on a burner, type a single coded phrase, and hit send:

Delta compromised. Moving to Echo.

The message pings once and dissolves. My contact will know what it means. No names, no locations, just the shift of ground.

The city hums outside, unaware. Inside, the last of my things go into a black duffel. Pain drags at me, but adrenaline keeps my hands steady. Victory Park is burned. Fort Worth cover is still alive. That's where I go next. I shoulder the bag, glance once at the skyline through the blackout glass, and lock the door behind me. Whoever planted that lily thinks they've rattled me. They're wrong.

They've just put me back on the hunt.

Chapter 22
Beau

The smell of smoke clings to everything — clothes, skin, the damp grass under my boots. Fire crews swarm the presidential house like ants, hoses arcing white against the night, sirens wailing over the low roar of collapsing beams. The second floor is gone. Leclair's wing, nothing but blackened ribs and flame.

The last time Harrington saw this kind of chaos was when Pastor Greene's affair with the choir director blew wide open. That circus had everything — late-night meetings in the fellowship hall, money gone missing from the building fund, half the congregation splitting to start their own church. For months you couldn't buy groceries without someone whispering about it in the checkout line.

But that stayed ours. Local shame, local gossip. This is different. This is fire on the university president's lawn, an international executive dead in his bed. Harrington won't be able to box this in. It'll go national before the sun comes up.

Before the questions start, I do my own sweep. The outer lawn is littered with glass and plaster, smoke curling from the windows like the building's still trying to breathe. I step over what used to be the front steps, boots crunching through debris, and let the noise of the scene fade until it's just me, the crackle of fire, and the hiss of ruptured pipes.

Leclair's wing is a ruin. The second floor's half gone, the roof peeled open like a can. I keep my flashlight low, sweeping the edge where the blast buckled the frame. The air smells of scorched wiring and something chemical—accelerant, maybe, but not standard fuel. The pattern's wrong for a gas leak. Too focused. Too clean.

I crouch near the debris field. Shattered glass, fragments of tile, a scorched fragment of desk—edges curled inward, not out. The detonation started inside. Someone wanted it precise. Contained.

I find what's left of a badge lanyard caught on the railing, melted plastic fused to the strap. The metal clasp still bears the logo: **Red Haven Foods.** I pocket it before anyone else sees. Proof of something that shouldn't be here.

The clipboards come fast after that. Campus security first, then the fire marshal, then suits flashing federal credentials like they own the ground. They all want the same thing—names, times, routes.

I give them mine clean, like I've done a hundred times before. North perimeter, across the quad, looped the south dorms, back up toward the presidential house. I write it once, repeat it under oath on another. I leave Clara out of it. Doesn't matter that I saw her. Doesn't matter that she moved like someone with fire in her veins. Saying her name now would only raise questions I can't answer.

The fire chief reads the tally: two staff injured bad enough for medevac, one confirmed dead pulled from the east stairwell, three unaccounted for. Leclair's assistant is alive, shocky, wrapped in a blanket. No sign of Leclair himself—except for what's left of his room.

I stand still, pen loose in my hand, watching smoke bleed from the roof. Heat radiates even from here, sweat prickling under my collar. I keep my face blank, my tone steady, but inside, the knot tightens.

They press harder. Did I notice anything unusual? Strange vehicles near campus? Students wandering where they shouldn't? I shake my head, keep my answers flat. My job isn't to speculate. My job is to hold the line.

But Clara's words echo anyway, the last thing she threw at me before she disappeared into the night: *Looks like you've got your hands full.*

Yeah. And she's part of the weight I'm carrying.

The questions keep circling until they all start to sound the same. Routes, times, whether I saw anything out of place. I keep my answers clipped, neutral. Professional. The fire chief thanks me, another suit checks my name off a list, and for the moment, I'm free.

That's when I notice the cameras.

They line the edge of campus now, vans stacked with satellite dishes, lenses glinting under the floodlights. Reporters with perfect hair, interns juggling cords, producers barking into earpieces. The swarm's already feeding, hungry for the story. "International executive killed in Harrington blaze" — I can hear the headline forming in their throats.

If one of them clocks me, they'll start asking questions I can't afford to answer.

I step back into the shadows, let the uniforms draw the spotlight while I angle away from the crowd. Past the cordon, through the line of campus SUVs with their tinted windows and government plates. Leclair's people won't be using them now, and the keys are still in the ignition of one. I slide behind the wheel, engine rumbling to life.

By the time the cameras turn my way, I'm already rolling north, the fire fading in the rearview.

Three hours later, the Dallas skyline breaks the horizon. I park the borrowed SUV in an underground garage and walk the last stretch to where my truck waits. Seeing it feels like home. I drop into the driver's seat, lean back, and let the weight of the night sink in. The glove box clicks open under my hand. I fish out a joint, spark it with the silver Zippo that's been riding my pocket since Kabul, and take a long pull. The smoke burns just enough to scrape the edge off.

I scroll to Benny's number and hit call. He picks up on the second ring, voice rough with sleep or whiskey. "This better be good, Beau. You know what time it is?"

"Early," I say, exhaling smoke. "Or late. Depends how you look at it."

He grunts. "Spare me philosophy. What happened?"

"Leclair's gone. His whole wing blew sky-high tonight. Fire crews are still digging through the wreckage, but they pulled at least one body out and it's not him. Media's swarming Harrington already. By morning it'll be national."

The silence on the other end stretches long enough that I wonder if the line dropped. Then Benny whistles low. "Jesucristo. *Jesus Christ.* That's not just an accident. That's a statement."

"Yeah. And the timing stinks." I rub a hand over my jaw. "I was on campus when it happened. Ran my route, got pulled into the aftermath. Answered what I had to, kept it clean. Left Clara out of it."

There's a pause, then the clatter of keys in the background. "You already had me pulling threads on her," Benny says slowly. "Now you're telling me she ghosted right after a bomb went off? *Coño, Beau.* That doesn't smell like coincidence."

"That's why I need you to push harder. Last time I told you she was too clean, too precise. Now I know it. She was moving like she had a mission tonight, and then she vanished. If she's tangled up in this, I need to know how deep."

"You're asking me to put trackers on an Orion rep."

"I'm asking you to keep me alive. Hayes isn't who she says she is, and if Orion's running two games in Harrington, I'm the one standing in the crossfire."

A long exhale rolls down the line. Then Benny's voice goes sharp, all business. "Entendido. *Understood.* I'll widen the net—bank records, travel pings, anyone she's touched in the last month. But Beau—if she's sitting on this blast, you may not like the answer I find."

"I already don't."

Silence stretches, then the faint strike of a lighter and Benny's dry laugh. "You still owe me breakfast. Extra hollandaise."

"You'd drown in it if I let you."

"Better hollandaise than fire, hermano." *Brother.* His tone drops low. "Stay alive, Beau."

The line clicks dead, leaving me with the smoke, the quiet, and Clara Hayes's name burning hotter than the wreckage still smoldering on campus.

I take one last drag, grind the joint out in the ashtray, and fire the truck to life.

Then I point the nose toward Orion. Marcus will want a report. And I need answers.

Answers Harrington won't give me.

From the street, Orion's Dallas office looks like any other tower of steel and glass. But when the elevator doors whisper open on the fourteenth floor, the illusion shifts. Same carpet. Same glossy photos of smiling workers plastered across the walls. Tonight, though, the polish feels wrong—too bright, too clean, like a hospital corridor playing at corporate warmth. Even the lilies on the reception desk cut sharper, their sweetness turned to knives.

Beverly glances up, headset tilted, smile automatic until she registers me. Her fingers twitch nervously against the keyboard. She doesn't ask questions. Just sends the message through, eyes darting away like she doesn't want to be caught looking at me too long.

"He's waiting," she says, voice a little thinner than usual.

"Thanks," I murmur, already heading down the hall.

The silence there is heavy, padded but not soft. Every step pulls me closer to the last door, the one with glass walls framing Dallas in neon teeth. Marcus stands inside, sleeves rolled, pen clicking sharp in his hand. He doesn't turn when I enter—just watches me through the reflection in the glass.

"What the hell happened in Harrington?"

I keep my voice even. "Leclair's residence went up. Second floor's gone. One dead, two injured, more unaccounted for. Fire crews are calling it unstable."

"That's the newsfeed version," Marcus snaps. "I want yours."

"I ran my route. Accounted for my time. Stayed clean when the questions came."

His jaw tightens. He circles me once, like a wolf testing a fence. "So the biggest explosion Harrington's seen in decades happens right under your nose, and all you've got for me are excuses about how clean you played it?"

I square my shoulders. "I gave you facts."

"No," he bites back, "you gave me excuses. A man with your background should have smelled this before it burned. You're supposed to be a step ahead, Beau. Instead, you're running mop-up while the whole country gets a front-row seat."

The words hit harder than I want them to. My hands curl loose at my sides, knuckles itching. "You think I lost my touch."

"I don't think," Marcus says, leaning in close, voice low and hot against my ear. "I know. Because the Beau I trusted wouldn't have let Leclair get blown to hell without knowing who lit the fuse."

I hold his stare, my pulse steady even as the fire builds in my chest. "Then maybe you should've put someone else on the ground."

For a second the silence stretches, taut as wire. Marcus studies me, eyes still hard as flint, searching for the crack he wants to see.

Then his mouth twists into something that isn't a smile. "You've got one chance to fix this, Beau. One. You bring me answers. You clean up your mess. Or I'll see to it you're permanently retired."

At Orion, *retired* doesn't mean a pension and a fishing trip. It means a bullet and a hole no one marks on a map.

I keep my face steady, even as the words burn down my spine. "You'll get your answers."

What I don't tell him is that Clara Hayes was on the ground that night, moving like someone with more purpose than a procurement rep has any right to. I don't mention the way she vanished just after Leclair's room went sky-high. I don't hint at the whispers about other divisions sniffing around Harrington, because if Marcus smells blood, he'll turn on anyone to keep Orion clean.

Right now, silence buys me space. And space is the only thing keeping me alive.

Marcus leans back, satisfied enough to let the tension ease a notch. "Clock's already running."

I give him a short nod, nothing more, then turn for the door. My reflection catches in the polished glass as I pass, a reminder of just how thin the line is I'm walking.

I don't look back.

If Marcus thinks I've lost my touch, I'll prove otherwise. But I'll do it my way. No Clara, no whispers of other departments, no loose threads for him to pull. Just the truth I can dig out before the clock runs out.

One chance. That's all he gave me.

And if I miss, I'm dead.

Chapter 23
Clara

Lilies. I've always hated the flower. I used to tell people I was allergic just to keep them away. They're not sympathy, not celebration—they're a warning. A doomsday omen. One I knew would come eventually but never thought would land here, now. After the hard drive went missing I figured that was my last free pass. Seems Orion still had a use for me—until today.

I lock the apartment behind me and head for the parking garage. Something gnaws at my gut, sharp and restless. They were here recently. They wanted me to feel it.

The air shifts as I step into the stairwell, cooler, echoing. I keep my head down, eyes up, tracking every shadow as I move. A glint off a handrail. A faint scuff on concrete. Someone was here, and maybe still is.

Just as I reach the garage entrance my phone vibrates once, low against my palm. I slip deeper into a pocket of shadow before checking it. Notifications flare across the screen—flags I set for myself. Shit. Someone's been digging into my background.

Definitely more than one player in the game now.

I slide the phone back into my pocket and move. Down the last flight, through the heavy metal door into the parking garage. The air is damp and smells of concrete dust and oil. Overhead fluorescents hum, flickering every few seconds. Every sound—footsteps, pipes creaking, a car door slamming two levels down—carries too far.

I slow my pace, scanning. Angles, shadows, blind spots. My Jeep sits near the back under a pillar, exactly where I left it. But something about the sight sets my teeth on edge.

I approach from the passenger side first, keeping low, eyes sweeping the perimeter. Under the bumpers, inside the wheel wells, behind the grill—standard counter-surveillance routine. My flashlight stays hooded in my palm, just enough of a beam to catch anything that shouldn't be there.

Then I see it: a small, matte-black tracker magnetized to the inside of the rear wheel well, blinking a heartbeat of red so faint most wouldn't notice. Someone's been following me longer than I thought. I pluck it free, palm closing over it until the light disappears, and slide it into my pocket without breaking stride.

I lean into the driver's side and the chemical tang hits under the leather. Wires where no wires should be. My gaze follows the line down, under the steering column, and my stomach drops.

Small. Compact. Taped neat to the ignition harness. A pressure switch spliced into the starter. Not a tracker, not a warning. A kill-switch bomb.

I pull back slow, breathing through my nose, counting heartbeats. One wrong move and the Jeep becomes my coffin.

My fingers find the notch I built into the trim months ago and the panel pops free on a soft click. Inside, tucked in the hollow as if it had always been waiting for this exact night, is the slim metal tool I keep for stupid road-side problems and a plain key. No fob. No brand. Clean. Good. Clean is useful.

I work slow, hands steady. The wiring here is neat and clinical, the sort of job that leaves no room for panic. I don't cut. I don't yank. I trace the feed, find the splice that ties the pressure switch into the starter, and use the tool to lift the tiniest clamp. It takes ten fingers and the calm of someone who has done worse things in worse places, but when the clamp slips free the circuit goes open and the starter is a harmless coil of wires again. The threat goes quiet.

I slide the panel back, tuck the tool inside my palm, and edge out. Two steps from the Jeep I crouch and peer under the chassis. There, bolted and banded to the rear crossmember, is a flat puck with a short aerial. A tracker. Someone who wants to know where I go even after the Jeep stops burning.

I strip the bolts quick and quiet, fingers working with practiced patience until the unit comes free. It's smaller than I expected, heavier than it looks. I pocket it. Leave with pockets full of trouble.

I drive. The city thins behind me, taillights swallowed by wet asphalt. The gravel pit comes up sooner than I like, a half-moon of broken stone tucked between trees the cops never bother to cut. I ease the Jeep into the center, far from the saplings, engine ticking as it cools.

I pop the hood, breath shallow, hands moving quick and sure. I do what I came to do without thinking too long about it—give the charge the one thing that will let it do its work without me in the blast radius. No heroics, no fiddling; just the clean push it needs and nothing more. The metal smells like ozone and oil, my glove sticking to the rim of the hood for a heartbeat.

Back at the driver's seat I leave a glove splayed over the passenger bench and tear a strip from my jacket, knotting it around the wheel as if I fought and lost. Little details make a story believable. I drop the unmarked key into my pocket and slide out before the Jeep cools.

My boots crunch over gravel as I step away. Each pace presses the plan into motion. I keep my face forward, shoulders tight, the bike waiting where I stashed it under the tarp a block off. I don't look back until the heat hits the back of my neck.

The blast rips the air open. Light blooms white and then orange, a sudden sun where there should be none. The sound follows, low and hungry, a freight train rolled into two seconds. Stone and dirt spray up in a heartbeat, and the shock hits my chest like a hand. I keep walking—faster now—boots slipping on grit, jacket slapping my ribs. The world behind me fractures into noise and light and the smell of burning rubber and plastic.

I let it happen without watching. Let them see the picture they want. Smoke fattens and curls into the trees. Somewhere a siren begins, thin and keening, but I keep going until the heat is only a memory and the city swallows the sound again.

I don't stop until the gravel gives way to cracked pavement and the trees thin into the row of forgotten warehouses. The tarp I stashed the bike under is a shadow among shadows, draped over a dented delivery crate two blocks off the pit. My breath fogs in the cooler air. My legs burn from the walk but the adrenalin keeps it steady.

I drop the tarp in one motion. The bike sits folded in darkness, sleek and patient, black like a held breath. My fingers trace the tank, feeling the faint warmth left from the last time I ran it. I strip the jacket and helmet from the canvas roll, the leather sticky with grit, and pull them on. The weight of the helmet lands like a decision.

I move with fast, efficient hands—check the chain, twist the throttle to feel the idle, thumb the kill switch, a ritual that keeps me honest. The engine answers, hungry and sure. Light bounces off chrome, reflecting the smear of smoke still rising from the pit on the horizon.

I swing a leg over and tuck the unmarked key into the slot. For a second I let the sound fill me, a small rightness in a world that's been wrong. The visor snaps down. The road snaps into place.

I roll off the lot, tires finding the alley with a soft hiss. The city breathes around me, streets waking, people unaware of the stage they're passing through. I ease onto the main and point the nose south, away from the blast and toward the logic of the plan. My shoulders loosen fractionally with the motion. The bike pulls like an animal reading the leash.

I don't look back again. Not for the smoke, not for the flames. Not for the picture they'll make of the night. Headlights cut a ribbon through the dim. I tuck into the lane and ride, every mile folding the danger into distance.

The bike spits a couple of tired coughs as I pull up curbside and kill the engine. The helmet snaps up with one hand. The city smells like gasoline, pretzel carts, and the faint curl of smoke still drifting from the gravel pit. My fingers are gritty from the pit, the unmarked key warm against my palm. The tracker is gone. So is the bomb. Both done and buried where they'll tell the story I need them to tell.

If they want me dead, fine. Let them have the picture. I might as well eat first.

I walk into the diner like I walk into every room where I need to be invisible. Head down, shoulders loose, eyes cataloging exits without looking like I am. The bell over the door sings the same tired note. Fluorescent lights wash the vinyl booths in an honest, ugly glow.

Every step pulls at the bruises blooming under my skin. My ribs ache with the memory of fists. My wrists throb where rope burned too deep. Even the weight of the leather jacket makes my shoulders scream, but I don't let it show. Pain is familiar. Pain is cover.

The place is quieter than it should be for this hour. A few regulars, a kid scrolling through a phone, Doris at the far end wiping a tabletop with the same slow, careful motion she uses on the world. She lifts her face and something soft passes through her expression. Recognition without curiosity. Safe.

I sit at the counter because booths invite conversation. I need crowd noise around me, faces to hide behind. I ease onto the stool slow, careful not to let my ribs brush the edge of the counter, and drop the helmet on the seat beside me. The motion alone makes my muscles scream, but I grit down on it.

The waitress sets a cup in front of me. I curl my hands around it before she can walk away, inhale like the heat might unknot the tremor living under my ribs. It doesn't. It just stabilizes it.

"Short stack, blueberry compote," I say, quick and firm, leaving no space for questions. The waitress nods and moves. Doris pads over with two napkins folded on her palm. She sets one in front of me without a word. There is a way people can ask what is wrong without saying the words. Doris asks like that and I answer with a posture.

I watch the street through the diner's long window while I wait for food. The city yawns by in small dramas. A man with a briefcase hails a cab. A woman with wind in her hair laughs at something on her phone. Life keeps going, unaware. None of it belongs to me. None of it can touch what I carry in my jacket.

The pancakes arrive on a chipped plate like a benediction. Butter melts into the warm fluff, the blueberry compote thick and generous, bruised fruit that tastes of summer and things I will never have. I stab my fork in like defusing a small ritual. The first bite is a memory of normal that sits heavy and impossible on my tongue.

The TV above the counter hums low, just background noise until the tone shifts.

Breaking News. The anchor's voice cuts through the clatter of plates. "Explosion reported at the Presidential House early this morning. At least five confirmed dead, including Victor Leclair, exe early this morning. At least five confirmed dead, including Victor Leclair, executive liaison for Red Haven Foods. Officials have not ruled out foul play."

The footage flickers—flames clawing at white columns, smoke spilling across the capital lawn. Sirens wail. The anchor keeps talking, but the words fade, replaced by the static rush in my ears. Victor Leclair. Dead.

The plate is warm beneath my hands, syrup pooling like amber glass. I cut another bite, pretending it's just breakfast, pretending the world hasn't shifted again.

Then he slides onto the stool beside me, close enough that the faint scent of leather, smoke, and coffee cuts through the sugar in the air.

"Pancakes do fix just 'bout everything," Beau drawls, voice low, rough around the edges, threaded with too many unspoken things. He leans an elbow on the counter like he owns it. "Though you are sittin' in my seat."

I don't look at him right away. My fork hovers, knife scraping lightly against porcelain. He's baiting me, waiting to see if I'll bite. Heat coils in my stomach—not from the pancakes. From him. From the way his gray eyes track me like he already knows my rhythm, my precision.

Finally, I angle my head, lips curving into a polite half-smile. "Is that so? I don't see your name on it."

"Don't need my name on it," he says easily, sipping from the mug the waitress sets in front of him. "Everybody knows it."

The banter is light on the surface, but my pulse betrays me. He shouldn't be here. Not tonight. Not now, when my cover is already splintering and every second is weighted with choices I can't take back. And yet—he is. Always sliding in when the edges fray, always watching.

The waitress tops off my coffee, drops the check without asking, and drifts away. I cut another neat triangle, though the taste barely registers. I can feel him watching more than I can taste the food.

"Funny thing," Beau says after a beat, tone casual, almost lazy. "We keep runnin' into each other in places most folks wouldn't expect. College towns. Warehouses. Now here." He stirs his coffee with a spoon he doesn't need, gaze steady on the swirl. "Almost like we've been circling the same table from different sides."

My fork pauses, then continues its path to my mouth. My smile is faint, controlled. "Some tables are big enough for more than one seat. Doesn't mean we're here for the same meal."

He chuckles, low and rich, like I've just said something funny when we both know I haven't. "Fair point. Still—funny how we seem to order off the same menu. Same night. Same city. Same target."

The word target hits like a blade pressed to the ribs. I keep my face still, sip my coffee as if it's nothing more than caffeine warming my chest. Inside, my pulse hammers. He knows more than he should. Or maybe he's fishing. Either way, he's too close.

"Targets are relative," I murmur, setting the cup down with deliberate care. "Depends who's paying the bill. Some people want compliance. Others want closure."

His smile never wavers, but his eyes sharpen. "And which one are you after tonight?"

"Neither." I cut another triangle of pancake, lift it slow. "I'm just here for pancakes."

The bite lingers on my tongue, syrup sweet and cloying. Too sweet. I chew slow, keeping my hands steady even though every word out of his mouth feels like a test.

"Well then," Beau says, smirk tugging at his lips, "guess I'm just here for coffee. Shame if anyone thought we were...comparing notes."

"Notes?" I tilt my head just enough to study him sidelong, keeping my tone mild. "About what?"

He shrugs, slow, easy, like none of this matters. "About how accidents sometimes ain't accidents. About how certain names draw too much attention when they show up in small towns. About how some folks are real precise, down to the second."

My fork stills halfway to my plate. Precise. He's watching me closer than he lets on. My smile doesn't falter, though my jaw is tight. "Precision keeps things clean," I say lightly. "You'd know that, wouldn't you?"

His grin fades into something steadier, more pointed. He leans in, close enough that the warmth of his arm brushes mine. "Reckon I would. Reckon you'd know too."

The air thickens, syrup and coffee suddenly heavy in my throat. To anyone watching, it's harmless banter—cowboy meets inspector, late-night flirtation at a counter. But beneath the words, I hear what he's really asking. *What side of Orion are you on, Clara?*

I sip my coffee to buy time, though it tastes bitter now. "Why would I compare notes, Beau? Few at our table can be trusted."

His eyes glint, like I've confirmed something for him. He sets his mug down with a deliberate clink, leaning back just enough to look at me fully. "Because some of us don't bother with cover stories. Beau isn't a name I cooked up—it's just who I am. Night terrors, ranch dirt under my nails, homemade remedies and weed to take the edge off. No polish. No mask." His voice dips lower, cutting through the noise of the diner. "Question is—who are you under all that precision?"

Heat curls low in my stomach, dangerous and uninvited. He shouldn't ask me that. I shouldn't want to answer. But the truth is, I don't know anymore. Clara Hayes is supposed to be untouchable, clean, disciplined. And yet here I am, pulse hammering at a cowboy who looks at me like he sees straight through the steel.

I force my lips into a smile, sharper than it feels. "I'm whoever I need to be."

His gaze lingers, slow and heavy, the corner of his mouth twitching like he knows exactly how much of a lie that is.

And damn him—I think he does.

Chapter 24
Beau

"I'll be who I need to be," she says, steady as a trigger pull, voice smooth enough to almost make me believe it.

But I don't.

I tip my coffee, let the bitterness burn down my throat, and keep my eyes on her. "See, that's the thing, Clara. I don't get to be whoever I need to be. Beau's all there is. Night terrors, busted knuckles. Weed and whiskey to take the edge off. Dirt under my nails that don't wash out no matter how many showers I take. No polish. No mask."

Her fork stills midair. She studies me like she's trying to decide if that's honesty or just another mask of its own. Then, quiet enough that only I can hear it, she says:

"They left me a lily."

The words land like a gunshot under the noise of the diner. Lily. My gut knots. Every Orion agent knows what that means. A lily isn't a flower—it's a funeral notice. End of service. End of use. End of you.

I set my mug down slow, the ceramic heavy against the counter. "You sure?"

Her eyes lock on mine—sharp, deliberate, like she's aiming for the part of me that still flinches.

"One bloom," she says. "And a note. Said mistakes are the only legacy that lingers. Even yours."

Legacy. My jaw tightens. They didn't just tag her—they branded her with her own bloodline. Orion never wastes ink unless they want the message burned in.

I lean a fraction closer, keep my voice low and even. "Then why the hell are you sittin' here eatin' pancakes like it's Sunday morning?"

Her smile is small, razor-thin. "Because if it is my last meal, I'm going to enjoy it. And if it isn't—" she taps her fork once against the plate, the sound sharp, decisive "—then it means Orion underestimated me. Again."

For a second, I almost smile. She's reckless, stubborn as hell, and already marked. But the fire in her eyes? That's not someone ready to lay down.

And that scares me more than the lily.

I lean in, let my arm brush against the counter, close enough that the heat between us feels like it could set the diner on fire. "You don't have to ride this out alone."

Her fork pauses mid-cut, hesitation flickering in her eyes before she shutters it. "And what—share notes over black coffee and cigarette smoke? You know as well as I do there aren't many tables in this world worth sitting at."

I shake my head slow, jaw set. "Ain't about notes. I got a ranch a few hours south, quiet as the grave. No one to ask questions. You need a place to breathe, to plan, to get Orion's knife outta your ribs—it's there. Open."

Her lips part like she's about to cut me off, but she doesn't. Not right away. The silence stretches, loud under the clatter of dishes and Doris pouring refills three stools down.

Finally, she exhales through her nose, low. "You don't know what you're offering, Beau."

"Sure I do." I meet her eyes head-on. "Sanctuary. For as long as you need it."

She studies me, searching for the angle, the catch. There isn't one. Just a man tired of watching Orion chew people up and spit them onto the concrete.

Her hand hovers over the coffee cup, knuckles pale where she grips the handle. The sleeve of her jacket shifts just enough for me to catch it — the faint ridged marks ringing her wrist like ghost shackles. Rope burns. Fresh. Her posture looks loose, casual, but her shoulders are tight, a stiffness she can't quite hide. She's hurting. Sore. Running on nerve and habit, not strength.

"Why are you doing this?" she asks quietly.

"We've been circling each other for days — same towns, same targets, different orders — and now you're offering me an escape hatch like we're not on opposite ends of the same gun." I let the words sit, eyes still on those wrists, on the way she forces herself to hold steady. I lean a little closer, voice dropping rough and steady. "Maybe because I'm tired of watchin' Orion stack bodies on the altar and call it efficiency. Maybe because I don't like seein' you lined up next."

Her mouth tightens, but her eyes betray the smallest crack, a sliver of something softer. She doesn't say yes. Doesn't say no. Just sits there, caught between instinct and exhaustion, and for the first time all night, I think she's actually considering it.

"And when Orion finds out?" she finally asks.

"Then they'll have to get through me first."

The words come out like a vow before I can dress them up. And by the look in her eyes—sharp, suspicious, but edged with something unguarded—I know she heard the part I didn't say out loud: *I don't want you to die, Clara. Not like this.*

Her eyes drop to her plate, tracing the rim of syrup like she's reading the future in it. For a heartbeat I think she'll tell me to go to hell, stand up, and walk out. Instead she says, almost to herself, "Every time I think I've got control of the board, Orion flips it over."

"Then maybe it's time you stop playin' on their board," I murmur, keeping my voice low, steady. "Come south. Days, not weeks. Clear your head. No lily. No knives."

She lifts her eyes to mine, slow, deliberate. "And do what? Hide out while the rest of the pieces fall?"

"Not hide. Breathe. Eat breakfast without lookin' over your shoulder." I let the corner of my mouth tug, a flicker of dry humor under the weight. "Hell, maybe even find out if pancakes really do fix just about everything."

That earns me the faintest ghost of a smile. "Blades over breakfast," she says under her breath, as if tasting the phrase. "That's more like it."

"Could be worse ways to start a day," I say, leaning in just enough to close the space between us. "Could be worse ways to start a fight."

Her fingers tighten on the mug, knuckles white. She looks at me like she's trying to see past the ranch dirt and busted knuckles to whatever's underneath. "You don't even know who I am under this."

"Don't need to." I tilt my head, voice a shade rougher. "I just know you're sittin' here with a lily in your hand and no good options. I'm offerin' you one."

The air between us hums—coffee, sugar, steel. To anyone else it's just a man and a woman at a diner counter. But every word we trade is a coded question, a test of where the other stands.

Finally she exhales, slow. "And if I come out there?"

"Then you'll have a door that locks behind you, a kitchen that don't serve lilies, and a man who's got no interest in puttin' a knife in your back."

Her mouth curves, almost sad. "You make it sound easy."

"It ain't easy. But it's real."

She hesitates, fork hovering over the last triangle of pancake. In her eyes there's still calculation, but there's also something else now—a flicker of wanting. Of exhaustion. Of maybe believing me.

I don't push. Just let her sit with it, let her decide if she wants out or if she wants to keep walking into Orion's teeth.

Her fork finally drops against the plate, the last bite of pancake untouched. She studies me for a long beat, something sharp and unreadable flickering behind her eyes. Then she leans in just enough that only I can hear it.

"Alright," she says, voice steady but low, like she's daring herself to believe it. "I'll come. But we have to make a stop first."

The words hang there, heavy. Not a refusal. Not surrender. A condition.

I search her face, but she gives me nothing—just the smooth, precise mask of a woman who's lived too long under Orion's shadow.

"Stop where?" I ask carefully, already knowing she won't give me the real answer.

Her lips curve into something faint, dangerous. "Someplace that doesn't serve pancakes."

I let out a breath, slow. She's not giving me details. Not yet. But she said *okay*. That's more than I expected.

"Fine," I say, leaning back, voice low and rough. "We'll make your stop. But after that, Clara, we're headed south. No detours."

Her gaze holds mine a second longer, testing, measuring, then she nods once. Agreement—or the closest thing I'm going to get to one.

I toss a couple bills on the counter, enough to cover her plate and then some, and follow her out into the night.

The parking lot hums with sodium lights, throwing long shadows across the cracked pavement. She heads straight for the far corner, and that's when I see it—the bike. Sleek, black, polished down to the bolts. A predator crouched on two wheels.

She doesn't glance at me as she pulls a leather jacket from the saddlebag, shrugging into it like it was made for her skin. The zipper slides up, hugging every sharp line of her frame, and for a second I forget to breathe. Helmet in hand, she finally looks my way.

"Follow me," she says, voice muffled as she pulls the visor down. No explanation. No plan. Just an order.

The engine roars to life, low and hungry, and she swings a leg over the bike with the kind of ease that tells me this isn't her first escape. For a heartbeat, the glow from the diner's neon catches on her helmet, painting her in firelight. And damn if it doesn't look like she was born for it.

I smirk to myself, sliding into the truck. Figures. I've met plenty of people who look good with a weapon in their hands. But her? She looks good leaving destruction in her wake.

I keep her tail-lights in view as she weaves out of Dallas traffic like the city bends to her rhythm. Me in the truck, her carving a line ahead—like two halves of something the world wouldn't understand if it saw it straight.

By the time we hit Fort Worth, the streets have gone quiet, the city's heartbeat slowing into late-night silence. She pulls up outside a nondescript house, the kind you'd drive past a hundred times without ever remembering. No porch light. No welcome mat. Just shadows and silence.

She kills the engine and swings off the bike, helmet tucked under her arm. "This is the stop," she says, tone final, like it's been waiting for her all along.

I park across the street, engine still rumbling low. My hand lingers on the wheel as I watch her walk toward the door, leather jacket cutting through the dark like a blade.

And I can't shake the feeling that whatever waits inside, it's about to cut both of us.

Chapter 25
Clara

The house waits in silence, every window black, the kind of quiet that hums louder than any city street. I kill the bike, swing off, and pull the helmet free. My hair clings damp to my temples, but I don't bother fixing it. No point in polish when the air already smells like secrets.

Behind me, Beau's truck idles for half a beat before shutting down. His boots hit pavement, steady and deliberate, and then he's at my side. Too close. Close enough that I can feel the weight of him even before he speaks.

"You sure about this?" His voice is low, gruff, but there's no judgment in it—just the weight of someone who's already bracing for the fallout.

"I'm sure," I answer, though the word tastes like glass. My hand slips into the pocket where the spare key rests cold and unmarked. I slip it into the lock, the click echoing louder than it should, and push the door open.

The smell hits first. Stale air, dust, faint soap—nothing that screams intrusion, but nothing that feels like home either. Beau follows me inside without hesitation, shoulders brushing mine as we step into the narrow entry.

We move together, silent and precise, the way two predators circle the same ground. He veers left, eyes cutting over the living room; I take the right, scanning the kitchen, the shadows under the table, the line of cabinets. Each step is measured, every corner cleared.

The tension hums under my skin. Not just the possibility of what we might find—but the press of him at my back, the way his presence fills the room, heavy as gravity.

I edge into the living room, penlight low, sweeping it across the floor in slow arcs. My ribs ache with each breath, wrists throbbing under the jacket cuffs where the rope bit deep. The bruises make everything feel heavier, slower.

That's when my boot catches — a cord strung too tight across the floor. Pain spikes up my side as my body pitches forward, the sharp edge of the coffee table rushing toward my temple.

Before I can brace, strong hands clamp around my waist and yank me back in one clean motion. The movement jolts every bruise, knocking a hiss out of me before I can swallow it. My shoulder hits his chest, hard and solid, and his arm locks around me, steadying me until my feet find the floor again.

The table edge misses by an inch. His heartbeat is against my back, his breath warm against my hair. For a second all I can do is stay there, trembling, hating that I'm trembling, fighting the pull between pain, adrenaline, and the unexpected steadiness of him holding me up.

"Careful," he mutters, voice hot against my ear.

I freeze, heart hammering, every nerve sparking at the heat of his grip. His breath ghosts over my cheek, steady, unshaken, while mine comes sharp and ragged.

"Cord wasn't here last time," I whisper, forcing the words out, though my focus is split between the warning and the feel of his hand splayed against my ribs.

He doesn't let go right away. His fingers flex once, almost like he's grounding himself, then he eases me upright, close enough that I still feel the warmth where he touched.

Our eyes meet in the dim light, too close, too long. I can read the unspoken question in his stare—how much of this is Orion, and how much is us.

I swallow hard, tear my gaze away, and crouch to trace the cord. Not an accident. Set there to trip someone. To mark that someone had been here.

"Looks like you were right," Beau says behind me, tone low, threaded with something darker. "House isn't clean."

Neither am I, I think, but I don't say it out loud.

The hallway feels narrower than it should, shadows pressing in on either side. My penlight skims along the walls, catching on old nail holes, a chipped frame, the faint scuff of boots that don't belong to me.

Beau moves just behind me, quiet for a man his size, but I can feel him there—the weight of him, the steady heat, the way his breath shifts the air.

I stop at the corner where the hallway splits, one path toward the bedroom, the other toward the back door. His shoulder brushes mine when he comes up beside me, solid as stone, close enough that I catch the low rasp of his breathing. Our lights overlap, beams colliding on the blank stretch of wall in front of us.

The air tightens. Too close, too quiet. His scent wraps around me—smoke, leather, a trace of whiskey he hasn't had tonight but lingers anyway. I tilt my head just slightly, and there it is—his breath mingling with mine, warm, steady, intimate in the worst possible place.

Every instinct screams at me to move, to push forward, to keep control. But control has been slipping since Dallas. Since the lily. Since the bomb under my ignition.

"Fuck it," I whisper, sharp, decisive.

Before I can think better of it, I close the distance, pressing my mouth to his. It's rough, urgent, not the kind of kiss you plan but the kind you fall into because the fire's already lit and you're done pretending you don't feel it.

His hand comes up, steady at my jaw, anchoring me. The wall at my back, the heat of him in front—it's like every ghost in this house vanishes for one impossible second.

Then I breathe him in, taste him, and I know there's no walking this back.

The kiss doesn't break. If anything, it sharpens, like flint striking steel. Beau doesn't hesitate, doesn't pull back—he leans into me, mouth firm, hungry, answering mine with heat that's been simmering under every sharp word and every look since Harrington.

I feel the hallway disappear around us as we stumble forward, mouths still locked, shoulders brushing the walls. My hand fists in the fabric of his shirt, dragging him closer, needing more. His arm wraps firm around my waist, steadying me, steering me without breaking stride.

We don't stop until the bedroom doorframe hits my shoulder. He nudges it open with the weight of his body, crowding me inside, never once letting go. The bed waits in the half-light, sheets still pulled tight from a life I don't live anymore.

We fall onto it in a tangle, the world spinning for a breath before he braces himself above me. His weight presses me into the mattress, solid, immovable, and my pulse hammers against every inch of him.

His mouth leaves mine just long enough for a gasp, then it's back—rougher now, teeth catching, tongue demanding. My hands slide up into his hair, pulling him down harder. His hat is long gone, tossed somewhere down the hall, and I don't care where.

The scrape of his belt buckle against my hip makes me shiver, sharp and electric. He groans low in his chest, a sound that feels like it was pulled from somewhere deep, and presses harder, hips grinding once against mine.

We're still clothed—jeans, jacket, leather, layers between us—but it feels like nothing. The heat cuts through it all, blurring the edges of thought until the only thing left is want.

"Clara," he breathes against my throat, low and ragged, as if saying my name costs him something.

I arch up into him, nails digging into his shoulders, and for the first time all night I stop thinking about lilies, bombs, or Orion.

For once, it's just this. Him. Me. The fire we've been circling finally set alight.

His mouth leaves mine, trailing lower, rough kisses pressing against my jaw, down the line of my throat. Each one steals a breath from me, each one setting my skin on fire. My head tips back, instinctive, baring myself to him, arching into the heat.

And that's when I see it.

The moonlight cuts through the thin curtains, silvering the nightstand. A vase sits there, glass clear, water catching the light. And inside—lilies. White, perfect, pristine.

Every ounce of heat drains out of me in an instant. My blood goes cold. The symbol is unmistakable. The message is clear.

Orion was here.

My body tenses hard beneath Beau, and his lips still against my skin. He feels the change in me immediately, lifts his head just enough to search my face. My eyes aren't on him anymore—they're locked on the flowers.

Lilies. My funeral notice. My death warrant. A reminder that no matter how far I run, they'll always be one step ahead.

My breath hitches, but not from his touch. My eyes go wide before I even realize it, the sound of my pulse drowning out everything else. The lilies stare back at me from the nightstand, white petals like open hands in the moonlight.

"Clara?" Beau's voice is low, still husky from the moment, but I'm already shoving at his chest. His gaze follows mine, tracks the line of my stare until it lands on the flowers. I feel the muscles under my palms go rigid as he sees them too.

I scramble out from under him, the sheets tangling at my knees. "No," I rasp, shaking my head. "I can't—God, I can't do this. Not with you."

"Hey." He's on his feet in a second, reaching out but stopping short, hands hanging open. "Clara—"

"They'll always find me!" My voice cracks, raw and ugly. "No matter how clean I run, how careful I am, they'll leave a lily and a note and they'll take everything I touch. Everything." I back up until my spine hits the cold wall, hugging my arms around myself like I can hold it all in.

Beau takes a slow step toward me, eyes flicking from my face to the flowers, reading more than I'm saying. The moonlight cuts across him too, silvering his jaw, softening nothing. "They put it here," he murmurs. "A lily in your safe house."

I nod once, sharp, breath shuddering out of me. "You don't get it. This isn't just a threat. This is a countdown. I shouldn't have brought you here."

He studies me, steady as stone, but there's something behind his eyes—anger, maybe, or the same vow he made in the diner. "You think I scare easy?"

"They don't leave survivors," I snap, softer but still shaking. "They don't leave...anything."

For a beat, it's just the two of us in the bedroom, the lilies bleeding their perfume into the dark, crowding out the heat that was there seconds ago. Every unsaid truth hangs heavy between us, thicker than the moonlight spilling across the bed.

Chapter 26
Beau

The words slice deeper than I expect. My chest still burns where her palms pressed. I drag a hand down my jaw, force my voice low and steady. "You think I don't know what it means to have Orion breathing down your neck?"

Her laugh is sharp, hollow. "You don't know what it's like to wake up every morning knowing you're already a dead woman walking."

I take a slow step closer, not touching her, but close enough that her shoulders tense. "No, Clara. I know exactly what that's like. I've lived with it for years."

Her lips part, like she wants to spit fire, but nothing comes out. Just the sound of her breath, shaky, uneven, mingling with mine in the dark.

"You're not alone in this," I say finally, the words rough, unsanded. "Not unless you choose to be."

The words hang there between us, heavy as a loaded gun. She's close enough that I can see the tremor in her fingers, the pulse jumping at her throat. Moonlight cuts across her face, throwing one eye into shadow, the other glinting like a blade.

I want to reach for her, to steady the tremor, but I hold back. If I touch her now, she'll bolt. If I don't, she might break.

Her breath hits my collarbone, quick and shallow. She whispers, almost to herself, "They'll always find me."

"Let 'em try," I murmur, stepping closer anyway. My boots scuff against the hardwood; her scent is all salt and adrenaline now, not perfume. "You think I don't know what that lily means? You think I'd still be standin' here if I didn't?"

She flinches at that, just enough to let me see the crack in her armor. "Then why?" she asks, voice fraying at the edges. "Why are you still here?"

"Because I don't run from ghosts," I say, softer than I mean to. "And because I don't leave people to die alone."

For a moment, she closes her eyes, and the fight drains out of her shoulders. We're so close our breath mingles, warm and uneven. My hand lifts before I can stop it, fingers grazing her jaw, thumb tracing the curve just below her lip. She doesn't pull back—but she doesn't lean in either.

"Let me help you," I say, low enough it's a growl. "Come back to the ranch. Just a few days. Get your head clear. Make a plan that doesn't end with a body bag."

Her eyes snap open at that, sharp again, but softer somewhere behind it. "You don't know what you're asking."

"Yeah," I whisper. "I do."

The air between us is razor-thin, her breath brushing mine, her eyes locked like she's daring me to push or daring herself not to fall. I don't. Not yet. Instead, I step past her, slow and deliberate, toward the nightstand.

The lilies lean in the moonlight, white petals too perfect, too clean. Death dressed as purity. My gut knots as I reach for the vase, fingers brushing glass slick with condensation. Something stiff catches against my knuckle.

Tucked beneath the stems, folded sharp, is another note. Small. Precise. Waiting.

I ease it free, the paper damp at the edges, and smooth it flat against my palm. The handwriting is careful, deliberate, like every stroke was meant to cut.

"Mistakes pile up. Legacies rot. You are finished."

My jaw tightens. Same message as before, only louder. Only final.

I glance back at Clara. She hasn't moved, but her knuckles are white where she grips the edge of the dresser, body strung tight like a bow about to snap. Her eyes flick to the note, then back to me.

"They want you to see it," I say, voice low, steady. "Want you to choke on it."

She swallows hard, throat working, but doesn't answer.

I fold the paper once, slide it into my jacket pocket, and meet her stare head-on. "Not tonight."

"What'd you come here for, Clara?" My voice is low, even, but it doesn't leave her any room to dodge. "'Cause you didn't drag me across half of Texas just to gawk at flowers."

Her lips press tight, jaw ticking like she wants to throw the question back. But finally she exhales, shaky, and crosses to the closet.

She kneels, fingers slipping under the floorboard until I hear the faint scrape of wood lifting. A small black duffel slides free, worn at the edges, zipper tab wrapped in red tape.

Her go bag. The kind of insurance you only keep when you never believe in safe havens.

"I stashed it after... him," she says, voice flat but strained, not looking at me. "Just in case I ever had to run."

She sets it on the bed and unzips it in one clean motion. Inside are stacked external hard drives and thumb drives tucked into labeled pouches, a compact encrypted laptop, a blacked-out power bank and spare batteries, a tangle of chargers, burner phone and extra SIMs taped to a card, laminated copies of IDs and a thin sheaf of emergency contacts, and a roll of cash. Not clothes, but data and lifelines — everything you need to vanish.

I step closer, eyes locked on hers. "So what's it gonna be? You running, or you finally letting someone watch your six?"

"I don't run," she says, flat, final. The words land like a fist in my gut more than anything else she's said tonight.

She moves before I can say anything, quick and efficient the way I've seen her move in the dock and at the pool table. Her hand leaves the duffel and goes for her phone. I watch the tilt of her shoulders, the way she breathes through it like she's counting off a checklist only she can see.

The screen wakes, thumb sliding with practiced speed. She types a short line, no flourish, no wasted words. I catch the words as they flash, brief and binary in the glow:

Latte: Lily. Echo. Compromised.

Sent. The phone chirps once and the display folds dark.

Then she does something small and violent. She yanks the lilies from the vase. White petals fall like confetti, soft at first, then wet and limp as she pulls. She doesn't pause to pity them. She drops the flowers onto the hardwood and presses her boot into them, grinding them into a smear of white and sticky water.

My mouth goes dry. That move is a calling card all on its own. Orion knows how to speak in symbols. A lily on the pillow meant one thing. A crushed lily under a boot says something else entirely. Intent. Defiance. Trash the omen and the omen no longer owns you.

She doesn't stop there. With her free hand she lifts the phone, flicks the little sim slot open with a nail, tears the tiny card free, and snaps it in half. The broken halves she drops deliberately into the vase, into the water that's still sloshing, sending a pale web of bubbles up and popping them with the soft sound of regret.

Then she lifts the phone and drops that too, face down, into the water. The glass takes it with a dull plunk. She watches it sink like she's watching a threat drown.

Silence hangs heavy for a second, the only sounds the small drip from the smashed stems and the quiet settling of the house. I step forward before I think about it, boots quiet on the rug.

"You okay?" I ask. My voice is no softer than it needs to be. I shouldn't be surprised by the ritual. I shouldn't be surprised she burned a line to Latte. Still, seeing a trained operator reduce her comms to ruin feels like watching someone set their own hand on fire to prove a point.

Her jaw works. For a moment she looks almost like the woman at the counter who ate pancakes calm as winter. Then she straightens, shoulders squared, and the work face slides back on like armor.

"Phone is wet," she says, dry. "Sim's toast. They'll listen to the line if it rings. If they don't get that message, then they're blind. If they get it, they'll move."

I digest that, then glance to the vase, to the soaked petals and the floating shards of plastic. The image, ugly and final, sits heavy between us.

"You could come to the ranch for a couple days," I say, the offer steady and immediate. "Lay low, plan. I'll keep the visitors list honest."

She looks at me and, for the first time all night, I see something softer under the steel. Exhaustion. A tether that's almost pleading.

"Two days," she answers, voice small but firm. "That's all. Then I finish it."

I nod once. "Two days," I echo, though the words scrape like gravel in my throat.

She squares her shoulders, steady as stone. "That's all I need."

The room feels smaller for it, air heavy with crushed lilies and the ghost of what almost happened between us. I should keep my distance. Hell, I *need* to. Getting close to her doesn't just blur lines—it paints a target over both our heads.

But the sight of her, standing there with her chin high and defiance written in every line of her body, does something to me I can't shake. I want to believe she can shoulder this on her own. I want to let her. And yet the thought of Orion gutting her life piece by piece makes my chest tighten in a way that feels too much like a promise.

She's fire and precision, a woman already marked for death. The smart move is to step back, let her burn on her own terms. Instead I find myself closer than I meant to be, voice low, almost betraying me. *Just don't forget—you don't have to do this alone."*

Her eyes flash at me, hard as steel, daring me to mean it.

And I already do. Too much.

We don't say much after that. The silence sits between us, thick with everything we haven't admitted and the lilies ground into the floor. She grabs her bag, movements clipped, controlled, and I force myself not to reach for it, not to reach for her.

Outside, the night air is cooler, cleaner. My truck idles at the curb, a low growl in the dark. She wheels the bike up beside it, and I lift it into the bed, the weight heavy but familiar. I cinch the straps down tight, checking them twice. She watches, arms folded, helmet under one arm, her face carved sharp in the moonlight.

"Won't scratch it," I tell her, giving the tie-downs a last tug.

"Better not," she fires back, but the edge in her voice is softer now, almost weary.

We climb in without another word. Her bag at her feet, her stare fixed on the road ahead. My hands on the wheel, knuckles pale where I grip it harder than I should.

The house disappears in the rearview, swallowed by shadow. Ahead, four hours of asphalt and silence, the dark road binding us. Past that, the ranch.

I don't know what happens when we get there. Tonight, for the first time, she isn't walking alone.

The headlights eat the highway. Four hours for silence to thicken and thoughts to sharpen.

She sits angled toward the window, arms folded tight, like she's holding herself together with will alone. I catch her reflection in the glass, jaw set, eyes rimmed in exhaustion. For a long time she does not move. Then her head tips against the doorframe. Her breaths go shallow and uneven, as if she is still fighting in her sleep. Fitful, restless.

I keep my eyes on the road and glance over every few miles. She twitches, murmurs something I can't catch, fingers curling against her thigh like she's bracing for impact.

I tighten my grip on the wheel. She is not safe here. Not with Orion on her heels. Not with me. And yet I keep driving south.

Four hours to the ranch. Four hours to figure out what the hell I'm doing.

Chapter 27
Clara

The rhythm of the tires lulls me under, and the cab dissolves into shadow.

I'm small again, standing in a hall that stretches forever, walls paneled in mirrored glass. Each reflection shows a different me—Clara Hayes in braids and school shoes, Clara Hayes with a clipboard and badge, Clara Hayes smiling too wide at neighbors who never looked past the surface. My name echoes like a mantra, drilled into me: *Clara Hayes will make her own way. Clara Hayes needs no legacy. Clara Hayes is enough.*

But behind the mirrors, shadows stir. The Orion crest burns faintly, pulsing like a heartbeat. My father's voice slips through the seams: *You are a legacy, whether they see it or not.* The mirrors shiver, cracking hairline fractures across the glass. My cover is supposed to be whole, but I see the splintering.

I run, barefoot across polished floors that ripple like water, and the Black Bible drive glimmers at the far end—small, black, humming with names. I chase it, but the hall stretches farther with every step. Then the drive flickers, changes shape, and becomes a lily. White. Waiting. A funeral I can't outrun.

Hands grab me from the dark—Travis's grip, warm and cruel, pulling me back. Cassandra's laugh spills behind him, sweet and sharp, while petals rain down like ash. Each one carries a word: *failure, liability, finished.* They stick to my skin, cold as ice.

I stumble, and suddenly I'm in a house I know too well—the Fort Worth cover home, couch turned to chains, coffee table to a slab. Lilies crowd every surface, growing from the wallpaper, pressing me back. Their perfume is thick, suffocating. *Mistakes can't be cleaned forever.* The note writes itself across the petals, over and over, until I can't breathe.

Then—firelight. A different heat.

Beau steps out of the smoke, not in a suit or a uniform, but dust-streaked, jacket open, eyes steady. No mask. No mirrors. He doesn't say a word, but his hand is there, outstretched. A choice.

I reach for him, and for a moment the lilies recoil, withering. But then they scream, white petals twisting black, vines coiling around his wrist, trying to drag him down with me. I shout his name—too loud, too desperate—and the dream buckles.

I jolt awake, breath ragged, hair plastered to my temple. The truck cab is real again—vinyl seat under me, night pouring through the window. Beau drives on, hands steady on the wheel, moonlight tracing the hard line of his jaw.

The steady thrum of the tires lulls me under again, though it's not sleep so much as slipping in and out, caught between memory and dream. My ribs ache with every breath, rope-burn stings when I shift, and the bruises from yesterday press sharp reminders into every nerve. The pain keeps me half-awake, but exhaustion keeps dragging me back under.

The world outside the window drifts in broken fragments. Neon bleeding into farmland. Farmland dissolving into shadowed trees. Trees thinning into wide, flat stretches of blacktop. It feels less like travel and more like layers of me being stripped away, card by fragile card, until there's nothing left but the fragile frame underneath.

Clara Hayes. Legacy agent. Cover life. Dead woman walking. The lilies whisper each of those truths back at me in my dreams, their perfume clinging even here, far from that room.

I stir, eyes hooded, not fully awake, and catch Beau's profile in the glow of the dash. Solid. Unmoved. Just being Beau. And I can't help wondering if maybe it's time—time to bury Clara Hayes, let her die with the flowers they left me. If he can just be himself, maybe I can drag my real name back into the light.

The thought flickers and fades as I drift again, bruises heavy, eyelids heavier. The truck hums on through the dark, carrying me farther from the ruins and closer to something I'm not sure I deserve.

The crunch of gravel pulls me up from the haze of half-sleep. My neck aches from the angle, ribs sore from the day before, and for a moment I don't know where I am. Then the scent hits: hay and damp earth, cedar carried sharp on the wind through the cracked window. Not Dallas. Not Harrington. Somewhere quieter.

Beau slows the truck as the headlights sweep over a wide iron gate strung with barbed wire. Fixed to the post, a weathered sign leans crooked, letters barely visible in the moonlight: Copper Creek Ranch. The name looks older than the metal it hangs on, worn soft by sun and storms yet still standing.

Beyond the gate, the land stretches out like a dark sea. Pastures roll in silver waves under the moon, fence posts marching steady into the distance. A barn squats against the horizon, tin roof glinting faint in the dark. Somewhere in the distance a dog barks once, sharp and lonely, before silence folds back over the fields.

The engine idles as Beau leans out the window, bracing his arm against the frame to punch a code into the battered keypad. Metal grinds as the gate drags open, the sound more warning than welcome.

We creep forward, gravel spitting under the tires. The truck's beams catch the eyes of cattle scattered in the fields, brief pinpricks of gold before they vanish back into the dark.

I press a palm to my thigh, grounding myself as the ranch opens in layers before me. The lilies, the wreckage, the lies—they still cling, heavy as ever. But Copper Creek smells different. Cleaner. Honest in a way that makes my chest ache.

Beau doesn't say a word. His hands stay steady on the wheel, jaw cut hard in the glow of the dash. The land itself seems to hold him together. Bringing me here feels like its own kind of vow.

For the first time all night, I let myself breathe. Copper Creek feels like a threshold. One I'm not sure I'll step back from.

The gate clanks shut behind us, swallowed by the dark. The road narrows into a single lane, gravel crunching under the tires as the truck winds deeper into the land.

On either side, pasture stretches wide and endless, broken only by the shadow of oak stands and the slow rise of hills. The air smells of damp earth, hay, and the faint copper tang of the creek the ranch takes its name from. Somewhere out there, water moves slow over stone, a quiet heartbeat threading through the land.

The headlights catch the edge of a wooden fence, paint long stripped by sun and storms, and a low barn with its roof patched in dull sheets of tin. Horses shift inside, the sound of hooves muffled, a snort breaking the stillness as the truck rolls past.

The drive bends once more, climbing a small rise, and then the house comes into view. Two stories, brick and timber, weathered but strong, its porch stretched wide with rocking chairs set like sentries. A single light burns above the door, golden against the night, throwing shadows long across the steps. It doesn't look like a place for secrets. It looks like a place that insists on truth.

Beau slows the truck, easing it to a stop in front of the porch. The engine cuts, leaving the chirp of crickets and the distant rush of the creek. For a long moment neither of us moves, the silence heavier than the night sky pressing down.

I shift in the seat, sore muscles pulling against bruises, eyes fixed on the glow spilling from the porch lamp. Every part of me wants to believe that light means safety. But I know better. Safety is a story told to children. Still, here, for the first time in days, the weight of running eases just enough to let me breathe.

Beau finally breaks the quiet, his voice low and steady. "Home."

The word lingers, simple and dangerous all at once.

He climbs out first, boots crunching on the gravel, and circles around to drop the tailgate. The scrape of metal against metal cuts through the night as he lowers the ramp, muscles moving easy as he starts on the bike. I force my stiff body to follow, every bruise reminding me of the hours before, the ropes, the chair, the fists that landed where clothes will hide. My wrists ache as I steady the ramp, the phantom burn of hemp against skin sharp as ever.

"Careful," Beau mutters, though he's the one taking the weight, rolling the bike down with practiced hands. His gaze flicks to me when I wince at a shift in my ribs, something unreadable sparking in his eyes before he looks away. He doesn't say more, but I feel the question there anyway.

Once the bike's secured under the lean-to by the barn, he jerks his chin toward the house. "Come on. You need rest."

I almost laugh—sharp, bitter. Rest. The word feels like a luxury I don't remember how to afford. But the porch light spills wider as we climb the steps, its glow catching the lines of his face, softening edges that war have carved hard. He unlocks the door, and it opens on a rush of air that smells faintly of cedar and smoke.

The inside is spare, worn, but steady. Wood floors scuffed by boots, a leather couch slouched into the shape of someone who actually lives here, a stone hearth stacked with kindling. No polish. No masks. Just a man's life laid plain.

My chest tightens. It shouldn't feel disarming, but it does.

He shuts the door behind us, turning the lock with a solid click. For a moment the quiet holds us there in the entryway, too close, our shadows tangling across the wall. His presence fills the space, broad shoulders, steady heat, the weight of someone who could catch me if I fell again.

I break the silence first, my voice low. "Doesn't look like a place for secrets."

His eyes catch mine, steady, unflinching. "Ain't."

And in that one word, I hear the promise—dangerous, reckless—that maybe here, for a little while, truth doesn't have to be a weapon.

Chapter 28
Beau

I climb out first, boots crunching the gravel, and drop the tailgate. The ramp groans as I lower it, metal on metal, and I roll the bike down with practiced ease. She steadies the side, and when she flinches—just a fraction, ribs pulling—I catch it. The bruises, the rope burns, the way she moves like every inch of her body's a reminder of what Orion lets slide. Something sharp sparks in my chest, but I keep my mouth shut. "Careful," is all I say.

Her wrists shift under the dim light, raw lines barely hidden by her sleeves. My jaw tightens. Whoever did that, whatever they thought they proved, left their fingerprints on her. And I'm looking right at them.

Once the bike's under the lean-to, I jerk my chin toward the porch. "Come on. You need rest."

The word tastes foreign in my mouth. Rest. For someone like her, it's not a gift—it's a truce. But I still want to hand it over, if only for one night.

We climb the steps, the glow from the porch lamp catching her face. She looks worn, edges frayed, but that light softens her too, in ways I don't let myself dwell on. I unlock the door, push it open. Cedar, smoke, and home wrap around us the second we step inside.

It's nothing fancy. Wood floors marked by years of boots, couch shaped by whoever sat here last, hearth stacked with kindling I haven't had time to burn. Plain. Honest. No gloss, no mask. My life, laid bare.

She lingers just inside the door, eyes roaming the space like it's disarming her piece by piece. For a second, I see it—how she fits here.

Too well. My chest knots tight. Wanting that, wanting her here, is its own kind of danger.

I lock the door behind us. The click echoes louder than it should, leaving us in the hush of the entryway, shadows tangling on the wall. She's close enough I feel her presence before I look. Close enough that if she stumbled, I'd catch her without thinking.

Her voice breaks the quiet, low, almost a confession. "Doesn't look like a place for secrets."

I meet her eyes, steady, no flinch, no lie. "Ain't."

One word. Simple. But it carries more weight than I mean to give it. And I know she hears it—that promise I didn't plan on making, the one that's reckless as hell.

Because in this house, with her standing here, truth feels dangerous. And for the first time in a long time, I want dangerous.

I hook her bag off my shoulder and set it just inside the door, leaving it there like it doesn't weigh a thing, even though I know it does. "Come on," I say, nodding toward the hall. "You should know the lay of the place."

The house opens easy around us, familiar shadows and scuffed floors guiding my steps. I point out the kitchen first—worn cabinets, coffee pot ready, cast-iron that's older than me. "Not much for pretty, but it does the job."

She lingers in the doorway, eyes sharp, taking in every corner like she's mapping exits instead of cupboards. Habit. Mine too.

The living room comes next, the couch sagged into comfort, fireplace stacked with kindling. "You could hole up here if you don't feel like climbing stairs."

Her gaze flicks across the mantle, catching the single frame turned face-down, but she doesn't ask. I don't offer.

Upstairs, I gesture to the spare room. Sheets tight, quilt folded neat, closet empty. Nothing personal to trip over. Across the hall, the bathroom waits, plain but steady. "Hot water takes a minute," I add.

I stop short of the last door. My door. The silence says enough.

When I circle back, she's standing in the guest room, hand resting light on the frame of the bedpost. Like she doesn't want to admit the place already feels steadier than it should.

"This is yours," I say finally, voice low. "For as long as you need."

I duck into the hall closet, grab a stack of clean towels, and bring them back to the guest room. She's already lowered herself to the edge of the bed, moving careful, stiff from bruises she won't admit to. For a second, I just stand there, watching her fingers smooth the quilt like she's testing if it's real.

I set the towels on the dresser, then pull the bottle of ibuprofen from my pocket and place it on top without a word. A small first aid kit follows, set beside it neat as if it belongs there. She doesn't need me to spell it out. She'll know what it's for.

Her eyes flick to the items, then back to me, but I don't linger long enough to read whatever's in them. "Bathroom's across the hall," I say instead, keeping my voice even. "Water runs hot if you let it."

She shifts on the mattress, moving slow, deliberate. I tip my head once, an unspoken goodnight, then step out and pull the door nearly shut behind me.

Downstairs, the house feels different—too quiet, too full. I move through it on instinct, boots soft against the worn floorboards, and into the office. The desk is stacked with files I should be working through. I drag them close, then push them back just as quick, the weight of them too heavy tonight.

The leather chair creaks under me as I lean back, eyes on the dark window. The reflection staring back looks older, more tired than I want to admit. Upstairs, there's a woman who shouldn't be here, who looks like she belongs here anyway, and that thought sits heavier than any file Orion's ever dropped on my desk.

The office smells faintly of leather and dust, the kind of space that holds years in its corners. I drop into the chair, lean back, and let the weight of the house settle around me. The desk's a mess—files half-open, notes scribbled, a catalog for tractor parts I don't remember ordering.

Except it isn't a catalog.

The envelope's too heavy, too stiff. Looks like a manual for farm equipment, down to the glossy cover stamped with a company logo. To anyone else it'd be junk mail. But the return address isn't a supplier—it's one of Benny's little tells, a fake outfit he's been using for years.

I slit it open with my thumb. Inside, neat pages, Benny's handwriting sharp in the margins. I flip through, and her life unfolds in black and white.

Clara Hayes. Orion inspection agent. Clean on paper. Too clean. The type of file meant to be skimmed, not studied. But Benny did more than skim. He circled the word *legacy*. No details, no names, just that one word burned into the margins. Legacy agent. That alone says enough. Born in it, bred for it, never really given the choice to walk away.

I set the file down slow, rub at the ache between my eyes. She's sitting upstairs right now with her whole life packed into a canvas bag, rope burns still raw on her wrists, and Orion's already put a lily on her table.

With a curse under my breath, I pull the battered tin from the drawer, roll one quick, and light it. The joint flares, smoke curling up into the still air. I take a slow drag, hold it until it burns low in my chest, and let it out in a long, bitter sigh.

The file sits there waiting, but I shove it aside, bury it under the real tractor catalog this time. If she's a legacy, the blood's hers to carry. Doesn't mean I won't keep her alive while she's under my roof.

I lean back, joint burning low between my fingers, and stare out the dark window. Copper Creek runs quiet outside, but my head's a storm.

The joint burns down to a crooked ash, but I don't stub it out. I let it smolder in the tray, the smoke curling lazy in the lamplight. My eyes keep drifting back to the file even though I shoved it under the catalog like that could make it disappear.

With a curse, I drag it out again. Benny never sends half-measures. If there's more in here, I need to see it.

The first few pages are Clara—her inspections, her assignments, the word *legacy* carved like a scar in the margins. I flip past them, jaw tight, until a different name catches my eye.

Victor Leclair.

The pages under his name don't read like Marcus's briefing—clean and careful, corporate polished. These are raw. Surveillance notes. Wire pulls. Things only someone who knows how to get their hands dirty could have put together.

Leclair's listed as Red Haven executive, but Benny's scribbles say otherwise: "Arms facilitation. Shell corps in Marseille, Quebec, Bogotá. Sons used as intermediaries. One defected. Son may hold *Bible*."

Bible. My pulse ticks hard. Marcus never said a damn thing about the drive being in play again.

I flip another page. Grainy photos, Leclair shaking hands with men I recognize from old ops—faces tied to weapons markets, off-the-books shipments, disappearances that never made headlines. His polished smile in each one looks the same, but the eyes don't. Cold. Calculating.

Marcus gave me a job: keep Leclair breathing. Protect the client. But this file makes him look less like a client and more like a fox Orion stuck in the henhouse to see what he'd do.

I lean back, smoke curling out my nose, head heavy with the weight of it.

So Marcus lied. Or he didn't tell me because he knew I'd ask the wrong questions.

I flip to the last page. A hand-scribbled note from Benny:

"Careful, hermano. They're not protecting him. They're using him. And if Hayes is on the board too, you're not just babysitting—you're sitting on a powder keg."

I stare at the words until they blur. Benny's right. The whole thing stinks like bait. And I've been shoved right into the middle of it.

I drag deep on the joint, the burn biting harsher this time. If Marcus thinks I'm just going to play his hired gun while he keeps the truth locked up, he's got another thing coming.

Chapter 29
Clara

The door clicks shut behind him, and for a moment I just stand there, staring at the towels folded sharp as a blade on the dresser. The bottle of ibuprofen sits on top, label turned out like an accusation. Beside it, a first aid kit, clean and white. No words. No questions. Just placed there like he knows exactly how bad the bruises go, how deep the burns bite.

My chest tightens. It shouldn't matter—field kits are standard, painkillers routine. But the thought of him noticing without asking, of him seeing without pressing, that burns hotter than any rope ever did.

I sit on the edge of the bed, the mattress dipping under my weight. Every muscle screams when I move, sore from the hours tied down, ribs pulling where fists landed. My wrists throb when I flex them, red bands etched like reminders of failure. Of weakness. I breathe slow, press my palms into my knees until the shake steadies.

This room smells faintly of cedar and soap. Clean. Honest. The kind of space you'd think someone like me never belongs in. And yet—I catch myself cataloging the window, the closet, the door Beau just walked through. Escape routes. Always escape routes. Even here, where the air feels... softer. Safer.

Dangerous words. Safety. Belonging. I can't afford to want them.

I push myself up, ignoring the stab of protest in my ribs, and cross to the small mirror hanging crooked over the dresser. My reflection stares back—dark hair mussed, eyes ringed in shadows, mouth set tight. Clara Hayes. Inspector. Cover. Legacy in hiding. The name they gave me when they said, *You'll make your own way. You won't use your bloodline.* A lie, of course. The bloodline always catches up.

The lilies proved that.

I bite the inside of my cheek until the copper taste fills my mouth. Legacy only buys time. That's what the note said. And time is something I've been running out of since the Bible vanished into smoke and betrayal.

Through the door, faint as a heartbeat, I catch the creak of floorboards. Beau moving through the house. Heavy, deliberate, like a man carrying weight he won't speak out loud. He's too close. Too steady. And for the first time in years, the thought of letting someone share the burden doesn't feel like weakness. It feels like surrender.

I press my fingers against the mirror's edge, my reflection wavering. Surrender is dangerous. Surrender gets you killed.

And yet, for a second, I imagine what it would be like to set Clara Hayes down here at Copper Creek. To let the name I've hidden all my life rise to the surface, like Beau lets his. Just Beau. No polish. No mask.

The thought terrifies me more than the lilies.

Steam still clings to my skin when I pull on the only things soft enough not to hurt—baggy sweats and a black tank top. The fabric hangs loose, swallowing me whole, but every movement still drags across sore ribs. I tug the drawstring tight, shove damp hair back from my face, and stare down at the elastic wrap clutched in my hands.

Three tries. Three failures. My fingers are too clumsy, my body too tender, and the ache sharpens every time I try to cinch it. I could leave it. I could crawl into bed and pretend the pain is just another ghost to carry. But the truth is, I can't afford sloppy right now. Not with Orion. Not with Victor's name still burning in my head. Not with lilies still fresh in my memory.

I shove the wrap under my arm, bare feet whispering against the floor as I pad down the hall. The faint glow under the office door leaks into the dark, curling smoke carrying the unmistakable bite of weed. Figures.

I knock once, low. My voice is steady when I speak, but quieter than I mean it to be.

"Beau... I need a hand."

"Enter," his voice rumbles from the other side.

I push the door open, and the haze hits first. Smoke curls in lazy ribbons around the room, carrying the pungent weight of something I recognize instantly. He's leaned back in his chair, boots up on the desk, joint smoldering between his fingers. The lamplight cuts him in half—face shadowed, eyes sharp, tracking me the second I step in.

His gaze flicks from my damp hair to the tank top, to the elastic wrap clutched in my hand. Something shifts in his expression, quick and quiet, before he masks it with a drag from the joint. "You look like hell," he says, low. Not unkind.

I cross the threshold, trying not to wince as my ribs remind me who's boss. "Good thing you're not my handler."

He smirks, lifts the joint. "Want a hit?"

I arch a brow, holding up the wrap. "Not exactly why I came in here."

"Didn't ask why." He tips it toward me, smoke curling from the cherry. "It'll take the edge off. Muscle aches, bruises, sleep that doesn't feel like you're being hunted. Nature's remedy."

I shake my head, jaw tight. "Last thing I need is to fog myself up."

His boots drop to the floor with a thud. He leans forward, elbows braced on his knees, joint pinched between two fingers like a dare. His voice drops, rough as gravel. "Fog clears. Pain doesn't. You been carrying it like armor, but even armor cracks. One drag won't kill you. Might even let you close your eyes without seeing lilies."

The word twists in me sharper than the bruises. He knows what he's saying, what it means. My instinct is to shut him out, to slam the wall back up. But my body aches like I've been broken in half, and exhaustion hums behind my eyes like a threat.

I exhale slow, steady, and extend my hand. "Fine. One drag."

His grin is small, wolfish, but there's no triumph in it. He passes it over like an offering, ember glowing in the dim.

I raise it to my lips, inhale. The burn scrapes my throat raw, earthy and sharp, and I cough once, trying to cover it with a smirk. "Happy?"

He leans back, smoke curling from his own lips, eyes steady on me. "Ecstatic."

The heat coils through me, loosening places I didn't realize were locked. My shoulders sag despite myself, and for the first time in days, the ache eases.

The smoke still clings to my tongue, bitter but oddly grounding, when I hold the wrap out toward him. "This was the reason I came in here. I can't... quite reach without tearing something open again."

For a moment, he just looks at me, the joint balanced between his fingers, eyes unreadable in the haze. Then he stubs it out in the ashtray and rises from the chair, slow, deliberate. His height fills the room, the weight of him pressing in until it's all I can do to keep my breath steady.

"Sit," he says quietly, tipping his chin toward the edge of the desk.

I perch there, feeling suddenly exposed in baggy sweats and a thin tank top, damp hair dripping cold trails down my back. My hands twitch against my thighs as he takes the wrap from me, unspooling it with practiced care.

When his fingers brush my side, light as a feather, it sends a jolt through me sharper than the pain. Electricity, crackling in every nerve ending. His touch isn't clinical—it's deliberate, gentle in a way that feels dangerous. He winds the fabric around my ribs, slow and precise, like the act itself is something sacred.

"Hold," he murmurs, and I raise my arms, wincing as the muscles stretch. His hands graze the underside of my arms as he pulls the bandage tight.

For a second, I forget how to breathe.

He finishes binding my ribs, hands lingering a beat too long before stepping back. I think it's over—that I can finally breathe again—but then he pulls open a drawer in his desk and takes out another kit. Not the neat, corporate first-aid box from earlier. This one is older, scuffed, the kind of kit you keep close because you know someday you'll need it.

"Wrists," he says, low and steady. Not a request.

My body goes rigid. Every instinct screams to pull the sleeves down, to hide the marks left by Victor's men, to pretend I'm still untouchable. But his gaze holds me, unyielding, until my hands give themselves up.

He crouches in front of me, big frame bent small, careful in a way no one his size should have to be. The sting of antiseptic sears into the raw grooves, makes me hiss through my teeth. He doesn't apologize, doesn't fumble. He waits, grounding me with the weight of his hand against my forearm until the tremor passes. Then his fingers smooth ointment across the burns, light as breath, deliberate.

The bandage comes snug, tied precise. And before I can look away, he presses his mouth to the gauze. A kiss, feather-soft. Once. Twice. Each one a vow I never asked for.

My chest aches, not from bruises but from the break he's forcing open in me.

"Ankles," he says next, voice like gravel, but gentler than I've ever heard him.

It takes everything I have to draw my legs up, to peel back fabric and show the damage there—angry rope burns carved into skin where Victor's men pinned me down, tied me to the chair until my bones screamed. His jaw hardens at the sight, a muscle twitching near his temple, but his hands stay steady.

The salve cools and burns all at once. His touch doesn't flinch, doesn't pity, just works with a tenderness that cuts deeper than cruelty ever did. When he finishes, he leans in again, his lips brushing each wrapped ankle. Not for comfort, not even forgiveness—something older, heavier, like he's swearing he won't let it happen again.

When his eyes lift, they pin me in place. Smoke curls between us, faint, but the charge in the air is alive, sparking, like the moment right before lightning cracks.

"You don't have to keep carrying Clara Hayes," he says, voice rough, stripped bare. "You can let her go. Be who you were meant to be. Whoever that is."

The words hollow me out. I want to laugh, to snap, to tell him I don't know who that is anymore. That Clara Hayes has been the mask I wore since childhood, and Victoria Montague is the ghost I buried so deep I almost forgot she existed. But his voice—it doesn't sound like a man asking for intel. It sounds like a man offering me a hand out of the grave.

My throat tightens. The silence between us is thick, heavy with antiseptic and cedar smoke and everything I've swallowed down for years. He's still so close, warmth lingering on my skin where his hands steadied me.

I draw in a breath that tastes like breaking glass.

"My name…" My voice splinters. But I force it through, syllable by syllable, soft and certain, like pulling a blade free. "Is Victoria Paige Montague."

The name hangs between us, sharp as a knife, fragile as glass. I haven't said it out loud in years—not since Orion made me Clara Hayes, not since my family made me legacy before I was even old enough to choose.

And now, in the low light of his office, with him looking at me like I'm not broken but alive, I almost believe it means something again.

For the first time, it doesn't feel like a forgotten life left behind — it feels like the beginning of one that might be mine.

Chapter 30
Beau

The skillet hisses as the sausage cooks down, the smell thick and sharp. I stir it slow, let the motion steady me. But my head's not on the pan. It's back in that office, her ribs under my hands, the tremor she tried to hide when the wrap tightened. The rope burns at her wrists and ankles—red, raw, nothing I could scrub clean with ointment and gauze. My fingers lingered longer than they should've.

Not doctor's work. Not agent's work. Just a man who didn't want to see her hurt anymore.

And the lilies. White petals glowing in the dark like open hands on the nightstand. Orion's way of signing a death notice. I've seen it before, on men tougher than both of us combined. Some ran. Most didn't live long enough to. She looked at those flowers and still had enough steel to grind them under her boot. I don't know if that makes her reckless or the bravest damn person I've ever met.

I crack eggs into the skillet, let the yolks bleed into yellow as they firm. Coffee gurgles behind me, the pot filling the air with something grounding. I set the creamer and sugar next to it without thinking. Not for me—black is all I need—but I've watched her at Doris's counter, cream first, three spoons of sugar, always the same. Details tell me more than words. She keeps precision like armor, but under it, she's flesh and blood, bruised and burning, still here.

I don't know how long she'll stay. I don't know if I should want her to. But as the biscuits rise and the gravy thickens, the thought I can't shake is simple: for the first time in a long damn while, I'm not cooking just for myself.

The oven timer dings soft, and I pull the biscuits free, steam rolling up as I set the tray on the stovetop. Golden, split easy, the way they should be. That's when I hear her—bare feet against the floor, the whisper of fabric moving as she crosses the hall.

I glance up just enough to catch her in the doorway. Hair loose, a little tangled from sleep, eyes heavy like she hasn't shaken the night yet. But she's upright. Breathing. Here.

"How you feelin'?" I ask, voice low as I reach for the pan, spoon cutting through thick gravy.

She doesn't answer right away, just steps further into the kitchen, the lamplight catching the bruises at the edges of her collarbone where the sweats don't hide them. My jaw ticks.

I nod toward the counter instead. "Coffee's ready. Creamer and sugar's there the way you take it."

Her gaze lingers on the setup, then shifts back to me. There's a flicker there—like she wants to ask how I know, but thinks better of it. I don't push. Just set the biscuits in a basket and let the quiet hang, the kitchen filling with more than the heat off the stove.

She moves quiet, almost careful, to the table. Three sugar packets tear open crisp, three pours from the creamer pitcher, all dropped into the cup before she even reaches for the pot. Coffee follows, dark folding into pale until it settles the way she likes it. She stirs once, slow, then takes her seat, shoulders drawn tight with the effort of moving.

I set her plate down in front of her—biscuits split, gravy rich over the top, eggs and bacon tucked alongside.

"Thanks," she says, voice low, fingers curling around the coffee. Her eyes flick to the food, lingering, like she isn't sure whether to dig in or keep her distance from the comfort of it.

She takes a long sip, gaze steady over the rim of her cup, watching me as I set my own plate down and pull out the chair across from her. Only when I sit does she lower the mug, lips curving faint at the edges.

"What—no pancakes?" she says, tone teasing, just sharp enough to poke.

I huff out a laugh, shaking my head. "Figured I'd spare you the sermon this mornin'. Didn't want you thinkin' pancakes were all I knew how to make."

Her brow arches, playful. "So what—you're trying to prove range now?"

"Somethin' like that." I gesture at her plate, smirk tugging at my mouth. "Though I gotta admit, I'm curious. You eat your burgers with a knife and fork—think you can actually handle somethin' as messy as sausage gravy?"

Her laugh escapes before she can stop it, warm and unguarded. "Please. I could drown in this gravy and come out cleaner than you do after breakfast."

I grin wide at that, the sound of her laugh sparking something in my chest I shouldn't be feeling. "That so? Guess we'll see. Gravy's got a way of humblin' the best of us."

She takes another slow sip of coffee, eyes dancing over the rim. "If that's your way of warning me not to ruin your table, you should've said so. Precision's kind of my thing."

I chuckle, leaning back in my chair. "Yeah, I noticed. Though I think this morning's the first time I've ever seen precision try to square off with biscuits."

Her laugh lingers, low and genuine, while she saws carefully through her eggs. I watch as she cuts around the yolk, neat little sections disappearing one by one. The whites first, the yolk untouched.

Between bites, she says, "We need a plan." Her tone has shifted—still light enough to pass as casual, but there's steel under it.

I nod, tearing off a biscuit and dragging it through the gravy. "Then maybe it's time we compare notes."

She doesn't answer right away, just keeps at her plate with that same quiet efficiency. When the whites are gone, she steadies the fork against the yolk, then lifts it whole onto her spoon. One smooth motion, deliberate, slipping it into her mouth without a single drop spilled.

I can't help it—I grin. "Even the way you eat eggs is precise."

Her eyes flick up, and there's a faint curve at the corner of her lips, like she's fighting not to smile. She swallows, wipes her mouth with the edge of her napkin, and mutters, "Better precise than sloppy."

"Guess that's why you're still here," I shoot back, leaning in just enough that she catches the double meaning.

She only shrugs, a small gesture of agreement, before chasing the last of her coffee with another long sip. When she sets the mug down, her gaze fixes on me, sharper now, stripped of the teasing.

"Alright," she says, tone quiet but cutting through the morning stillness. "You know how I work. Clean. Precise. But I don't know you. Not really. So give me the short version. Orion. This mission. Why you're here."

I lean back in my chair, fork idle against the plate, and exhale slow. Cliff notes. Nothing more. "I've been with Orion longer than I'd care to count. Started out overseas. Protection. Extraction. Cleaning up other people's mistakes." My jaw flexes, the memories bitter even in shorthand. "Came home to the ranch between jobs, but Orion's grip doesn't loosen easy. Marcus calls, I go. That's the deal."

I pause, meet her eyes head-on. "This time, it was Leclair. File said protection detail. Make sure he breathes through the week, walk him out clean. Nothing more, nothing less."

Her brows lift, faint but telling. "That's it?"

"That's it," I say, though the weight in my chest makes it sound like a lie.

She doesn't look away. Doesn't blink. Just leans back in her chair, fork balanced neatly across her plate like she's dissecting me instead of breakfast. "You're leaving something out."

I grunt, shake my head. "Already told you, cliff notes."

"Cliff notes don't come with that much grit in your voice," she counters, eyes narrowing just a fraction. "So either you're bad at summaries, or you're hoping I'll stop asking."

I smirk, but it's hollow. "Maybe both."

Her stare pins me harder, unrelenting. "You work protection, extraction, cleanup. Fine. But men like you don't get called in for nothing. If they wanted a babysitter, they'd have sent anyone. Marcus sent you. That means something. So—what aren't you saying?"

The air between us sharpens, and I catch myself tightening my grip on the edge of the table. For a long beat, I don't answer. Then I sigh, low, resigned. "What I'm not saying is Marcus doesn't tell me everything. Never has. And when he does call, there's usually more blood in the water than the file admits."

The silence stretches, the kind that creaks like an old floorboard. I lean back in my chair, scrub a hand down my face. "You really wanna know what's not in the file?"

Clara doesn't flinch. "Yes."

My jaw works, the words dragging out of me like they don't want to come. "There was a job. Bogotá. Marcus pulled me in when I was younger, meaner. Supposed to be routine—extraction, escort, clean exit. Only it wasn't routine. Not even close."

Her fork stills, but she doesn't interrupt.

"I damn near lost myself in that city. Watched good people bleed out in alleys because someone higher up decided bodies were cheaper than backup. And I... I didn't stop it. Hell, I didn't want to stop it, not in that moment. That's how close I came to turning into the thing they warned me about." My voice drops, rough enough it almost cracks. "Since then, I've lost too many. Partners, marks, bystanders—doesn't matter. Orion always calls it collateral. But it ain't collateral when you see their faces every time you close your eyes."

The tension between us hums, sharper than the smell of coffee still rising from our cups.

I force a laugh that doesn't land. "So yeah. Cliff notes. Bogotá was the chapter where I almost didn't make it back. The rest? Just a man doing his time until the next page tears out."

The weight of Bogotá still hangs there, thick between us, until I push back from it with a crooked grin. "But that's enough about ghosts. Your turn, Vicky. What's your actual story?"

Her head snaps up, fork clinking against the plate. "What did you just call me?"

I let the grin widen, slow and deliberate, dimples cutting deep. "Vicky." I draw it out, savoring the syllables. "Fits you better than Clara ever did. Sharp, stubborn, got a sting if you don't handle it right."

Her eyes narrow, but there's heat under the glare, the kind that makes me want to poke the bear again just to see what happens.

Chapter 31

~~Clara~~
~~Vicky~~

Victoria

I set my fork down carefully, but my voice comes out slow, sharp, like I'm cutting glass. "My name is Victoria. Or Tori."

Beau doesn't even blink. He just leans back in his chair, that lazy cowboy posture, the corner of his mouth curling. "Nah. I like Vicky. Suits you better."

Heat crawls up my neck. "I'm not some damn valley girl, Beau."

That's when he does it—full smile, dimples on full display, like he knows exactly how close I am to throwing my coffee at him. It stirs something low in my core, dangerous and unsteady. He tips his chin, grin steady as sin. "Now tell me, Vicky… what do you know?"

I sigh hard, the kind that drags out of me like surrender, and roll my eyes toward the ceiling. "Fine." Pushing back from the table, I stand and busy myself with the coffee pot—three sugars, three pours of cream, then the coffee. The ritual buys me a second to decide just how much of the truth to hand over.

By the time I turn back, mug in hand, my voice is flat, clipped. "Cliff notes. Legacy agent—Orion carved that into me before I could spell the word. Clara Hayes has been my mask since I was twelve. On paper, I ran inspections, procurement, acquisitions. But that was just the cover. My real work?" I take a long sip, swallow hard. "Cleaning house. Quiet removals. Accidents that weren't accidents. Targets Orion decided the world didn't need anymore."

I set the cup down with a soft clink, meeting his eyes head-on. "Made me look useful without spilling too much blood in public."

Beau leans back, one arm draped loose over the backrest, eyes steady on me. A humorless smile tugs at his mouth. "That's why I never heard of you. They didn't just keep you in the shadows,

Victoria. They pulled you behind 'em. Buried you so deep you were a ghost even to the rest of us."

He's not wrong. His voice lands heavy, matter-of-fact.

He tips his mug toward me, coffee gone cold but his gaze hot as ever. "So tell me, what changed? What pulled you out now, sittin' at my table instead of rotting in some file marked classified?"

I set the mug down harder than I mean to, ceramic clinking against the wood. "Victor Leclair. His son, Alexandre. Three years ago, he stole something he should never have been able to touch—the Black Bible drive. My program. My security. My failure, according to Orion."

The words burn like acid in my throat, but I force them out. "Doesn't matter that I wasn't the one who opened the door. Doesn't matter that the leak came from higher than me. Legacy agents don't get mistakes. They get blame. They branded me with it, let me carry the weight while he disappeared into the wind with everything inside that drive."

I draw in a sharp breath, force myself to meet Beau's eyes. "Every time I think I've climbed out from under it, they drag me back. Harrington wasn't about food inspections. It was about closing the loop. Find Victor, squeeze him until the son surfaces, recover the drive, and prove I'm not the weak link they want me to be."

A bitter laugh slips out, brittle as glass. "Three years later, and I'm still paying interest on a debt I never owed."

I push back from the table, chair legs scraping lightly against the wood. The weight of my own words sits too heavy in the air, so I force myself upright, smoothing the front of my tank as if that will iron the crack out of my voice. "I'll be right back. I've got intel that might make this cleaner."

Beau studies me for a beat, unreadable, then gives a slow nod. "Good. I'll grab mine. Benny's been feeding me more than I asked for."

The way he says it—the faint rasp in his drawl, the quiet weight behind Benny's name—tells me there's more in those files than he plans to hand over. But I let it go. For now.

I step down the hall, the creak of the old boards muffled under my bare feet. When I return, a folder tucked under my arm, the kitchen feels changed. Not warmer, not softer—just fuller. The table's crowded now: his scrawled notes in a loose stack, a thick equipment catalogue masking what anyone else would mistake for junk mail, two coffee cups gone half cold. No Beau in sight, just his presence stamped into the paper and the lingering steam rising faint from the mugs.

For a moment I stand there, folder pressed against my ribs, eyes catching on the breadth of his handwriting across the pages. Precise, but not clinical. Direct. Ink from someone who's bled over too many reports to bother making them pretty. And for reasons I can't name, that feels heavier than any intel I brought back with me.

The scrape of boots on wood pulls me out of my head. Beau steps back into the kitchen, another stack of files in hand. He drops them beside mine, then lowers himself into the chair opposite, the weight of him grounding the air. He doesn't say anything at first, just nudges my fresh cup toward me like that's the opening move.

I flip my folder open, lay out the notes I've been building since Harrington. "Red Haven's clean on the surface. Too clean. Deliveries logged down to the minute, compliance forms polished. But every one of them hides something. Re-tagged crates. Routing codes that circle Dallas before landing back local. And their drivers—nervous in ways men only get when they're moving more than lettuce and frozen peas."

I set the dagger on the table between us, the steel catching the low light. The weight of it drags the air heavier, like it knows it was never meant to be here, on this table, between the two of us. Beau's gaze flicks down to it, then back to me, sharp, waiting.

"My recon wasn't for show," I say, voice even. "I've been inside their routes. Watched how they move shipments. They're not unmarked trucks—they blend in, same logos, same manifests. Nothing sloppy. If you weren't looking, you'd swear they were just another Red Haven load. But there's a tell." I tap the hilt of the dagger with my finger. "A flower. Black Bloom. Quiet as a whisper unless you know it's there. That's how they separate real freight from the mask."

Beau doesn't move, just studies me like he's weighing every word against the steel on the table. "And the freight?" he asks finally, low.

"Women," I answer, steady, even as my stomach knots. "Special request. Coastal Maine." My throat tightens, but I force the last word out. "Driftwood."

His head snaps up, eyes locking on mine. "Driftwood?" The way he says it is sharp, dangerous, like I just pulled a pin out of a grenade and dropped it between us.

I hold his stare. "I don't mishear, Beau. They said Driftwood. Out loud. I was close enough to feel the breath off the woman's lips."

The silence after stretches, thick with things we're not saying. The clock ticks loud, the coffee pot hisses, and that dagger gleams between us like a third player at the table.

Beau pushes back from the table so fast the chair legs screech against the floor. He starts pacing, heavy boots dragging grooves into the silence. One hand rakes through his hair, the other flexes like he doesn't know what to do with it.

"This is big," he mutters, voice low but sharp enough to cut. "I heard coastal Maine—women, candy, weapons. Thought I had the shape of it. But Driftwood?" His laugh is bitter, humorless. "Driftwood isn't just another pin on a map."

I lean back in my chair, watching him carve the air with every step. "What does it mean to you?"

He stops, shoulders tight, back to me. For a long moment I think he won't say it. Then he turns, jaw clenched hard enough I can see the muscle jump.

"My sister's there. Quinn."

My stomach flips so hard it feels like my ribs might crack. Quinn. He didn't just tell me his sister's there—he said her name.

I know that name. Of course I do. Quinn Maddox. Not just a name in a file, not just another ghost in the system. She was my battle partner, my sister-in-arms—the one who covered my blind spots when the world went to hell. When she walked away from Orion, I thought she'd finally found peace. Driftwood was supposed to be the kind of quiet people like us never get.

I made sure she had a shadow. Someone I trusted to keep an eye from a distance. Latte. Always watching, never interfering. Safety disguised as coincidence.

Quinn Maddox. Not dead. Not lost. Alive. And Beau just called her his sister.

"Shit." The word scrapes raw from my throat. "Shit, shit, shit." My fingers dig into the edge of the table, the wood biting back. Driftwood isn't just a waypoint—it's a goddamn convergence. Quinn. Latte. The shipment. The Black Bloom. Every thread I've been pulling just knotted in the same place.

My pulse spikes, sharp and unsteady. "You said Quinn," I manage, the words catching. "Your sister's name is Quinn?"

He nods once, jaw tight.

The full weight of it hits—my two worlds colliding, no seams left between them. His sister. My asset. Same town. Same storm. Same fuse already burning.

I look up at him, heart pounding. For the first time tonight, the board isn't mine. The way he watches me—measured, wary—I realize it never was.

The silence between us stretches thin, humming with tension and something dangerously close to panic. I push back from the table and pace to the window, needing space, air, anything that isn't the four walls closing in around this revelation.

The night outside is pitch-black, the ranch swallowed in quiet. No lights from the road, no neighbors for miles. Just reflection—me and him, caught in the glass. Two ghosts from the same machine, trying to outrun its shadow.

"I thought I'd done enough," I whisper, more to myself than to him. "I thought she was safe."

Beau's chair creaks. "You couldn't have known."

I turn, sharp. "That's the problem. I should have. I should've seen this coming."

He stands, slow and deliberate, closing the distance between us until he's a few feet away. His voice is steady, but there's an edge under it. "You think blamin' yourself makes this easier? You did what you had to. We both did."

I meet his eyes, something tight unraveling in my chest. "You don't get it. Every move I've made since Orion pulled me out of the field has been about control. About keeping people alive by staying two steps ahead. And now—" I gesture to the papers, the dagger, the whole mess between us. "Now it's chaos again. And Quinn's in the middle of it."

He doesn't argue. Doesn't have to. His silence says he feels the same twist of helpless fury I do.

I pull a shaky breath, forcing my voice low. "If Driftwood's part of Red Haven's network, that means the women, the shipments, the whole operation—it's already in motion."

He nods once. "Then we find the link before it moves."

The words are simple, but they anchor me. I can breathe again. Barely.

I walk back to the table, stare down at the dagger gleaming in the lamplight. Its reflection warps my face, splitting it into pieces. "Whoever's behind this," I say quietly, "they're using the same playbook Orion wrote. They just stripped the name off the cover."

Beau steps closer, voice low. "Then we rewrite it."

Chapter 32
Beau

For a second, neither of us moves. The air between us is wired, hot, the kind that tastes like the start of a bad idea that's already too far gone to stop.

She's the one who breaks it—of course she is. "We can still make this clean," she says, already pacing, already calculating. "I go back in tonight, same entry point as before. One last recon. You stake out the highway. Stop the truck before it clears Harrington."

I stare at her, disbelief flattening my tone. "You're talkin' about splitting up."

"It's efficient." Her hands move as she talks, sharp gestures that match the clipped rhythm of her voice. "I'm the only one who can move through the site without raising alarms. They already saw me walk out alive. If I show up again, they'll assume I'm tying up compliance paperwork. I can get eyes on the cages, mark how many guards, where they're loading from."

"Vicky," I say, low, warning in my voice, "you were *caught*."

"I was *released*," she snaps back. "Big difference."

"Yeah? From where I'm standing, the difference looks a hell of a lot like rope burns and bruised ribs."

Her jaw tightens, but her chin lifts, defiant. "I took the hits because I had to. You don't get to judge that. My cover held. They didn't see through me—they let me go." She meets my eyes, sharp as a knife. "Which means it worked."

I cross my arms, shifting my weight, doing my best to keep the temper out of my tone. "Or it means they're watchin' to see where you run next."

Her glare cuts quick, but there's something flickering under it—fear, maybe, or the kind of anger that hides it. "You think I don't know the risks?"

"I think you're still breathin' because you got lucky," I counter. "You go back in there, luck's gonna run out."

That lands. Her mouth opens, shuts. For a second, she just stares at me, eyes bright with the kind of fury that's born from being seen too clearly.

When she speaks again, her voice is quieter. "You don't understand. I can't just sit here and wait. Every hour that passes, those women get closer to the coast. Driftwood gets closer to becoming another goddamn ghost town. I'm not going to let that happen."

I scrub a hand through my hair, fighting the urge to slam my fist into the wall. "And you think I am? You think I'm gonna sit back while they run my sister's town through Red Haven's pipeline?"

That stops her. For a moment, we're both just breathing, the heat of it fogging up the air between us.

Finally, I exhale, voice rough. "We do this together. No split missions. No solo heroics. You got that?"

Her mouth twitches, half smirk, half surrender. "You always this stubborn?"

"Only when I'm right."

The edge softens just enough for the tension to shift—still sharp, but different now. The kind that hums low under the ribs.

She finally nods, slow, reluctant. "Fine. Together."

But I can already see it in her eyes—the flicker of someone who's not used to staying put, who's already planning her next move even as she agrees.

And that scares me more than the mission itself.

The word *together* hangs between us like smoke that won't clear. She said it, but I don't buy it—not fully. Victoria's a born operative; controls her oxygen. The only thing more dangerous than losing it is pretending she hasn't.

I push off the counter, breaking the tension before it eats us alive. "Then we do it smart. No guns blazing, no cowboy bullshit."

"Funny," she mutters, "I was about to say the same to you."

Her tone's sharp, but there's a curve to her mouth she doesn't quite hide.

I shake my head, moving past her to the back hall. "Come on. Armory's in the office closet."

She follows, barefoot, silent. Even like this—hair tied back, eyes hard—she moves like she's built from shadows and muscle memory.

When I open the closet door, she exhales low. Racks of rifles, tactical gear, a handful of Orion-grade sidearms from the days when my badge still meant something.

Her eyes flick over the weapons, calculating. "You've been busy."

"Old habits." I grab two pistols, slide one across the desk toward her. "You favor a Glock?"

Her lips twitch. "Some things don't change."

She checks the chamber, movements precise, almost ritualistic. It's muscle memory—same as mine.

I start packing the duffel: ammo, weapons, a spare set of plates. "We take the back road out past Copper Creek. Head north through the service route behind Red Haven. You'll guide us from there."

She nods. "I can get us to the secondary entrance—where they stage overnight loads. That's where the lift is. I'll get it open."

I glance at her. "And if there's company?"

"Then we improvise." Her tone's calm, too calm.

I pause, the gear strap half buckled in my hand. "That mean you got a plan or a death wish?"

"Maybe both," she says, but it's softer this time.

There's a quiet between us after that—charged but not hostile. Just two people about to step back into the kind of hell they swore they'd left behind.

When I zip the duffel shut, she's already at the counter, strapping her knife to her thigh. The dagger—the Black Bloom blade—rests beside her coffee cup like it belongs there. She slides it into her boot without a word.

I reach for the comms units on the counter, both clipped and charged from the night before. "Channel four," I say, handing her one.

She fits the earpiece in, taps twice to test the signal. Static hums, then clears. "Got you," she says.

I check mine next, adjusting the mic until her voice comes through clean. "Backup on seven if this one cuts out."

She gives me that look—half impatience, half understanding. "It won't."

"Good," I answer, slipping the unit into place. "Let's keep it that way."

She pulls on her jacket, checks the weight of the dagger in her boot, and nods once. The air between us hums—quiet, tense, waiting for the next move.

"You ready?" I ask.

She looks up, eyes catching the low light, and for a second, I forget how to breathe.

"Ready enough," she says. "You?"

"Never am," I admit, grabbing the keys from the hook.

Outside, the air's gone cool and damp. The sky's just starting to turn violet at the edges, that in-between time when night hasn't let go but day's already pressing in. I load the duffel into the truck bed, and she swings her leg over the bike seat like it's second nature.

"You're takin' that?" I ask.

She grins, small but wicked. "I move faster alone."

"Together, remember?"

She arches a brow. "Then try to keep up."

I can't help the half-laugh that breaks out of me. "You're impossible."

ble."

"I'm alive," she fires back, kicking the engine to life.

The growl of the bike echoes off the barn. I follow in the truck, headlights cutting a path through the dark. Gravel spits under the tires as Copper Creek disappears behind us—its porch light fading to a pinprick in the rearview.

She leads the way north, her taillight flickering red against the horizon.

I keep one hand on the wheel, the other drumming against my thigh, running the plan through my head in loops.

Warehouse Twenty-Seven. Hidden level. Thirteen women. One French voice threading through it all.

And somewhere inside that, a fuse ready to burn through both our lives.

For the first time in years, the mission feels personal.

And that's exactly what scares me most.

The road from Copper Creek to Harrington isn't built for speed. It's a patchwork of gravel, dirt, and cracked two-lane stretches where the asphalt's been losing its war with time. The kind of road that rattles your bones and keeps you awake, whether you want to be or ttles your bones and keeps you awake, whether you want to be or not. Headlights sweep over barbed-wire fences and the ghost of fields long gone to weed.

Victoria rides ahead, black helmet catching the moonlight, tail-light flicking in and out of view as the road curves. Every bump makes me feel the ache of the last few days—sleep lost, nerves tight—but she rides like she was born to outrun everything that chases her.

The plan's simple on paper. We go in together—she finds the hidden level, I cover the exits and keep the way out clean. No hero moves, no split routes, just in and out before anyone knows we were here. Simple enough. But simple plans have a way of catching fire once the doors close behind you.

By the time Harrington's outskirts rise out of the dark, my hands are tight on the wheel, the hum of the tires syncing with my pulse. We kill the lights a mile out, take the last stretch in silence. Gravel spits under the tires, dust curling in the beams of the moon.

The Red Haven compound sits ahead, lit up in that too-perfect way that makes my stomach knot. Floodlights wash the warehouses in amber, and the generators hum like a warning buried in the night. It looks routine—clean, quiet, maybe even harmless—but I've seen too many calm fronts to trust the silence.

I park the truck behind a cluster of trees just off the access road and kill the engine. The air hits thick—metal, rain, and that faint oil tang that never leaves a place like this. Feels like every op I swore I was done with.

Vicky's bike hums to a stop beside me. She moves like a ghost through the low light, and I can tell every breath still hurts. But she doesn't hesitate. Not once.

"You're sure this is the one?" I ask, though I already know her answer.

"Warehouse Twenty-Seven," she says, eyes locked on the north bay. "Hidden level under the compressors. Lift disguised in the wall. I found it the night before they took me."

I study her profile—jaw tight, eyes lit by that stubborn kind of fire. The one that got her through hell and back. "And you're still walking back in."

She just pulls her gloves tight. "If they move those women tonight, we lose them."

I move closer, close enough to feel her tension. "Then we do it together. No solo hero runs this time."

A flicker of something—gratitude, maybe guilt—crosses her face before she nods.

We cross the lot low and quick, keeping to the shadows. The badge she cloned flashes green at the side door. Inside, the air drops ten degrees. Smells like coolant and rust.

I check the corners, the rafters, the vents—old habits dying hard. Every sound feels amplified in here. The hum of the compressors, the low whine of lights, the distant tick of machinery. Too steady. Too controlled.

"Stay sharp," I murmur. "Places like this go quiet right before they burn."

She glances back, mouth curving faintly. "Good thing I stopped believing in easy roads a long time ago."

Almost makes me smile. Almost.

We move deeper down the corridor, side by side. Her stride is sure, but I can feel the edge of it—pain, anger, resolve all tied together. The metal walls reflect us back like ghosts, two figures walking into the same nightmare for different reasons.

And even as the unease crawls higher, I know one thing for sure. I'd follow her in again. Every damn time.

Chapter 33
Victoria

The warehouse looms ahead, its Red Haven logo barely visible beneath the glare of security lights. The hum of the compressors carries through the night, steady and mechanical, like a heartbeat that doesn't belong to anything human.

I cut the engine and roll the bike to a stop just inside the tree line. Gravel shifts under my boots as I swing off, every muscle still remembering what it cost to walk out of this place last time. The bruises pull, a dull throb beneath the wrap at my ribs.

Beau's truck eases up behind me, lights off, motor purring low. He kills the engine, steps out, and joins me at the edge of the lot. The night air smells faintly of rain and metal.

"You're sure this is the one?" His voice is low, steady, but I can hear the weight behind it.

"Warehouse Twenty-Seven," I say, eyes fixed on the glow of the north bay. "That's where they're moving from. There's a hidden level under it—behind the compressor units. Lift disguised in the wall. I found it the night before they took me."

He studies me for a long beat, jaw flexing. "And you're still walkin' back in."

"Someone has to." I pull my gloves tight, check the small sheath at my hip. "If they move those women tonight, we lose our shot."

Beau steps in close enough for his shoulder to brush mine. "We do this together. You're not goin' in alone again."

I nod once, the smallest movement, because I know arguing will waste time neither of us has.

The side door is unguarded, same as before. The badge I cloned flashes green. Inside, the air hits cold and sharp, heavy with coolant and oil. It's quieter than I expected. Too quiet.

We move as one—me ahead, Beau covering the rear, his footfalls a silent echo behind mine. The corridor stretches long and narrow, metal walls gleaming faint under the industrial lights. Every step down this hall feels like walking back into a nightmare I didn't escape from so much as outrun.

The compressor room looks the same: humming machinery, frost clinging to the pipes, condensation streaking the walls. I lead him to the far end, where the units meet the concrete. My gloved fingers trace along the seam until they find it—the thin break where the wall isn't a wall at all.

"Here."

Beau leans in, flashlight angled low. "That's damn near invisible."

"Not if you know what to look for." I press the latch. The hydraulics sigh, the disguised door swinging open without a sound. A draft of cool, sterile air rolls over us.

"Underground?" he mutters.

"Yeah. Big enough for vehicles. Smells like medical-grade filters."

We step through. The concrete slopes downward, the light fading as we descend. The hum grows louder, pulsing through the floor. I keep my breathing steady, the rhythm of my pulse syncing with the machines.

The first door on the right reveals the weapons room—open crates, stacked rifles, and the faint shimmer of stamped metal. I glance in long enough to see the Black Bloom symbol burned into the lid of a crate, then look away. "They're not just moving people," I whisper. "They're arming someone."

Beau's eyes narrow, voice low. "Thirteen women. That's not random cargo. It's a message."

We push deeper. The second corridor opens wider, the air thickening with chemical sterilizer and the metallic sting of fear. The cages are still there, but fewer this time. Chains hang loose from where the others were. The women that remain are silent, heads bowed, like they've already learned silence is safer than screaming.

A guard crosses the room, clipboard in hand, checking each cage before moving toward the lift at the far wall. I recognize the sound of it—the soft mechanical hiss of the same hidden system that brought me here once before.

"They're already transferring them," I whisper.

Beau's gaze tracks the guard. "Then we stop the transfer."

I shake my head. "We can't just storm the dock. Too many unknowns. But if we cut the power to the lift, we trap them here long enough to extract the women."

He looks at me like he's measuring whether I've lost my mind or finally found it. "You think we can move thirteen bodies without drawing every gun in this place?"

"I think chaos is our best shot," I whisper. "You cut the line outside, I take care of the circuit in here."

His jaw works, the muscle ticking once. "You get caught again—"

"I won't."

He doesn't believe me, not completely. But he doesn't argue, either.

I meet his eyes, steady and sharp. "We do this fast. In and out. If it goes wrong—"

"It won't." He cuts me off, voice rough. "Because this time, I'm right behind you."

The hum of the lift starts up again, faint but growing. We exchange one look—no words, no hesitation. Then we move—two shadows slipping back into hell to drag someone else out.

The hum deepens — that low, steady growl of machinery spinning to life — and it's enough to raise the hair on the back of my neck. Timing is everything. Once the lift starts, we'll have seconds before the next rotation of guards swings back through.

I nod once to Beau and slip along the wall toward the control room. It's half glass, half concrete, with a narrow door left on a careless latch. Typical. Men like this never expect their monsters to bite back.

The faint red glow of the monitors washes the space in static light. Readouts scroll across the screens — manifest numbers, shipment codes, biometric scans — all feeding from the same central system. I find the circuit board tucked behind a grated panel, cables bundled tight and labeled with corporate precision.

One switch to power the freight lift. One to control the locks. One for the main lights. I count the wires twice, mark their sequence, then pull my knife from my boot. The blade catches a sliver of red light as I slide it under the insulation.

Outside the glass, Beau moves through shadow, slow and deliberate. I can see the tension in the line of his shoulders — ready to strike, but patient. Always patient. The guards have started to circle the cages again, two men checking the locks, one logging something on a clipboard. The women keep their heads down, but I can feel their eyes. They sense the shift in the air too.

I whisper under my breath, "Three... two..." and cut the wire.

The lights die with a pop, plunging the entire level into darkness. A chorus of shouts erupts — boots scraping, radios crackling, flashlights snapping on. Sparks spit from the severed connection, and I jam my knife back into its sheath.

"Beau, move," I hiss into the comm clipped to my collar.

Static crackles, then his voice comes through, low and sure. "Already on it."

Gunfire barks in the distance — not aimed, just panic. The kind of noise that comes when men with power suddenly lose control.

I shove open the door and step into the dark. My pulse beats in my throat, a steady drum as I make for the cages. One of the guards swings a flashlight across the floor, catching the gleam of my boots. I drop low, sweep his leg, and drive my elbow into his throat before he can yell. His light hits the floor and rolls, painting a pale arc across concrete.

The women shrink back, eyes wide, silent. I crouch by the nearest cage, run my fingers along the lock — standard pad, reinforced, but old. I pull a pick from my pocket and work fast. Each click feels too loud, too slow. The first door snaps open.

"Go," I whisper. "Stay low, stay quiet."

They hesitate — of course they do. No one expects salvation from the same shadows that held them. "Now," I press, and the first one slips free, then another.

A burst of light floods the hallway — Beau's flashlight, I realize. He's back, gun raised, jaw set. "We're burnin' time, Vicky."

"I know," I snap, unlocking another cage. "Two more."

He moves in beside me, covering the corridor as I work. The lift hums again — backup generator kicking in. Of course they'd have redundancy. Nothing this big runs on one cord.

"New plan," I breathe. "You keep them covered. I'll overload the main."

Beau grabs my wrist, firm. "You go near that core with live power, it'll cook you."

"Then you'd better be ready to drag me out," I shoot back, breaking free.

I sprint to the far end of the corridor where the generator's warning lights flicker. It's older tech, tucked behind steel casing. I rip the cover open, grab a wrench from the rack, and jam it straight into the converter. The lights flare white-hot, then die with a crack like thunder.

The lift slams to a halt.

For one perfect second, there's silence — just the smell of ozone and burning metal. Then chaos. Boots thunder. Voices shout orders. Beau fires twice, clean, controlled.

"Vicky, move!"

I spin, grab the nearest woman by the arm, and shove her toward the service door. "Follow the others! Don't stop for anything!"

The air is thick with smoke and noise, every breath heavy with ash and burning metal. Shadows move through the haze — not all of them running.

The first man comes at me from the left, face half-hidden by a balaclava. I duck the swing of his rifle and drive my elbow into his ribs. He grunts, doubles over, and I grab the strap of his vest to yank him forward. One hard knee to the gut, one quick shove, and he's on the floor gasping. I scoop the weapon before it clatters away and bring it up just in time for the next one.

The second guard barrels toward me through the smoke, shouting orders I can't make out. I fire a short burst, controlled, low — two to the leg, one to the shoulder. He collapses into a table that goes up in a spray of splinters. Heat rolls through the hall, the lights flickering as fire chews at the walls.

Another shape breaks through the haze — closer this time. He's fast, heavy, trained. He grabs my arm mid-aim, twisting hard. The rifle jerks out of my hands. I slam my head back, feel the crack of his nose against my skull, and tear free with a hiss. Blood streaks down his face as he lunges again, but this time I'm faster. I draw the knife from my thigh holster and drive it across the inside of his forearm. He howls, clutching the wound, and I finish it with a heel to the knee that drops him cold.

The fire alarm screams overhead, a shrill counterpoint to the gunfire echoing down the corridor. I push forward, shoulder first, through the heat and chaos, smoke curling around my face.

Beau's at the far end, half-silhouetted against the orange glow, ushering people toward the stairwell and firing short bursts to keep the path clear. He's bleeding from the temple, jaw clenched, still steady. I cut through what's left of the hallway, stepping over debris and the men I left behind.

Another figure lurches from the corner — wild-eyed, desperate — and I react on instinct. The knife flashes once, catching light and shadow both, before he's down.

I reach Beau just as the last two women disappear into the stairwell. He turns, catches sight of me through the smoke, and for a heartbeat the noise drops away — just the two of us, standing in the ruin, the flames closing in.

A bullet ricochets off the wall near my head. We both drop, instinct in sync. His hand closes around my arm, pulling me against the wall, close enough I can smell the smoke on his skin.

"You alright?" he shouts over the noise.

"Ask me when we're topside!" I yell back.

We move — two shadows slipping through fire.

By the time we hit the surface, the warehouse is alive with alarms. Sirens wail, lights strobe against the night sky. The women huddle near the tree line where we left the vehicles. Beau motions them toward the truck, his movements crisp and efficient.

I pull the dagger from my belt, hands shaking, the metal hot from where it sat against my skin. I glance back once — the warehouse framed in red light, the sound of chaos rolling out into the dark.

Beau steps up beside me, breath ragged but steady. "That's one hell of a first date, Vicky."

I huff a breath that almost becomes a laugh. "Next time, I pick the venue."

Chapter 34
Beau

I don't wait for the flames to settle. There's no time. I haul open the truck's door, adrenaline still pounding through my veins. "Go!" I shout over the roar of the alarms.

Victoria doesn't hesitate—she's already straddling the bike, engine growling to life. The heat from the explosion paints her in flickering red and gold as she guns it toward the front gate, smoke curling behind her like a ghost that refuses to let go.

I throw open the tailgate, helping the women climb into the back, one by one. They're dazed, trembling, eyes wide with fear and disbelief. A few clutch each other's hands like lifelines. I toss a tarp over them—won't fool anyone for long, but maybe long enough.

When I hit the ignition, the truck grumbles reluctantly before the engine catches. Gravel spits under the tires as I swing it around and gun it for the service road. Ahead, the faint red glow of the bike cuts through the dark, weaving in and out of the shadows.

She doesn't look back once. Just keeps moving, head low, body tight to the machine. She's bleeding determination, the kind that doesn't quit even when it should.

"Hold on," I mutter to the women in the back as I floor it.

The dirt road narrows, alternating between gravel and hard-packed earth. Branches whip the sides of the truck. My headlights catch the glint of her taillight just before it vanishes around a bend.

When we hit the old service bridge, I spot her waiting on the other side, bike idling, scanning the road. The second she sees me, she signals—a sharp twist of her wrist, the kind that means *follow and don't ask questions.*

The backroads bleed into open country, the horizon stretching black and endless. The night air whips through the cracked windows, thick with the scent of gasoline, dirt, and smoke.

Finally, when the glow of the warehouse fades into a distant smear of red, she slows, coasting to a stop at a turnout. I pull the truck in behind her, kill the headlights, and step out.

She takes off her helmet, hair wild, eyes fierce. There's soot on her cheek and a smear of blood along her jaw, but she's grinning—wide and feral.

"They're alive," she says, breathless.

I nod, leaning against the door to steady the rush in my chest. "Yeah. For now."

Her grin falters, just a little, replaced by the quiet weight of what we both know—this was only a delay, not a victory.

The women in the truck whisper among themselves, the soft murmur of disbelief and relief threading through the night.

Victoria looks toward them, then back at me. "We can't take them to town. Not yet. It'll draw too much heat."

"I know," I say, jaw set. "Copper Creek. It's secure enough for now."

She studies me, eyes narrowing slightly. "You're sure?"

"Safer than out here."

A long breath escapes her, slow and shaky. "Then let's move before the wrong people start counting bodies."

I glance once more toward the fading plume of smoke, then back at her—smeared in ash and firelight, every inch of her carved from defiance.

"Reckon we just painted targets on our backs," I say.

Her lips twist into something that isn't quite a smile. "Good. Makes it easier for me to aim back."

And with that, she kicks the bike into gear and tears down the dark road ahead, the sound of her engine bleeding into the night.

We take the long way back—an hour's drive stretched into two because we can't risk the highways. The main routes out of Harrington are crawling with eyes, and the last thing I need is Orion, Red Haven, or whoever else tracking a pickup full of frightened women to my front gate.

Victoria rides point on the bike, a black streak ahead of me cutting through the dark. Her taillight flashes steady—one red pulse at a time. To anyone else it'd look like distance. To me it's rhythm. Focus. The one heartbeat keeping this drive from unraveling.

The women in the truck bed are quiet now. Wrapped in blankets, heads down, the hum of the tires and the smell of diesel filling the silence. Every so often, one shifts, and the sound tugs at me—proof they're still breathing. Proof we actually pulled this off.

The road snakes through pine and low fog, gravel giving way to cracked two-lane blacktop. We're twenty miles from Copper Creek when the hair on the back of my neck stands up.

Headlights.

Far back at first—just a glow between trees. But they don't fade when we turn. They stay locked.

Victoria's voice crackles through the comms. "You see that?"

"Yeah," I murmur. "Been there since we cleared the ridge."

"Could be a local," she says, though her tone says she doesn't buy it.

"Could be trouble."

The light behind us dips once, then levels out. Following.

I shift the truck into a higher gear, gravel spitting from the tires. "We'll stay north another five miles, cut down by the feed mill. If they're still with us then, we'll know."

Her engine revs through the headset. "Copy that."

The miles crawl by. The road narrows—trees pressing close, shadows reaching across the asphalt. The headlights shrink, vanish for half a breath—then flare bright again.

"Still there," I mutter.

"Yeah," she says. "And closing."

The first round hits the tailgate. A clean metallic crack that makes the women scream.

"Shit," I hiss, instinct snapping in. "We've got gunfire!"

"Keep driving," Victoria snaps through the line. "Don't slow down."

Her voice cuts through the panic, firm and steady. I grip the wheel, muscles locking as another shot punches through the rear glass. Shards scatter across the seat. "They're not trying to scare us—they're trying to stop us."

"Then we make it damn hard to catch us."

Her bike jerks left, kicking gravel into the dark, and she shouts over the comm, "They want the truck, not me. I'll lead them off."

"Like hell you will."

"Beau—listen. You've got the cargo. Thirteen women in the back of that truck. They'll follow the bike; it's louder, smaller, easier to chase. That's how this works."

"No," I snap, heart hammering. "You're still beat to hell from last week. I'm not letting you run into the line of fire."

"I took those hits because I had to," she fires back, voice sharp as glass. "Because I had to sell the cover. They think I'm a clipboard, remember? Harmless. It worked. They let me walk. You don't get to decide that was for nothing."

The silence that follows hums between us—electric and dangerous.

"Vicky—"

"Get them home," she says, softer now. "That's an order."

"Don't pull rank on me, Victoria."

"Then do it because you're the one who can."

Before I can stop her, she guns the throttle. The roar of the engine rips through the comms, then she's gone—cutting left down an unlit side road. The pursuing headlights pivot after her, one by one, tires screeching as they follow the bait.

"Victoria!" I shout into static. "Goddammit—"

The line hisses, dead.

The forest swallows her taillight before I can even curse again. Just one red blink—gone—and the dark settles thick around us.

I grip the wheel hard enough to ache, knuckles white in the wash of the dashboard light. The comms are nothing but static now. Not even breathing on the other end. Just wind.

"Come on, Vicky," I mutter. "Answer me."

Nothing.

The road stretches ahead, gravel grinding under the tires, the truck rocking with every rut. Behind me, one of the women whimpers; another murmurs something soft and foreign, soothing her quiet. I glance at the rearview, the tarp shifting like a heartbeat, and force the engine steady.

They're counting on me. On us.

I push the truck harder, hugging the curve of the two-lane, every mile widening the gap between the rescue and whatever hell Vicky's drawing fire from. She's reckless as sin—but she's not stupid. If she's baiting them, she's got an exit. She has to.

Still, the silence eats at me.

The ranch gate looms out of the dark sooner than I expect—Copper Creek, my only patch of earth that still feels like mine. I kill the headlights, ease the truck down the long gravel drive, and stop just short of the barn.

The air here smells of cedar and smoke. Safe. Almost.

I climb out slow, boots crunching against the dirt. The women huddle closer together, eyes wide, tracking me with a mix of fear and hope I don't know how to answer.

"It's over," I tell them quietly. "You're safe now."
I don't know if it's true. But it's all I've got to give.

The youngest—couldn't be more than nineteen—nods, clutching a blanket tighter around her shoulders. I force a smile that doesn't reach my eyes and guide them toward the house, one by one, through the back door.

Once they're inside, I lock up, check the windows, and make sure the curtains stay drawn. The air smells like coffee gone cold and old wood polish. I grab the comms mic from my vest. Static. Cold. Empty.

"Vicky, come on," I mutter, pacing the kitchen. "You said you'd make it back."

A flicker of interference crackles—half a breath, half a voice—and then nothing.

"Goddammit."

I drag a hand down my face, eyes burning with exhaustion and something meaner underneath. She's out there alone, running interference with half-healed ribs and a temper that doesn't know when to quit.

Old instincts take over. I head into my office, rip the map off the wall, and spread it across the kitchen table. Routes, back roads, dead zones, cutoffs—anywhere the feed lines disappear. If she's alive—and she's too damn stubborn not to be—I'll find her.

The house settles around us, old boards creaking with the wind. The women whisper prayers in a dozen languages. And outside, dawn starts bleeding through the trees.

One hour from Harrington. One hour from Copper Creek.

She bought us that time.

Now it's my turn to use it.

Chapter 35
Victoria

The night splits open around me—gravel and wind, the scream of the bike beneath me, the pulse of headlights too close behind. The comm's been dead since the first turnoff, nothing but static hissing in my ear like a ghost that won't let go.

Beau's truck is long gone by now. It has to be. That was the deal. I draw them off, he gets the women clear. Clean break. No witnesses. No second chances.

The road narrows from asphalt to gravel, then dirt—each shift rattling through my ribs until it feels like my bones are singing. Pain hums under my skin, sharp where the bruises never healed, but adrenaline burns hotter. I keep the throttle wide open, leaning into every curve like it owes me something.

Headlights flood the trees behind me—two vehicles, maybe three. Bigger engines. Trucks. They're not losing ground.

I cut my headlight, drop low over the bars, and veer off the main road into the service path that winds through the pines. The branches claw at my helmet as the path dips and narrows, roots grabbing at the tires. The engine growls, protesting the incline, but I don't let up.

The first shot cracks past me, tearing bark from a tree to my right. Another follows, closer, whining past my knee. They're firing blind, but all it takes is one lucky round.

I gun the throttle and throw the bike into a hard left turn, the back tire skidding before it catches. A flash grenade arcs from my hand without hesitation. It detonates in a burst of light that turns the woods white for a heartbeat, then drops everything back into darkness.

I don't look back.

The trail spills onto an old quarry road, uneven and slick with loose rock. The tires struggle for grip as I hit the slope, gravel spraying behind me. My heart pounds steady in my ears. Each second I stay alive is another second Beau gets closer to the ranch. Another second those women get to breathe.

I don't notice the chain until it's too late.

The headlight catches a glint of metal strung low across the road—too perfect to be chance. I yank the handlebars, but the front tire hits full force. The world snaps sideways.

Impact.

Dirt.

Sky.

Then nothing but pain.

I hit the ground hard, shoulder first, roll until I slam into something solid. The bike crashes somewhere behind me, metal shrieking before silence swallows it whole. My lungs fight for air, the world tilting in and out of focus.

Footsteps. Slow. Confident.

Voices carry over the hum of cooling engines—three, maybe four men. One laughs, the sound ugly and close.

I drag myself toward the wreck, fingers brushing cold steel—the dagger still strapped to my thigh. The motion makes my vision go white for a second, but I don't stop.

The first man rounds the corner of the fallen bike, flashlight beam cutting across the dirt. His shadow falls over me before he even realizes I'm not down for good. I move before he can speak—low, silent, blade flashing in an upward arc. The dagger bites deep into his thigh, and his shout splits the quiet.

He goes down hard. I rip the weapon free and spin, catching his wrist before he can grab the gun at his belt. One twist, one shot—his own round takes the man behind him.

Gunfire erupts in answer. I drop behind the wreck, heart hammering. Bullets slam into the metal, ringing it like a bell.

Pain flares in my ribs every time I breathe, but it's better than the alternative. I return fire, short bursts, enough to make them duck. Then silence.

They're repositioning.

I glance at the treeline. The only way out is forward. My body's shaking, the kind of tremor that comes when adrenaline burns through faster than blood can replace it. I press a hand against my ribs—wet, sticky. Doesn't matter. Not yet.

A truck engine roars to life somewhere behind the ridge. Headlights flood the road ahead, washing over the wreck, the trees, me.

For one split second, I let myself think about Beau—about the gravel roads between us, about the truck full of women who might finally have a chance.

Then I grit my teeth, tighten my grip on the dagger, and whisper into the dead comm,

"Keep them safe."

I step into the light.

The light hits like a punch. For a heartbeat, everything goes white—no sound, no air, just the hollow echo of my own pulse. Then rough hands close around my arms.

The dagger's gone before I even register it, booted away into the dark. I kick, twist, land one hit that earns a grunt and a harder blow in return. My knees buckle. Gravel grinds into my skin.

"Got her," a voice barks. "She's breathing."

Something cold snaps tight around my wrists. Metal. A chain. The sound of it locking into place is worse than any shout—it's memory, replaying itself like punishment.

When the bag goes over my head, I stop fighting. Not from surrender. From calculation. There's only so much you can do when the odds are this high and the air this thin.

They throw me into the back of a truck. The ride is short but violent—every turn slamming me against the wall until my ribs scream. By the time they haul me out, I know exactly where we are.

The smell gives it away first. Metal. Ozone. The faint, sour tang of fear that never leaves a room like this.

The chain bites deep into my wrists when I shift, metal grinding against bruised skin. The room smells the same as it did before—chemical cleaner, copper, stale sweat. I know this place. I swore I'd never breathe its air again.

The door opens.

Heels click, steady, measured.

She steps through like she's walking into a photoshoot.

Cassandra.

Same blonde hair, now pinned into a tight twist. Same red mouth that used to laugh too loud at every one of Travis's jokes. But her eyes—those are new. Cold. Surgical.

"Well," she says softly, her French accent curling around the edges of the word. "If it isn't the woman of the hour."

My pulse spikes, acid flooding my throat. "You've got to be kidding me."

Cassandra's smile widens, lazy and cruel. "You always did underestimate me, chère. It's adorable." She peels off a pair of black leather gloves finger by finger, then slips them back on, snug. "Did you think all I could do was play arm candy? Look pretty and pour wine?"

She picks up a small metal baton from a tray, turning it in her hands. "Travis used to tell me you were so very *careful.* So precise. Until the end."

My breath catches. "Travis?"

Her grin turns knife-sharp. "Oh, sweetheart. You still don't know?"

She touches the baton to my ribs and flicks a switch. The current lances through me, white-hot and clean. My muscles seize, my jaw clenches hard enough to hurt, and she watches it all with academic interest.

When the jolt stops, she steps closer, voice soft, almost kind. "Travis never loved you. He was a plant. Black Bloom wanted a key to the Bible, and you were Orion's precious little locksmith."

The world narrows to the sound of my pulse pounding in my ears. "He didn't—"

Cassandra cuts me off with a backhand across my face—clean, efficient, like she's correcting a mistake. My head snaps sideways, the chain rattling above me.

"Oh, he did," she purrs. "He courted you because you were useful. He stayed because you were effective. And when Alexandre Leclair needed access to the Bible drive, Travis opened the door for him. You never even saw it."

The words hit harder than the strike. I shake my head, breath ragged. "You're lying."

She drags the tip of the baton down my sternum, cold metal skimming sweat-damp skin. "Am I? You think Montague means something? You think Orion raised you because of your name?" Her voice lowers, almost reverent. "There was never a legacy, Victoria. You were raised to *kill*. You are a manufactured product, a prototype polished for perfection. Orion doesn't build legacies. It builds weapons."

The baton hums again, catching the inside of my thigh, and this time I don't bite back the sound—it tears out of me raw, sharp, echoing off the concrete.

Cassandra sighs, satisfied. "There she is. The truth hurts, doesn't it? That's how you know it's real."

She steps behind me, fingers sliding into my hair, twisting it until my scalp screams. Her breath ghosts my ear. "I told Travis once that you'd break beautifully. He didn't believe me. But I always see the potential."

I spit blood, shaking. "You're nothing but a parasite in designer heels."

She laughs, low and delighted. "And you're still clinging to the illusion that you had a choice."

A pause, then her voice drops, smooth as silk.

"Do you know what I love about Orion's experiments?" she murmurs, leaning close enough that her perfume—something floral and expensive—slides beneath the copper tang of blood. "No matter how hard they fight their conditioning, they always come back home."

She releases my hair, steps around to face me again. For a heartbeat, her expression softens—not pity, not affection, but curiosity. Then she leans in and presses her lips to mine.

It isn't deep. It isn't even cruel. Just *chaste*. A scientist testing the temperature of her creation.

When she pulls back, her smile curves slow and serpentine. "You did always have a certain appeal about you," she says, almost wistful.

"A potential we could have explored, if you hadn't been so busy pretending to be normal."

Her fingers trail down my cheek, feather-light, before she withdraws completely, eyes glinting. "Tell Beau when you see him," she says, tone turning mock-sweet, "that Travis sends his love. He always did like your fire."

Then she flicks the switch one last time.

The shock rips through me—light, pain, static. The edges of the room blur. When the current cuts, I hang limp from the chain, chest heaving, breath shallow but alive.

The door slams shut, the echo long and hollow.

I taste blood, iron and salt.

Travis. Cassandra. Alexandre. The Bible.

All threads of the same noose tightening around my throat.

But under the pain, there's something else. Rage.

Slow. Solid. Unbreakable.

They think they made me.

They think they still own me.

They don't.

I lift my head, voice a rasp against the dark.

"You're going to regret not killing me."

And for the first time since the chain went up, I smile.

Chapter 36
Beau

The map's folded in my vest, but my head's already upstairs. Four rooms. Four walls that used to mean family, quiet, normal. Now they're housing twelve broken women and everything I can't afford to lose.

Caleb's waiting in the kitchen, one hand around a mug gone cold, eyes heavy but alert. He doesn't need the details — he already sees it in my face. Still, I give them anyway, short and sharp.

"Guest room, Quinn's old room, and the spare," I say, counting them off with my fingers. "Lock the hall door from the inside once they're settled. You sleep in the living room — keep the shotgun close but out of sight."

He nods once. "And the master?"

"Off-limits," I say. "They need space that feels safe, not like they're trespassing." I grab a set of keys off the counter, toss them to him. "Main gate's locked. I moved the old Ford up by the trees — makes it look like nobody's been home in weeks."

"Food?"

"Pantry's stocked. Dorinda's casserole still in the freezer. Warm it slow. They're not gonna have much appetite, but they need something hot in their stomachs." I pause, watching the twitch in his jaw when I say it. "And keep them away from the windows. Curtains closed. Lights low."

He sets the mug down. "You expect company?"

"I expect trouble," I say simply. "If anyone shows — suits, uniforms, doesn't matter — you tell them Beau Maddox ain't takin' visitors. You don't open the damn door."

"Understood." His voice goes rough, tired. "And her?"

The question hangs heavy. I don't have to ask who he means.

"I'm goin' after her," I say. "She bought us time, Caleb. I'm not wasting it."

He studies me for a second, weighing the risk. Then: "You sure you're not walking straight into the same mess?"

"Wouldn't be the first time," I mutter, pulling the map from my vest. I spread it flat across the counter. "Routes are circled. Backroads into Harrington. Benny's still feeding me coordinates — says one of the secondary shipping lanes dead-ends near an unmarked lot. Could be where they took her."

Caleb leans in, scanning the marks. "The one past the old quarry?"

"Yeah." I fold the map once and slide it into my vest. "If I'm not back by sundown, lock everything down tight and keep the generator running. Nobody leaves. Nobody talks."

He nods again, slow, the way you do when there's nothing left to argue. "You really think she's still alive?"

I meet his eyes. "She's too damn stubborn not to be."

Caleb exhales through his nose. "Then bring her home."

I grab the keys, hand on the door. "Keep channel three open. If it goes quiet too long—don't wait. Take the women and head north through the pasture. The old trail meets the highway."

He nods once, solid. "Understood."

Outside, dawn is just brushing the treeline — pale gold and cold as bone. The air smells like cedar and diesel, like the kind of morning that starts before mercy wakes.

I tighten my grip on the map, glance once back at the house — four rooms, too small to hold the ghosts I'm leaving behind — then head for the truck.

"Hold tight, Vicky," I mutter as the engine growls to life. "I'm comin'."

The building looms gray against the rising light. Every instinct I've got is screaming trap, but that's never stopped me before. The side entrance is chained but not locked. Old habit makes me test it twice. The metal gives with a low grind. Inside, it smells of oil and ozone, that chemical-clean scent meant to hide something fouler underneath.

The first corridor's empty. Crates stacked floor to ceiling, tarps draped over half-finished shipments. Same pattern as before—too neat, too staged. But the temperature drops the deeper I go. Not the cold of storage, but of recycled air. Ventilation from somewhere below.

I follow it.

The hallway twists once, ending at a steel door half-hidden behind a row of shelving. No keypad. No code lock. Just a latch worn smooth by use. I press my ear against it—silence. Then, faintly, the hum of generators. And beneath that... a voice.

Female.

Measured.

French.

My pulse stutters. I've heard that voice before. The first night at Red Haven, drifting up from Victor Leclair's office. A woman talking to him like she owned the place.

Now she's here.

I draw my knife, easing the latch open. The hinges groan softly as I slip inside. The air hits me like a punch—thick with the stench of blood, sweat, and bleach. Chains rattle somewhere ahead, metal against concrete. My grip tightens.

I edge closer, slow and deliberate, until the dim light resolves shapes. Tables. Equipment. And a figure hanging from the center of the room, arms bound overhead.

Vicky.

She's conscious. Barely. Skin slick with sweat, wrists raw where the cuffs bite in. Her head lifts when the door creaks. I catch the faintest spark of recognition before her gaze shifts past me—to the woman standing in front of her.

The one speaking.

She's tall, sleek, wrapped in a long coat that glints faintly under the fluorescents. Blonde hair pinned back, posture elegant as a blade. She paces around Vicky with the kind of calm that only comes from control. And that voice—smooth, detached, clinical—cuts clean through the hum of the machines.

"Legacy can't be erased," she says. "Only repurposed."

My chest tightens. Whoever this woman is, she's the root of it all.

I move to the edge of the shadows, close enough to hear but not enough to draw attention. Waiting for my opening. Every muscle in me screams to rush in, to tear those chains down, to put a bullet between the stranger's eyes. But timing is everything.

Because right now, the only thing keeping Vicky alive is that voice still talking.

"You're going to regret not killing me."

Her laugh is all teeth and defiance, and for a heartbeat the room tightens around that one sound. Then I move.

There's no slow build. No thinking it through. My feet find purchase on the concrete, and everything else is a series of muscle memories that swallow the little voice that says don't. I charge.

The first guard sees me a hair too late. His eyes go wide, realization and regret mixing in the same instant his mouth opens. My shoulder barrels into him like a freight train, and the rifle in my hands becomes a club—crack, the world goes black at the edge of his vision—and he folds without grace. The second swings, slow and uncertain, and I meet him with an elbow into the ribs and a heel to the knee that floors him. There's no elegance, only the geometry of blunt force. The clang and thud are loud and useful.

The woman turns at the noise—only then do I catch her face in the half-light. It's smooth and calm in a way that makes my blood boil. No surprise, no scuttle. She expected this might come. Maybe she even wanted it to. Either way, she doesn't move to stop it; she lets me be the one to break the room.

I catch her under the arms before she can hit the floor, taking most of her weight while my other hand works the bolt. The metal bites into my palm, slick with rust and blood. "Hold on," I mutter, bracing her against my chest as I wrench. The chain fights back, screaming against the strain. Sparks jump where steel grinds on steel, my forearms burning from the effort.

She spits blood, curses—low, feral. The bolt shifts a fraction, then holds. I dig my heels in and twist again, every muscle locking down until the world narrows to metal and breath. Then, with a sharp crack, the link gives.

The chain snaps free, falling away in a clatter of steel. The sudden release sends her sagging against me, her body limp, trembling. I tighten my grip, steadying her before she slips, and pull her close, feeling the rough drag of her breath against my neck.

She's shaking, eyes half-rolled but alive. I press my jacket against the raw skin at her collarbone, blood seeping through the fabric, and listen for her heartbeat—uneven, defiant, still there.

She's still shaking when I ease her down, guiding her to the wall where the smoke's thinner. "Stay low," I tell her, pressing the rifle into her lap just in case. Her hand curls weakly around the stock, but she nods once, eyes glassy and stubborn.

I turn back toward the sound of boots on concrete.

I don't get far before the room erupts.

Two more men come at me from the flank, and I meet them full on. The first throws a wild swing—too slow—and I catch his wrist, twist, drive my shoulder into his chest, and send him skidding across the floor. He hits hard enough that the sound carries.

The second pulls a pistol; reflex takes the rifle from my hands, the butt slamming into his jaw. He staggers, drops the gun, and I stomp it away with the heel of my boot. He lunges again, running on adrenaline and bad judgment. I meet him in muscle and bone—knee to sternum, elbow to jaw—until he's staring at the ceiling and breathing slow.

Boots pound the mezzanine. Someone yells into a radio. I catch the echo and time my next moves around it. There's no room for hesitation; hesitation gets you dead. I shove a crate into the path of an oncoming guard, body-check him into the stack; the wood groans, splinters. My ribs smart from the impact, but it's worth the debt.

A man with a length of chain swings low; I duck, feeling the leather buzz against the back of my neck, and come up inside his guard—arm over his shoulder, hand around the throat—tight enough to make him gag. Adrenaline makes my hands precise. I pull, twist, and the man jerks forward, losing balance. The chain clatters from his grip and I use it like a whip, cracking it against the concrete to keep the others off for a second that stretches like a lifetime.

They try numbers. They try coordination. I try getting to her.

She's slumped against the wall now, the broken chain still looped around her shoulders and one arm. When one of the men crashes into the support post, the vibration jolts through the floor. She jerks, a low sound tearing from her throat, head snapping back against the concrete. For a second her eyes roll white, and panic bites at the back of my throat—sharp and metallic.

I move fast—drop low, shove the loose length of chain aside so it can't catch, check that she's breathing. She is, barely, chest rising in short, uneven pulls. "Stay down," I mutter, bracing her back against the wall before I turn.

Another guard barrels into me from the side, driving his shoulder into my ribs and slamming me against the post. Pain flares hot through my chest, but I twist, catch him by the vest, and ram my knee up into his gut. The air leaves him in a hard grunt. I shove him off and drive an elbow into his jaw for good measure. He drops, motionless.

I turn back to her. She's trying to push herself up, trembling, one arm tangled in the chain. I drop beside her, pull the metal free before it drags her down. "I've got you," I tell her, even if I'm not sure she hears it.

I slide an arm beneath her knees, another behind her back, and lift. She's too light, too warm, shaking from exhaustion and shock. Her head drops against my shoulder, breath hitching once before falling into a shallow, uneven rhythm.

The warehouse erupts behind us—boots pounding, radios barking, orders shouted—but I don't look back. Sunlight slices through the high windows, thin and blinding, painting everything in harsh gold. It catches the blood along her jaw, the torn links still dangling from her wrist, and the smoke curling up behind us as we move.

I keep moving. Every step's a hammer, every breath a curse. The air outside hits hot and sharp, thick with dust and the metallic tang of morning heat. Trucks idle somewhere down the row, men shouting into radios, but all I see is open space and the glint of my own tailgate.

I get her there, set her gently against the seat. She stirs—barely—eyes fluttering beneath lashes caked with sweat and grime. "Got you," I mutter, hand brushing her shoulder before I slam the door and circle around to the driver's side.

The sun's climbing fast, burning away the haze, and by the time the tires hit the road, the warehouse is just a glare in the rearview mirror.

Chapter 37
Beau

The road unspools in front of me, a thin ribbon of asphalt winding through scrub and sunrise. My knuckles are white on the wheel, every muscle locked to keep from looking at the passenger seat more than I already have.

She's there—barely conscious, head lolling against the window, blood drying along her collarbone where the chain bit deep. The morning light makes her look ghost-pale except where her shirt's torn, revealing the bruises blooming dark beneath. Each one feels personal, like I should've stopped it before it ever started.

The engine hums steady, the tires humming their own rhythm over the cracked road. I take the long way—gravel to dirt to narrow county backroads—because quiet buys time. We've both learned the same thing: speed means nothing if you're visible.

Her breath catches, small and sharp. I reach over without thinking, steadying her shoulder, fingers brushing skin that feels too hot. She flinches, then relaxes, like even in her half-conscious haze she knows it's me.

"Hang in there, Vicky," I murmur, keeping my eyes on the road. "Almost home."

Home. The word sounds strange in my mouth. Copper Creek isn't a refuge—it's a patch of earth I've tried to make mean something. Now it's the only place I can take her.

A few miles later, she stirs again, voice rough and paper-thin. "You came."

The words hit harder than they should. I let out a breath I didn't know I was holding. "'Course I did."

Her eyes crack open, glassy with exhaustion. "You shouldn't have."

"Yeah, well," I say, tightening my grip on the wheel, "you shouldn't've tried to play decoy with half-healed ribs, but we both make dumb choices."

Her lips twitch like she's trying to smile, but it hurts too much. "Did you get them out?"

"Women are safe," I tell her. "Caleb's with 'em. He's keepin' them at the ranch until we figure the next move."

That gets a faint nod. Relief softens the line of her mouth before her head tips back against the seat again.

The rest of the drive is all heat and silence. The world blurs into shades of dust and gold, the sun crawling higher, the weight of everything we've done pressing down on both of us.

By the time the Copper Creek gate comes into view, her breathing's evened out again. She's not asleep—too restless for that—but she's quiet. The kind of quiet that comes after pain has burned itself clean.

I slow the truck, gravel crunching under the tires, and glance at her again. The blood. The bruises. The small tremor still running through her fingers.

I've seen people come apart before. Soldiers. Operatives. Agents who thought they could outrun what was done to them. But seeing it on her—someone who's built from fire and precision—it does something to me I can't name.

"Almost there," I say again, softer this time.

Her lashes flutter. "Good," she murmurs, barely audible. "Because if you say 'hang in there' one more time, I might shoot you."

A hoarse laugh breaks out of me before I can stop it. "There she is."

She doesn't smile, but her breathing eases. I take the last turn slow, the ranch rising ahead—quiet, solid, waiting. Morning light stretches thin across the porch, catching the dew on the railings. Everything looks calm. It's a lie.

The truck crunches to a stop in the drive, gravel spitting under the tires. I kill the engine. The silence that follows is thick enough to choke on. For a second, I just sit there, listening to her shallow breaths beside me—steady but strained, each one scraping her raw.

Her lips part. "We made it?"

"Yeah." My voice comes out low, worn. "We made it."

She gives a small nod that probably costs her more strength than she'll admit. Her eyes flutter, but she's still awake—because she doesn't know how to stop fighting, not even now.

"Stay put," I tell her, already out of the truck. Gravel crunches under my boots as I come around to her side. When I open the door, she blinks against the light, one hand instinctively moving to her ribs.

"I can walk," she mutters.

I shake my head. "You could, if I was an idiot."

Before she can argue, I slide an arm under her knees, the other behind her shoulders, and lift. She's lighter than she should be—blood loss, exhaustion, adrenaline finally fading. She makes a soft sound in her throat that's half protest, half surrender, but she doesn't fight me. Not this time.

The porch boards creak beneath our weight as I carry her through the door. The house smells of cedar, old coffee, and faint lavender from the soap Caleb must've used cleaning up. I glance toward the hall—voices murmur behind closed doors, the rescued women tucked away and resting, or trying to. Every room's full. Every soul accounted for.

All but hers.

So I carry her into mine.

The door swings shut with a soft click. Morning light slants through the curtains, cutting stripes across the bed. The space smells like home and gun oil—neither of which she belongs to, but both seem to fit her anyway.

I ease her down onto the mattress. She tenses once, then sinks into the sheets like they're foreign terrain. For a long moment, she just stares at the ceiling, chest rising and falling, the ghosts of pain still chasing through her ribs.

"Didn't have to bring me in here," she says, voice frayed at the edges.

"Didn't have another bed," I lie, quiet.

She lets out a breath that might be a laugh. "You're a terrible liar, Beau."

"Only when I'm tellin' the truth."

That earns me a faint smirk—there, and gone again. I grab a towel and a bowl of water from the dresser, wiping away what blood I can before it dries. Her skin's clammy, her pulse thin but strong. When I press the cloth to her shoulder, she hisses but doesn't pull away.

"I've got it," she murmurs.

"I know," I say, wringing the cloth out. "Just humor me."

When the worst of it's cleaned, I grab the blanket off the foot of the bed and drape it over her. Her hand catches mine halfway through, fingers trembling, grip still sure.

Her eyes find mine, sharp even through the haze. "You shouldn't have come for me."

"Yeah," I say, settling on the edge of the bed. "That's probably true."

She studies me for a long beat, breath shallow, jaw tight like she's holding in the pain—or the words that want to cut through it. "They could've killed you," she whispers.

I give a small shrug. "They could've killed you. Figured we'd even the odds."

Her lips twitch, but it's not quite a smile. More like she's too damn tired to argue. "That's not how this works, Beau. You weren't supposed to—"

"Wasn't supposed to what?" My voice comes out rougher than I mean it to. "Give a damn?"

Her gaze drops away, focusing somewhere past my shoulder. "You don't understand," she says quietly. "Cassandra was there."

That stops me cold. "The woman you mentioned before?"

She nods, barely. "Yeah. Only this time, she wasn't playing secretary or arm candy. She was running the room."

Her voice breaks, raw at the edges. "She said Travis sends his love. That he always liked my fire."

The name hits like a gut punch. "Travis—the same one you—"

"Yes," she cuts in, sharp but shaking. "The same one who called me boring and walked out with her on his arm like I'd already stopped existing." Her eyes glint in the dim light, and something like shame threads through the anger. "Turns out, I didn't lose him. I was *handled*."

I lean forward, elbows on my knees. "Handled how?"

Her voice lowers, thin but steady. "He wasn't some bored accountant looking for adrenaline. He was theirs. A plant. Someone Cassandra sent in to keep tabs—on me, on Orion's movements, maybe both. He didn't love me. He was making sure I stayed close enough to trust him, and blind enough not to see what he was really after."

"The Bible."

She nods once. "Access. Not the drive itself, but the security clearance that opened the door. He gave it to Alexandre Leclair. Cassandra made sure I knew it."

I drag a hand over my face, fighting the burn in my chest. "You think she's telling the truth?"

"I know she is," she says. "Because that's how she wins—she only lies by omission."

For a moment, the silence stretches thick between us. She lies there half in shadow, half in morning light, all defiance and damage. It hits me then—what it costs her to keep breathing like this, to keep fighting when everything she trusted has turned to rot.

I reach for the blanket again, tuck it higher over her shoulders. "You're safe now," I tell her. "At least for the morning."

Her eyes flick toward me, tired but still sharp. "Safe's a temporary condition, Beau."

"Yeah," I admit. "But it's the one I'm best at providing."

She exhales, the smallest sound that might be a laugh. "You and your damn hero complex."

"Call it habit."

She doesn't answer. Just watches me for a beat longer, eyes softening at the edges before they finally close.

I stay there, listening to the rhythm of her breathing until it steadies—until I know she's really asleep. Only then do I let the tension drain from my shoulders, lean back in the chair, and look toward the pale light filtering through the curtains.

Travis. Cassandra. The Black Bloom.

Every name feels like a fuse waiting to burn.

And if they think they're going to finish what they started—they're about to learn what happens when you come after what's mine.

I wait until the light thins, the day leaning toward evening before I step out on the porch. The ranch looks different in that low gold — softer around the edges but no less dangerous. My thumb hovers over the sat phone longer than I want, then I hit the name I've kept for when things get ugly.

"Turtle," I say when he picks up, voice low. The line crackles. "Got us thirteen women. Pulled them out of a Red Haven run near Harrington. Need them gone, quiet."

A beat, then the low whistle I know too well. "Afternoon, Beau. Figured you'd call me when the sky got heavy. You need them moved tonight?"

"Tonight," I answer. "As in, before anything else moves. No windows."

He hums, thinking. "I can shift a rig. Two drivers who don't ask questions. They can be at your coordinates in—give me three hours. You got containment and cover?"

"I've got them inside the house. Locked down," I say.

"Good." His voice tightens. "I'll reroute the rig. They'll be on site by dusk. You keep them steady, I'll make the trail disappear."

The line clicks. I stand there a moment longer, watching the first long shadows crawl across Copper Creek. The women will move tonight. It's not perfect, but it's enough.

Inside, she breathes slow, shallow. The blanket rises and falls like a small, steady flag. "Rest," I whisper to the room and to her both. "Help is on the way."

Chapter 38
Victoria

The first thing I notice is the cold.

Not the kind that bites—just the kind that tells me he's not there.

For a week, I've woken up pressed against the same steady warmth, the rhythm of his breathing syncing with mine until I almost forget how to sleep without it. Now, the space behind me is empty, the sheets still dented where his body should be. My fingers find the hollow instinctively, tracing the faint imprint of him like muscle memory.

The scent of him lingers—cedar, smoke, and the ghost of coffee. It's grounding and dangerous all at once.

Somewhere down the hall, floorboards creak. Footsteps—measured, unhurried. A skillet scrapes metal, followed by the soft crack of eggshells. Then bacon. I'd know that sound anywhere. My stomach twists in protest before it growls, reminding me I've eaten little more than soup and stubbornness for days.

I stretch, slow, every muscle catching up with the reality of being alive. The ache in my ribs has dulled to something I can breathe through, the bruises yellowing out at the edges. The rest... the rest I try not to catalog.

The sheets smell like him. The room smells like coffee and morning. And for one fragile second, it almost feels normal.

Then the door opens.

He fills the frame like he always does—broad shoulders, messy hair, a dish towel thrown over one shoulder, the scent of breakfast following him in. His eyes find mine before anything else, and whatever sharp thing sits behind them softens.

It shouldn't make my chest tighten the way it does. But it does. Every damn time.

There's something disarming about him like this—barefoot, sun spilling across the lines of his forearms, stubble catching the light. The kind of man who looks built for danger but somehow manages to make domesticity look like a second skin. The contrast burns slow and deep in my gut, like I'm trying to remember what it feels like to want something that isn't survival.

His shirt is half unbuttoned, collar loose enough that I catch the edge of a scar I've never seen before. My eyes linger too long. He notices—of course he does—and one corner of his mouth curves, not quite a smile, but close enough to make my pulse jump.

"Morning," he says, voice low and rough with sleep, like he hasn't used it yet.

It rolls through me in a way that has nothing to do with the pain in my ribs and everything to do with the man standing in the doorway looking at me like I'm something fragile and dangerous at once.

I force myself to look away, to break the spell before I forget how to breathe. But it's too late. The warmth crawling under my skin isn't from the sunlight. It's him. It's always him.

He crosses the room, that lazy, unhurried stride that says he's exactly where he wants to be, and sets the tray on the nightstand beside me. Steam curls from two mugs and a plate stacked high with pancakes glistening under blueberry compote. Bacon, eggs, the works. It smells like a memory I don't remember having.

"Figured you'd be hungry," he says, sitting on the edge of the bed.

I blink at the tray, at the way he's gone and made it look like a goddamn Sunday morning instead of the aftermath of hell. "You made this?"

I shift upright, settling back against the headboard as he grins and reaches across to steal a piece of bacon from my plate before I can even grab a fork.

"Don't sound so surprised. I do eat, y'know."

I shake my head, trying not to smile as he chews like a man proud of his theft. "You're a menace."

"Depends who you ask." He leans back on one hand, easy and comfortable, like this is normal—like we haven't been bleeding and running and burning for weeks.

I spear a bite of pancake, scoop it through the syrup and compote, then hold it out without thinking. He hesitates a second, eyes flicking from the fork to my face, and then he leans forward, lips closing around the bite. His tongue brushes the edge of the fork before he pulls back, slow, deliberate.

"Damn," he murmurs, licking a bit of syrup from his thumb. "That's good."

"Homemade compote?" I ask, because words are safer than the heat crawling under my skin.

He nods. "Found the berries out by the creek. Figured you deserved somethin' better than ration bars and adrenaline."

I take another bite, slower this time, and wash it down with a sip of coffee. The first taste stops me cold. Perfect balance—cream first, three sugars. Exactly how I make it.

"You remembered."

He glances up, eyes catching mine over the rim of his mug. "Hard thing to forget."

The quiet stretches, easy and warm. I let it. For once, I don't fight it. I just sit there beside him, tasting blueberries and coffee and a peace I've never earned, and let myself think—maybe, just for a second—that this could almost be something like home.

He reaches out, his calloused thumb brushing lightly over my cheekbone, and the touch sends a shiver straight through me. His gaze catches mine—intense, searching—and in its depths, I see a question I don't have words for yet. My own hand rises, like it's caught on an invisible thread, and covers his, pressing it gently against my skin. The silence between us thickens, charged with unspoken things, with the lingering scent of breakfast and the sudden, overwhelming awareness of him. He leans in, slow and deliberate, and I meet him halfway, breath catching in my throat. His lips—warm, soft—find mine in a kiss that starts tender, exploratory, before deepening into something hungrier, something desperate and utterly, irrevocably real.

His control is maddening, every movement deliberate, like he's memorizing me one heartbeat at a time. His kisses trace fire—first feather-light, barely brushing my lips, then down along my jaw, to the sensitive curve of my neck. Each touch fans the spark higher until my heart pounds a frantic rhythm against my ribs, a wild drumbeat to the heat coiling deep in my core. A soft, involuntary sound escapes me, a plea more than a moan, as he returns to my lips, nipping, teasing, pushing me right to the edge of reason.

My hand slips beneath the open collar of his shirt, fingertips grazing the rough edges of a still-healing scar. The contact is intimate, grounding—an acknowledgment of the pain he carries and the trust I'm offering. My other hand fists in the fabric of his shirt, tugging him closer, needing more of him, all of him. The world narrows to this—his scent, his skin, the slow, burning slide of his mouth against mine—and for one impossible, perfect moment, nothing else exists but us.

He breaks the kiss, pulling back just enough for our foreheads to touch, his breath mingling with mine. His eyes, dark and heavy-lidded, search mine, still holding that question. "Vicky," he murmurs, his voice a low rumble against my ear, and the sound of my name from his lips feels like a confession. I don't answer, can't. My fingers are still tangled in his shirt, my heart still racing. I just look at him, letting the moment hang, letting the unspoken weight of everything we've been through settle between us, and in the quiet, I finally understand. It's not just about survival anymore. It's about this. It's about us.

And as if reading my thoughts, he leans in again, this time his lips finding the hollow of my throat. A soft gasp escapes me, and I arch into his touch, a silent invitation, a surrender I never thought I'd be capable of. The world outside the bedroom fades, the echoes of danger and despair momentarily silenced by the overwhelming thrum of connection.

This isn't just about solace; it's about a fierce, undeniable yearning that has taken root in the barren landscape of my heart. His hand slides from my cheek to cup the back of my neck, his thumb stroking my skin, sending shivers down my spine. The intensity in his gaze deepens, mirroring the raw emotion that twists within me. We are two broken pieces, fitting together, finding a fragile kind of completeness in the wreckage of our lives.

"Yes," I whisper, lifting my lips to meet his. "I want this." And this time, there's no hesitation, no holding back. Just the fierce, desperate certainty of a woman who has finally found something worth fighting for, something worth living for, in the arms of a man who makes her feel both seen and safe.

"More than anything," I whisper, my voice trembling but sure, "this is something for me. For us."

His eyes search mine, slow and deliberate, like he's reading every word I don't say aloud. Then his mouth finds the hollow of my neck again, lips brushing skin still tender, still healing. The breath he exhales is molten against me, a silent promise of more. He trails a line of fire up my throat, my jaw, until his lips finally capture mine in a kiss that is both gentle and demanding, a searing exploration that leaves me breathless and wanting.

"Then let me turn your pain into pleasure, Vicky," he murmurs, voice low and rough enough to make my whole body tighten.

My breath catches, and for a moment, everything—every scar, every ache, every ghost—melts beneath the weight of that promise.He kisses the sensitive skin there, working his way up my jawline until his lips claim mine once more. This kiss is deeper, a silent conversation of longing and need. His hands are everywhere, gentle yet firm, tracing the curves of my waist, gliding up my sides, fingers ghosting over the bruised hollow of my ribs with exquisite care. He murmurs against my mouth, a soft, indistinct sound of adoration, and I answer with a desperate sigh, my fingers burying themselves in his hair, holding him to me as if he might disappear.

He pulls back slightly, just enough to look into my eyes, and the intensity there steals my breath. "Every inch," he whispers, his thumb brushing over my trembling lower lip. "Every single inch of you is beautiful, Vicky."

He lowers his head, his lips trailing a path of fire down my throat, across my collarbone, pausing to linger at the delicate pulse point where my heart hammers against my skin. His touch is reverent, worshipful, stripping away layers of doubt and fear with each soft press of his mouth. A tremor runs through me, not of cold, but of pure, unadulterated sensation.

He pushes the sheets down, slowly, deliberately, his eyes never leaving mine, a silent question in their depths. I nod, barely, a silent invitation, and he continues his tender exploration, his kisses scattering over my shoulders, down the slope of my arm, to the inside of my elbow.

Every touch, every lingering brush of his lips, feels like a reclamation, a defiant act of beauty against the ugliness I've known. His gaze, still locked with mine, dips to the flannel shirt I wear, his own from yesterday, still carrying the faint echo of cedar and smoke. With slow, deliberate movements, he undoes the buttons one by one, each soft click a counterpoint to the accelerating beat of my heart.

The fabric falls open, revealing the swell of my breasts, already aching for his touch. His hand, warm and calloused, cups one, his thumb circling the peak until a gasp escapes my lips. Then, he lowers his head, his mouth finding the other, tasting, suckling, a low growl rumbling in his chest that vibrates through me, a primal chord struck deep within my core.

Chapter 39
Beau

I lower my head, tracing the curve of her collarbone with my tongue, then moving lower to the swell of her breast. The soft skin yields beneath my lips, and I tease the peak with the tip of my tongue before drawing it fully into my mouth. She gasps, a soft sound that vibrates against my lips, and her fingers tangle in my hair, pulling me closer. I suck gently, eliciting another moan from her, and

I can feel her hips instinctively bucking against mine. Her body is a symphony of soft cries and shudders, and I want to play every note.

Slowly, deliberately, I release her breast and begin a trail of open-mouthed kisses down her stomach, across her navel, and lower still. Each kiss is a promise, a soft caress against her skin as I descend. Her breathing hitches, quick and shallow, as I reach the delicate skin of her inner thigh, gently parting her legs with my hand. I press my face into the warmth between her legs, inhaling her scent, a potent mix of arousal and her unique sweetness. Her muscles tense, and her body trembles as I finally reach her slick, pulsing core.

My mouth closes over her, and she's already slick and hot, her scent intoxicating. Her hips arch into my face, urgent and demanding, and her fingers tangle in my hair, pulling me closer still. I taste her, deep and sweet, and the small, desperate sounds she makes are a symphony in my ears. I suck gently, flicking my tongue against her pulsing core, and her body tenses, then shudders.

She's unraveling, piece by piece, beneath my touch, and I want to devour every exquisite inch. Her nails dig into my scalp, a sweet pain, as she moans my name, a broken whisper that fuels my hunger. I lift my head for a moment, just long enough to see her face, flushed and beautiful, her eyes wide and unfocused. Then I descend again, losing myself in the taste and feel of her, consumed by the need to bring her to the edge, and then over.

I slowly, deliberately slide a finger inside her, her wet heat a fiery mark against my skin. She gasps, a sharp intake of breath that's music to my ears, and her hips lift, subtly, seeking more. I push a little further, her body yielding, clinging, and then I add another, her inner walls clenching around me, a sweet, possessive grip. A soft moan escapes her, a throaty sound that sends a shiver down my spine, and then she's arching, her body a taut bow, as another wave of pleasure washes over her.

I push into her with my fingers, hard and fast, riding the wave of her pleasure, feeling her tighten around me. Her breath hitches, a small cry tearing from her throat, and she convulses around me, her body arching off the bed. I hover at her entrance, devouring her lips with a slow, teasing kiss that deepens with raw hunger.

She comes again, her touch scorching, leaving trails of fire across my skin. This time her fingers twist in my hair, tugging hard until my head tilts back and our eyes lock. There's a predatory glint in her eyes, a hunger that mirrors the one churning in my gut. Her free hand descends, a whisper against my hip as she reaches for my belt. Deftly, her fingers navigate the buckle.

In one swift, fluid motion, she shoves my jeans and boxers down, the rough denim scraping against my thighs as they fall to my knees. The sudden exposure of my cock to the cool air sends a jolt through me, a mixture of vulnerability and thrilling anticipation. I can feel the blood rushing, a frantic drumbeat echoing in my ears as her eyes linger on my exposed flesh, a slow, appreciative smile playing on her lips.

I watch her hands, mesmerized, as she takes me in her palm, her touch a searing brand against my skin. A low groan escapes my throat, and I lean back, giving her full access, my body trembling with anticipation. Her fingers curl around me, a gentle squeeze that sends a jolt of pure pleasure straight to my core. Her eyes meet mine, dark and knowing, and a wicked smile plays on her lips as she slowly, deliberately, begins to stroke. With a sudden, swift motion, she flips me onto my back, her body pressing against mine, pinning me to the bed. I gasp, a thrill shooting through me as she straddles my hips, her weight a delicious pressure. Her eyes never leave mine as she lowers her head, her soft hair brushing against my thighs, and then, her warm, wet mouth closes around me, sending me spiraling into a haze of pure, unadulterated bliss.

I groan, a deep, guttural sound, as her mouth works its magic, a combination of firm suction and teasing flicks of her tongue that drives me wild. My hands tangle in her hair, gripping just tight enough as I push my hips upward, meeting her rhythm. I can feel the exquisite friction, the warmth of her mouth, the soft pull and release that threatens to shatter my control. Each stroke is a jolt, an electric current that sizzles through my core, making my vision swim. I'm teetering on the edge, utterly consumed by the sensation, by her, by the raw, unbridled pleasure she's giving me. Her lips are a wet heat, a tantalizing dance that pulls me deeper into the haze. I'm lost in it, lost in her, and there's nowhere else I'd rather be than right here, on the precipice of oblivion, with her.

A small gasp escapes her as she guides my cock to her opening, slick and ready. The soft, hot skin yields as I press forward, slowly, deliberately. I feel myself sink into her, inch by exquisite inch, a perfect fit that makes my muscles clench and my breath catch. Her body shudders around me, a silent welcome, as I fill her completely. She finally pulls away from me, a soft gasp escaping her as she rises. Her hips sway gently, a silent invitation, as she straddles me, the heat between us practically radiating in the cool afternoon air. Our eyes, dark with a shared desire, meet and hold, a wordless conversation passing between us that speaks of hunger and yearning.

Then, with a low growl that rumbles deep in my chest, our mouths meet once more. This kiss is deeper, hungrier than before, a frantic seeking, a desperate taking. Tongues dance and duel, each seeking to dominate, to consume. Her fingers tangle in my hair, pulling gently, demandingly, as she guides me, a slow, exquisite pressure, to her entrance. The world outside our intimate bubble ceases to exist, replaced by the symphony of our breaths, our heartbeats, and the intoxicating scent of our combined desires.

As her internal muscles contract around me, I'm struck by the sound that escapes her lips—raw, helpless, almost stunned. It sends a shudder down my spine so fierce it feels like it might snap me in half. It's a sound I've heard only rarely, in the spaces between nightmares and waking, in the brief unguarded minutes just before sleep claims her. But never like this, never beneath my hands, never because of me. The noise vibrates through the air and marks me; it's a wound, a brand, a desperate prayer. I want to fill the rest of my days with it, to build my house and my world from the sound of her surrender. With a grunt, I flip her onto her back, never leaving the warm sheath of her body.

As she's beneath me, Victoria's legs are shaking around my waist, and her fingers are gripping tighter with every move. She throws her head back, letting out a soft sound as I go deeper, both of us slick with sweat and wanting more. She arches her back, moaning again, a primal noise that just revs me up, and I keep driving into her, feeling us get closer with each thrust.

We lock eyes, having a silent chat, and I can see Victoria's eyelashes getting dark with unshed tears, showing just how intense this is. She's taking short, ragged breaths, her chest heaving like she's reaching for something just out of reach. I lean down to kiss her neck, tasting that mix of sweat and salt and the last bit of her holding back. Her skin is flushed, her heart pounding under my lips, a frantic drumbeat pushing me on.

With one last, powerful thrust, I pull out, and it's a bit of a shock, but I don't go far. My attention shifts, drawn to the delicate curve of her inner thigh, then up to her clit. I lean down, my tongue tracing a path of fire, licking and sucking and fingering, wanting to stretch out this pleasure, to make this exquisite torture last, to hear those breathless sounds again. Her hips buck without thinking, her fingers now tangled in my hair, pulling me closer, deeper into the building storm. Her moans get louder, more demanding, a melodic plea that

I'm more than ready to answer. The climax is right there, a tangible presence, building and building until it feels like it's going to shatter us both into a million glittering pieces of pure ecstasy.

I can feel her pulse quicken under my tongue as I move lower down her body, sucking on each nipple before trailing kisses along her stomach. Victoria squirms beneath me as I move further south until I reach her wet core. My tongue dances around her entrance before flicking back up towards her swollen clit.

Every breath she takes is a promise. I feel myself getting closer to the edge but I don't want to let go just yet; I want to make sure Victoria reaches the peak first. As I continue lavishing attention on her clit, sliding two fingers inside of her and curling them upwards, I find that sweet spot that makes her cry out in ecstasy. The raw, shivering sounds she makes send up an echo in my own throat, an answering rumble of possessive hunger that drives out every last doubt.

I don't realize I'm speaking, didn't mean to say anything at all, but the words are dragged out of me: "I want you. I want you always." I'm almost afraid to look at her, terrified that she'd see just how badly I've been unraveled, but when I do her pupils are blown wide and her face is open, unmasked, for the first time since I've met her. It's something new and old at once, a secret only the two of us have ever known.

Withdrawing my fingers from within her, I slide back up Victoria's body, aligning myself with her entrance. Slowly, intimately, I push back inside of her as we share breathless kisses. I slide an arm beneath her, cradling her body like it's something breakable and precious and mine alone. Her legs wrap tightly around me, urging us onward as we move together in perfect harmony. I want to stay here, inside the moment, until the rest of the world goes quiet. My whole body feels wrung out and electrified at the same time, every nerve on fire. I've never wanted anything more than to keep her like this—wild and open and safe, with me. As our pace quickens and our bodies strain towards a shared climax, I can feel it—the connection between us transcending into something more powerful than either could have imagined.

The quiet after feels unreal. The air between us hums with leftover heat, our breaths tangled, bodies slick and trembling. For the first time in longer than I can remember, the silence doesn't feel like something waiting to break.

Victoria shifts closer, her head finding the hollow of my chest, her hair sticking damp against my skin. My arm slides around her instinctively, holding her there, keeping her heartbeat pressed to mine until they find the same rhythm.

Neither of us speaks. We don't need to. The language now is breath and touch—the way her fingers trace slow, aimless shapes over my ribs, the way my thumb brushes circles at the base of her spine. Every motion says the same thing: *we're still here.*

Victoria's head rests against my chest, her breath steady, warm against my skin. The morning light filters through the curtains in thin, gold ribbons, catching on the curve of her shoulder where my arm lies draped. The air still smells like us—heat, coffee, and something soft I don't have a name for.

She shifts in her sleep, murmuring something I can't quite catch. My fingers find a loose strand of her hair, twirling it absently. I should close my eyes, let the quiet win for once, but I don't trust it. Not after everything. Not when the world's got a habit of kicking in the door the second I start to breathe.

The phone on the nightstand buzzes. Once. Twice. Persistent.

I tense, careful not to wake her, and reach for it. The name on the screen freezes me where I am.

Quinn.

"Shit," I whisper under my breath. My thumb hovers a second before I swipe to answer. "What do you need, Quinn? Make it quick. I'm in the middle of something important."

Vicky's eyes snap open. "Quinn?" The word is a raw curse, tearing from her throat. "What the hell, Beau? You didn't tell her, did you? You absolute ass, she's going to kill me."

Static, then her voice—sharp as a whip and twice as fast.

"Beau Sloane Maddox—what the hell are you doing? No, scratch that. Don't answer. I don't need the visual."

I groan, dragging a hand down my face. "Quinn Blaire Maddox, if you don't get to the fucking point, I'll come through this phone myself."

"Fine," she snaps. "Sorry to interrupt your... extracurriculars. But I need your help. Someone killed Kat, Beau."

That hits me square in the chest. I sit up a little, careful not to jostle Victoria. "Shit," I mutter, voice low. "I'm sorry, sis. What do you need?"

"I need you to run a list of my jobs for the last ten years. Someone's framing me, Beau. They used my fucking kill signature—right down to the halo of blood at their feet."

The words sink in slow and heavy, like stones in water. "Fuck."

"Yeah," she says, voice frayed. "It's bad. And to make it worse, some detective's crawling up my ass because I was the one who found her. In my shop."

I let out a long breath, pinch the bridge of my nose. "Fuckkkkk," I drag it out, shaking my head. "Goddamn it, Quinnie, what the hell did you get yourself into?"

"Don't you dare use that awful nickname."

That earns a half-smile from me. "Still easy to rattle you. Focus—we need to cut this call. I'll send an encrypted file tomorrow. Pulling a decade of jobs takes time. You've been a busy little fuck."

"Yeah, I know." Her sigh cracks in my ear. "Thanks, bub. Talk soon."

"Yeah," I murmur. "Always."

The line goes dead. I set the phone face down on the nightstand and scrub a hand over my face. The house is quiet except for the soft tick of the old clock in the hallway. Behind me, the sheets rustle—she's already awake, sitting up against the headboard, waiting for the call to end.

When I glance over, her eyes catch the faint blue of moonlight spilling through the window. "That was Quinn," she says flatly. Not a question.

"Yeah," I admit, leaning back against the headboard. "She's in trouble."

Her jaw tightens. "She usually is."

"Not like this."

The silence stretches until I feel it in my chest. She pushes up halfway, the sheet slipping from her shoulder, hair tousled from sleep. "You going after her?"

I shake my head. "Not yet. Not until I know more."

Her gaze flicks to the phone on the nightstand, then back to me, sharp now. "She doesn't know I'm here, does she?"

"You already told me to go to hell for answering," I say, voice rough, a hint of a smile ghosting through. "Didn't seem like the moment to make introductions."

That pulls a low breath out of her—almost a laugh, almost not. "I just didn't want to hear her voice. Not after everything."

"Vicky—"

She cuts me off with a small shake of her head. "I know she's your sister, Beau. And I'm glad she's alive. I just... I don't know how to tell her what's coming."

I watch her for a moment, the weight of it sitting between us. "Then don't," I say finally. "Not yet."

Her lips press together. She looks away, jaw working like she's trying not to bite back words that'll hurt us both.

I reach for the joint sitting in the ashtray, light it, take a drag, and hold it out to her. "Here," I say, smoke curling between us. "You look like you could use it more than me."

She hesitates, then takes it, our fingers brushing. "You think this fixes anything?" she asks, voice softer now.

"Nah," I say, watching her take a slow pull. "That's pancakes. This just makes the fire burn slower."

She exhales, the smoke a ghost twisting through the dark. "You and your damn metaphors."

"Better than your damn temper," I mutter, and she finally, actually laughs—quiet and real, the kind that hits me somewhere deep.

For a minute, we just sit there passing the joint back and forth, the silence turning into something almost peaceful.

Then she leans back against me, head resting on my shoulder, and says quietly, "If Quinn's in this... we don't have much time."

I rest my chin on her hair, breathing her in. "No," I murmur, feeling her heartbeat against my ribs. "We don't."

The clock ticks. The smoke fades. And for the first time since I got that call, I let myself believe we might still have a fighting chance.

Chapter 40
Victoria

The morning feels too still for everything we've lost. Sunlight filters weakly through the curtains, striping the floor in pale gold. I've been up since before dawn, elbows buried in Beau's desk, surrounded by files and half-drunk coffee. The place smells like paper, cedar, and the faint ghost of last night's heat.

Beau moves behind me, quiet but heavy in presence. He's reading over my shoulder, the scrape of his thumb against the edge of a file the only sound between us. "You sure this is all of it?" he asks finally, voice rough, low.

"Everything Quinn's done for the last ten years," I answer, scrolling through the database I built overnight. "Official kills, ghost ops, wiped contracts. Nothing that explains why someone would bother framing her."

He nods, slow. "Driftwood's when she dropped off the radar. About three years ago."

"Smart move." I lean back, eyes aching from hours of staring at the screen. "She earned peace and took it. I thought she had it."

The silence stretches. Beau's still reading, jaw tight, eyes narrowing at something I can't see from here. When he speaks again, his tone's careful, like he already knows it's going to hurt. "This Kat Quinn mentioned last night—the one who got killed."

My stomach turns to ice. "What did you just say?"

He looks up. "She said someone killed Kat. Body staged with her kill signature."

I stand so fast the chair legs screech against the floor. "No." My pulse spikes, a pounding between my ribs. "No, no, no."

"Who was she, Vicky?"

My throat's dry when I say it. "Latte."

Recognition flashes in his face. "Your contact?"

"My protégé." The word cracks on its way out. "Kat was assigned to me when she was nineteen—fresh out of training, all nerves and brilliance. I trained her, shaped her, sent her into the field when she was ready. When the Bible went missing, she got burned by association. I pulled strings, got her placed in Driftwood under civilian cover." My voice softens, the ache catching in my chest. "I wasn't protecting Orion's asset. I was protecting my kid."

Beau exhales hard, dragging a hand over his mouth. "And now she's dead."

I force myself to nod, but the motion feels foreign. "Whoever killed her used Quinn's signature—same radius, same halo pattern. That's not coincidence. It's precision. They wanted to send a message, and they wanted it to hurt."

Beau settles across from me, elbows on his knees, voice low and calm. "You think this ties back to the Bible?"

"It has to." I grab one of the folders and slap it open on the desk. "Kat was one of the last people who knew the file structure. She helped encrypt the backup before it vanished. If she's gone and

Quinn's framed, that means they're closing the loop. Every person with access is being erased."

He studies me for a long beat, eyes steady, unreadable. Then he says, "So what do we do?"

I look down at the stacks of names, dates, contracts. The ghosts of our past lives. "We get ahead of it," I say. "We figure out who's pulling the strings before they erase us too."

Beau's hand finds mine on the desk, rough, grounding. "Then we don't stop 'til we do."

The words hit harder than a promise—they sound like a vow.

For a moment I just breathe, the smell of coffee and cedar filling the silence between us. I should feel steady. Focused. But all I can see is Kat's laugh, the way she used to bite her pen when she was nervous. The way she called me *boss* even after I told her to stop.

And all I can hear is Quinn's voice from Beau's late-night call—tired, afraid, still fighting.

I press my palms flat against the desk, forcing my voice to stay level. "If they've started killing my people, Beau... then it's already begun."

He nods once, slow. "Then we hit back first."

The days start to blur.

Morning after morning, I wake up in Beau's bed, his heat still clinging to the sheets even when he's already up. The first thing I smell is coffee, the second is cedar, and the third is frustration rolling off him in waves. We've turned his bedroom into a war room—laptops, maps, flash drives, notes scrawled across legal pads and receipts. Every time I clear a space, it fills back up with new dead ends.

We chase every thread we can find. Old Orion kill orders, Red Haven manifests, Black Bloom's phantom routing numbers. Quinn's jobs. Kat's last movements. It's all there in fragments but nothing locks together. Every lead either loops back into itself or vanishes into nothing. A week ago I would've told you I could smell patterns in the dark. Now all I smell is smoke.

Beau's different when he's hunting. Quieter. He moves around the room like a storm front—steady, heavy, deliberate. Sometimes he'll reach over and slide my coffee closer without looking, like his hands know where I am before his eyes do. Sometimes, late at night, he'll lean back against the headboard, close his eyes, and mutter a curse so low it sounds like a prayer.

I keep my head down, fingers flying over keys, scrolling through old encrypted logs, reaching out to every ghost contact I still have. "This is bullshit," I mutter one afternoon, shoving a file away from me so hard it slides off the desk. "We're not missing something—we're being blocked."

Beau crouches to pick it up, lays it back on the desk without a word. "Blocked or baited," he says finally. "Could be both."

I rub a hand over my face. "Quinn's signature. Kat's name. Driftwood. Someone's running a narrative and we're dancing to it."

His hand lands warm on the back of my neck, grounding me, even as my pulse spikes. "Then we stop dancin', Vicky. We change the beat."

But changing the beat isn't easy. We run through Quinn's old contracts a second time. A third. Every connection she's had in the last decade, every city she's set foot in, every job I can dig up from old Orion archives. Nothing. The only constants are the Bible, Black Bloom, and bodies.

It's past midnight on the third day when Beau pushes back from the desk hard enough to make the chair screech. "This isn't working," he says, voice low but edged. "We're chasing ghosts while they're stackin' bodies."

I glance up from my screen, eyes gritty, heart aching. "Then we stop chasing. We make them show themselves."

He tilts his head, studying me. "You got somethin' in mind?"

I lean forward, hands clasped, the glimmer of an idea sparking like a match in the dark. "Yeah. But it's risky."

"Good," he says, a flicker of a smile breaking through the exhaustion. "I'm gettin' tired of bein' careful."

It's the fourth day of my search, but it's been more than a week since the explosion at Harrington, and the footage still runs on every network — grainy loops of smoke spilling from the Presidential House, firefighters dragging hoses through the wreckage, commentators speculating in low, urgent tones about gas leaks, structural failures, terrorism. Every theory but the truth.

Beau mutes the TV halfway through the segment, jaw tight. The silence that follows feels heavier than the smoke ever did.

We've moved the search to the dining room. The farmhouse table between us is buried in files. Quinn's job lists, Red Haven manifests, map routes — all jumbled together like none of it can make sense without the rest. I've been combing through it for hours, eyes burning, trying to find the connection that keeps slipping just out of reach.

"You were on the grounds when it happened," I say, not looking up. "You saw it."

Beau grunted. "I heard it first. Thought a generator blew till I saw the fireball. Second floor went up like kindling." He looked at me, his voice raw. "I was arguing with you in the quad when it hit."

My throat was dry, but I nodded. "You asked what the hell I was doing. I told you it looked like you had your hands full."

That earns me the faintest flicker of a smile — quick, gone again. We don't have to say what really happened that night. He was watching the world burn while I was crawling out of my own hell, wrists shredded, ribs cracked, adrenaline the only thing keeping me upright. Both of us in the same city, both running from ghosts named Victor Leclair.

I slide another file across the table. "They still haven't found a body."

He looks down at the photo — what's left of the Presidential House. Charred bricks, glass, ash. "Maybe because there ain't one."

"Maybe because he walked out before it went up," I counter. "The east wing cameras went dark three minutes before detonation. The feed cut clean. That's not random, Beau. Someone pulled it."

He leans back, rubbing a hand over his jaw. "Victor planned his own damn funeral."

"Wouldn't be the first time," I mutter. "He's been playing both sides for years. Red Haven gave him resources. The Black Bloom gave him cover."

Beau's eyes flick toward me. "You think he's still alive."

"I know he is." I tap the article on the tablet between us — *Authorities Still Searching for Victor Leclair's Remains.* "They're looking for a corpse that doesn't exist."

The line of his mouth hardens. "If he's breathing, he's still moving pieces. Maybe even calling shots."

"Exactly. And the timing—" I drag a finger across the map — "the same week the shipments stopped moving, the same night the Presidential House burned. He staged the blast to bury the trail."

He exhales through his nose, slow and heavy. "And he damn near buried you too."

The words hang between us. True. But not the whole truth.

I meet his eyes. "He underestimated me. They all did."

He doesn't argue. Just reaches across the table, fingertips brushing mine. The gesture is small, grounding. "You think Victor's back in play?"

"I think he never left."

Beau nods once, slow, like he's already building the plan in his head. "Then we find the proof. Before the world writes him off for good."

Outside, the last of the evening sun fades behind the trees, throwing the room into the amber hush of twilight. The news replay continues silently on the muted screen — fire, rubble, chaos. The world thinks the story's over.

But Beau and I know better.

Victor Leclair's not a ghost. He's the match that lit everything.

And he's still out there.

The knock comes just as I'm starting to speak.
Three hard raps. Then silence.

Beau and I lock eyes across the table. He doesn't move for a second, head tilted, listening. The sound comes again—two this time, quicker, sharper. Not neighborly.

No one drives this far out unless they mean to.

He's already up, chair scraping against the floor. "Stay here."

I rise anyway, ignoring the pull in my ribs. "Not a chance."

He doesn't argue, just grabs the pistol off the counter and crosses the room in long, silent strides. The floorboards barely creak under his boots. I stay close, my hand brushing the dagger at the small of my back—habit more than fear.

The third knock never comes.

Beau flips the lock and wrenches the door open.

Two figures stand on the porch, haloed in the porch light and the rising dust of the long drive. Both look like they crawled straight through hell.

Quinn Maddox leans against the rail, hair wild, knuckles split, one eye swollen nearly shut. Her flannel's torn, streaked with blood that isn't all hers. She's thinner, sharper—stripped down to muscle and stubbornness.

Beside her stands a man I don't recognize—tall, broad-shouldered, exhaustion clinging to him like armor. He's got one arm braced around Quinn's waist to keep her upright, the other holding a gun that hangs loose but ready. His shirt's half open, his jaw shadowed with days of travel, and his eyes are the hollow kind that have seen too much.

Beau's voice drops, low and rough. "Quinn."

She gives him a look that's half relief, half accusation. "'Bout time, brother." Her voice cracks in the middle, the edge fraying. For a second she looks less like the soldier I remember and more like someone who's been barely holding it together.

eau's already moving, stepping out to steady her. "What the hell happened?"

"We got a lead," Quinn rasps, her voice sandpapered raw. "Word was, Kat was alive. Someone said she'd been seen near the docks—hurt, hiding." She swallows hard, leaning more of her weight into him. "It was a setup. They were waiting for us."

The man beside her doesn't correct her or introduce himself. He just scans the tree line, eyes sharp and restless. "We barely made it out. Whoever's running Red Haven's cleanup—they're not hiding anymore."

Beau's jaw tightens. "You're tellin' me they ambushed you?"

Quinn nods once, slow. "They wanted me to find her. They used her name to draw me out." Her voice cracks, quiet and vicious all at once. "Kat's gone, Beau. They made damn sure of it."

The world narrows to that word.

Kat.

My chest goes tight, air catching on the name like a blade.

"She's gone," Quinn says, confirming what I already knew but couldn't say out loud. "And it wasn't random."

The silence that follows is suffocating. The air feels thick, heavy with salt and smoke and grief. Beau guides her inside, the gentleness in his movements something I've never seen before. He settles her onto the couch, grabs a blanket from the armrest, tucking it around her shoulders like muscle memory.

I crouch near the coffee table, my gaze tracing the bruises on her arms, the tremor in her hands. "Where were you hit?"

Her head lifts at my voice. The recognition hits like a gunshot. "Tori?"

"Yeah," I say quietly. "It's me."

A broken laugh leaves her throat. "You've got to be shitting me."

"Long story." My mouth twists. "You're not the only ghost that came back."

Her face softens for just a breath before the weight of the moment slams back in. She leans against the couch, letting Beau clean the cut on her temple.

The man stays standing near the window, gun still in hand, shoulders squared. His eyes keep flicking to the treeline like he expects it to move. "They're not going to stop," he says. "Driftwood was just the first cut. They're moving something bigger—and they wanted her out of the way first."

Beau looks over Quinn's head at me, his eyes steady, grim. "Victor."

It's not a question.

I nod once. "He's alive."

Quinn's eyes widen, confusion breaking into fury. "Wait—you're saying Victor Leclair's still breathing?"

Beau answers for both of us. "That's what we're about to find out."

The air tastes of smoke and endings. Quinn's eyes, Beau's steady breath beside me, the weight of everything we've lost—it all feels like the start of something that won't let any of us walk away clean. We sit in the wreckage of what's left—blood drying, hearts still beating, the promise of vengeance brewing hotter than the coffee gone cold on the table.

Morning will come. It always does.

And when it does, there'll be blades over breakfast.

About the Author

Yvonne Hamilton is a fantasy author, world-builder, and co-founder of Golden Light Publishing House, where myth, madness, and meticulous storytelling collide. Based in West Virginia, she writes the kinds of stories that blur the line between beauty and ruin—realms forged in fire, characters stitched together with secrets, and worlds that refuse to stay quiet.

With a background in business management and data analytics, Yvonne brings the same precision she uses in spreadsheets to crafting sprawling universes filled with celestial bloodlines, shadowed magic, and rebellions that burn brighter than the stars. Her work—spanning dark fantasy, romantic thrillers, and multi-realm sagas—often explores redemption, betrayal, and the cost of truth in worlds built on lies.

When she's not writing, Yvonne can usually be found buried in coffee, orchestrating publishing schedules, or chasing down the next story that won't let her sleep. She believes good fiction should set something on fire—preferably expectations. She's not a pyro... promise.

To my husband, Ricky. You are my rock and my biggest supporter through every wild dream I chase. Thank you for believing in me and for coming along on this journey. Thank you for standing by me through three degrees, through endless drafting sessions and late-night brainstorming calls, and for your patience when I get completely obsessive over a story. None of this would be possible without your love and support.

To my partners at Golden Light Publishing House, B. Wills and Charletta. Thank you for the random, no-context messages, the late-night brainstorming sessions, and the endless planning calls that somehow blend into our everyday conversations. I am grateful to call you not just friends, but chosen family. This journey would be so much duller without your energy, laughter, and support.

To my alpha readers, M.A. and Ashlee. Your feedback was invaluable. Yes, I did ask for it, and you absolutely delivered. I cannot wait to share the rest of the series with you.

To my fellow authors. Thank you for smiling politely while encouraging my insane plans and goals, even when the big picture sounds far-fetched. What can I say? Organized chaos at its best. I am honored to watch each of you thrive on your own creative paths.

And finally, to the readers. Thank you for opening these pages and stepping into this world with me. I hope you found something here that resonated—something that made you laugh, ache, or hold your breath. Whether you saw yourself in the shadows or in the light, may this story remind you that even in the darkest moments, there is always a spark worth chasing.

www.ingramcontent.com/pod-product-compliance
Lightning Source LLC
Chambersburg PA
CBHW060813120726
47909CB00006B/1906